G.I. JOE

COBRA

SON OF THE SNAKE

COBRA
SON OF THE SNAKE

WRITER:
MIKE COSTA

ARTISTS:
ANTONIO FUSO AND
WERTHER DELL'EDERA

COLORIST:
ARIANNA FLOREAN

LETTERS:
NEIL UYETAKE

SERIES EDITORS:
JOHN BARBER AND
CARLOS GUZMAN

COVER ARTISTS:
JOE EISMA AND
JUAN CASTRO

COVER COLORIST:
SIMON GOUGH

COLLECTION EDITORS:
JUSTIN EISINGER AND
ALONZO SIMON

COLLECTION DESIGNER:
NEIL UYETAKE

Special thanks to Hasbro's Aaron Archer, Derryl DePriest, Joe Del Regno, Ed Lane, Joe Furfaro, Jos Huxley, Heather Hopkins and Michael Kelly for their invaluable assistance.

IDW founded by Ted Adams, Alex Garner, Kris Oprisko, and Robbie Robbins

ISBN: 978-1-61377-547-9

16 15 14 13 1 2 3 4

IDW

Licensed By: Hasbro

Ted Adams, CEO & Publisher
Greg Goldstein, President & COO
Robbie Robbins, EVP/Sr. Graphic Artist
Chris Ryall, Chief Creative Officer/Editor-in-Chief
Matthew Ruzicka, CPA, Chief Financial Officer
Alan Payne, VP of Sales
Dirk Wood, VP of Marketing
Lorelei Bunjes, VP of Digital Services

Become our fan on Facebook **facebook.com/idwpublishing**
Follow us on Twitter **@idwpublishing**
Check us out on YouTube **youtube.com/idwpublishing**
www.IDWPUBLISHING.com

Originally published as COBRA Issues #13–16.

Even while Cobra orchestrated a war in Southeast Asia, Cobra High Command began to fall apart: Tomax and Major Bludd plotted to eliminate the new Cobra Commander with information provided by Serpentor. But when Tomax found out that the Cobra Council was being eliminated, he quickly made his escape. Major Bludd was betrayed by Serpentor and forced to flee as well, ending up in the custody of United Nations troops.

Meanwhile, G.I. JOE has seen some of its facilities closed, its operating budget severely limited, and a major change in command as Hawk was replaced by Duke. Now, Duke must rebuild...

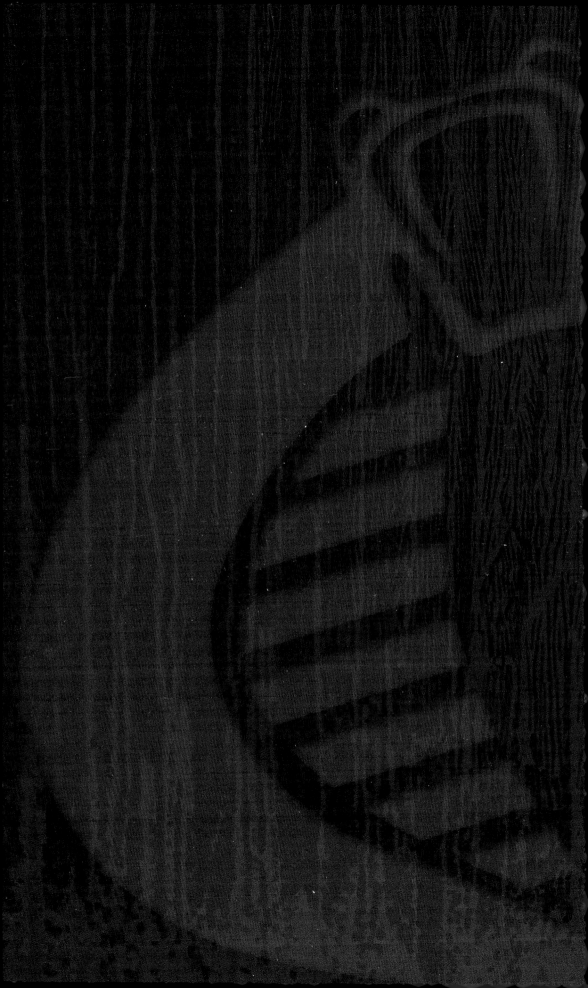

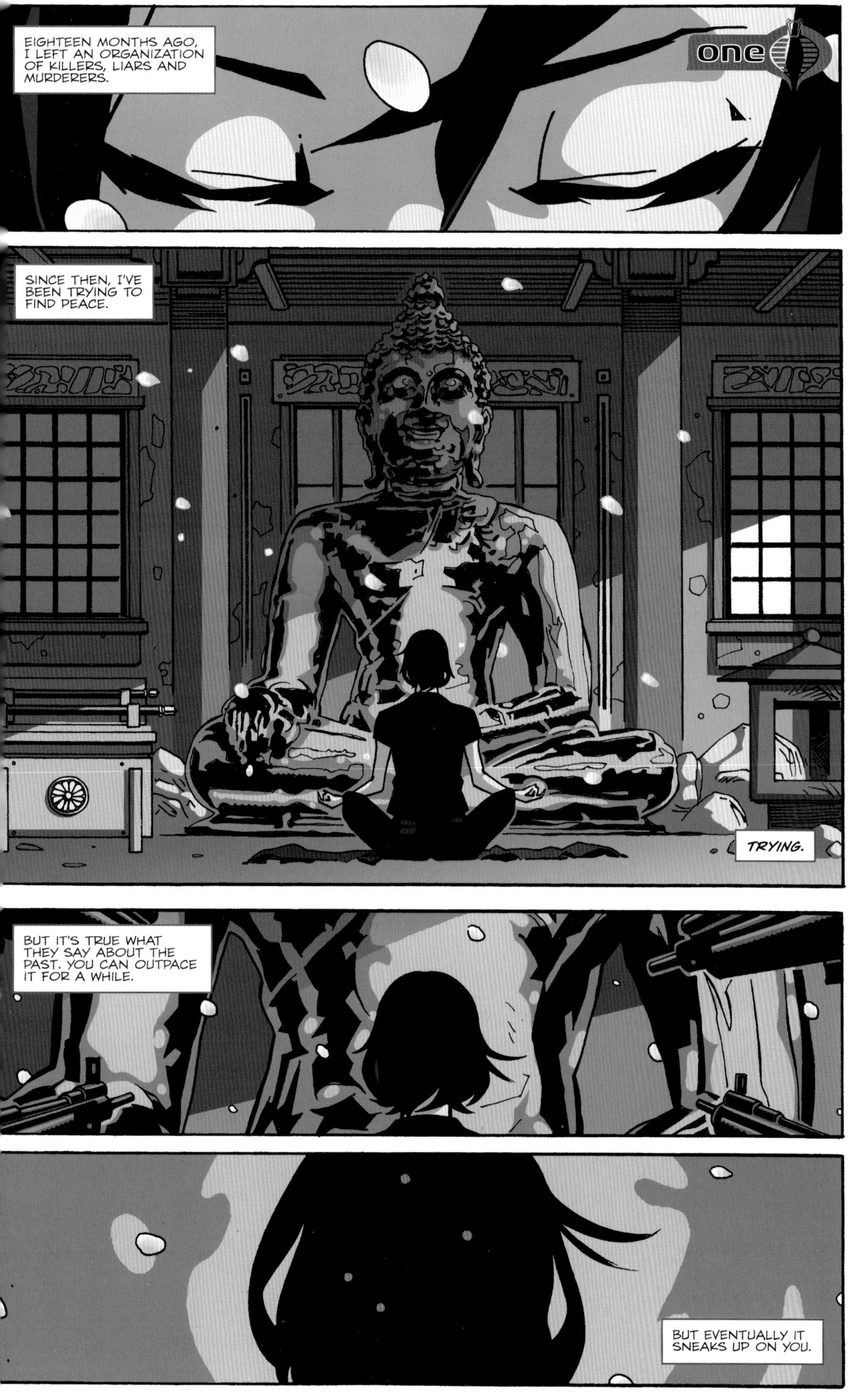

EIGHTEEN MONTHS AGO, I LEFT AN ORGANIZATION OF KILLERS, LIARS AND MURDERERS.
one
SINCE THEN, I'VE BEEN TRYING TO FIND PEACE.
TRYING.
BUT IT'S TRUE WHAT THEY SAY ABOUT THE PAST. YOU CAN OUTPACE IT FOR A WHILE.
BUT EVENTUALLY IT SNEAKS UP ON YOU.

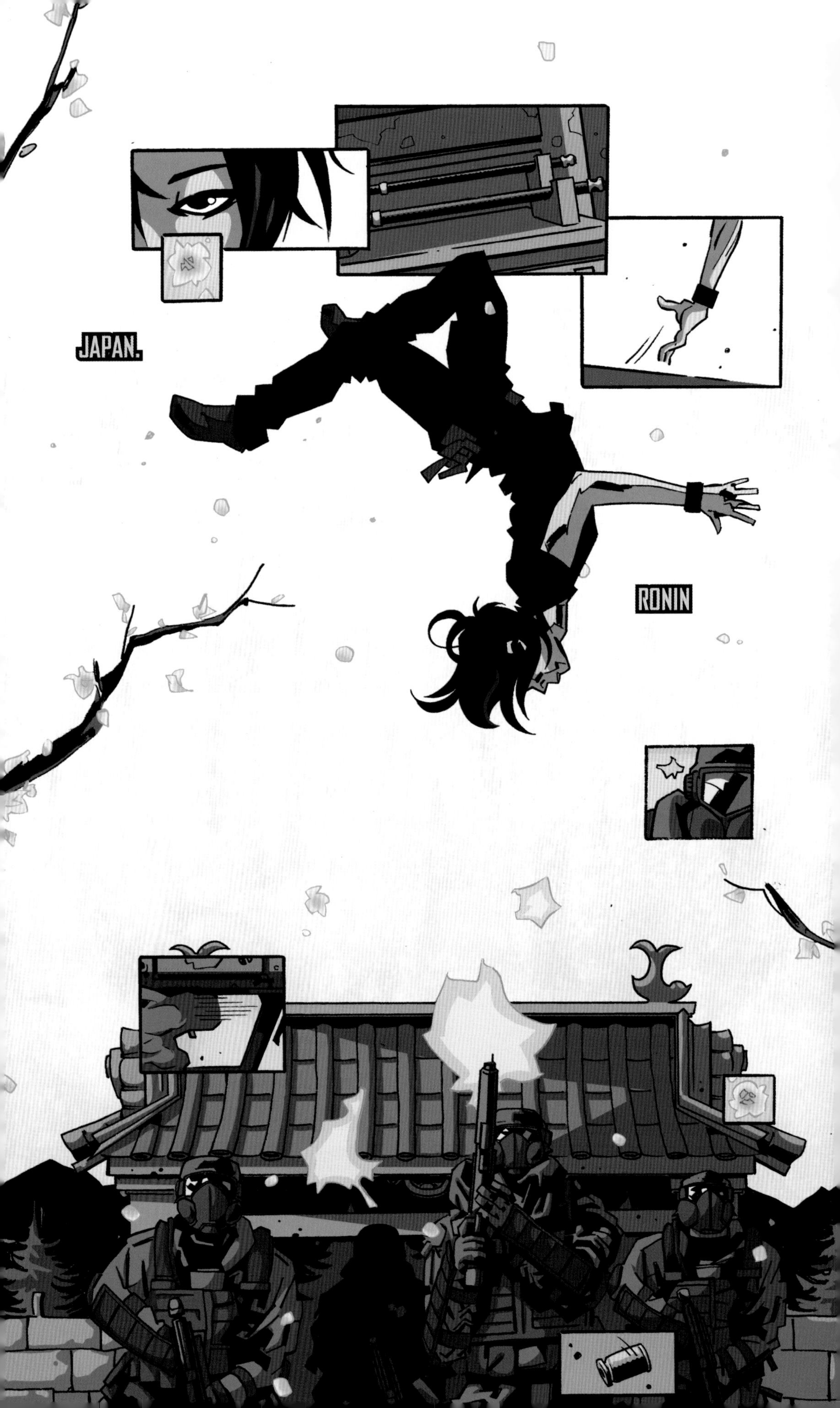
JAPAN.
RONIN

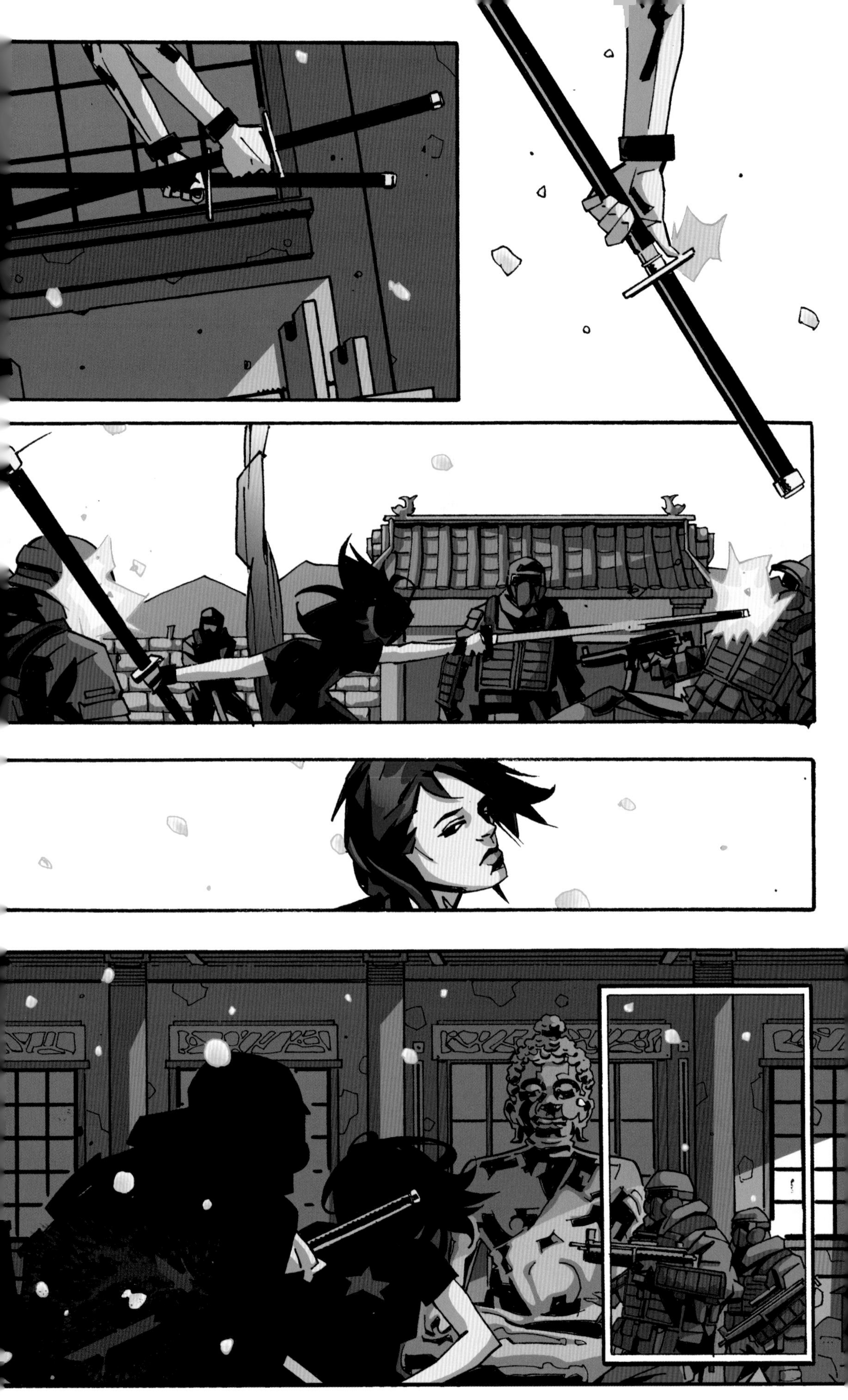

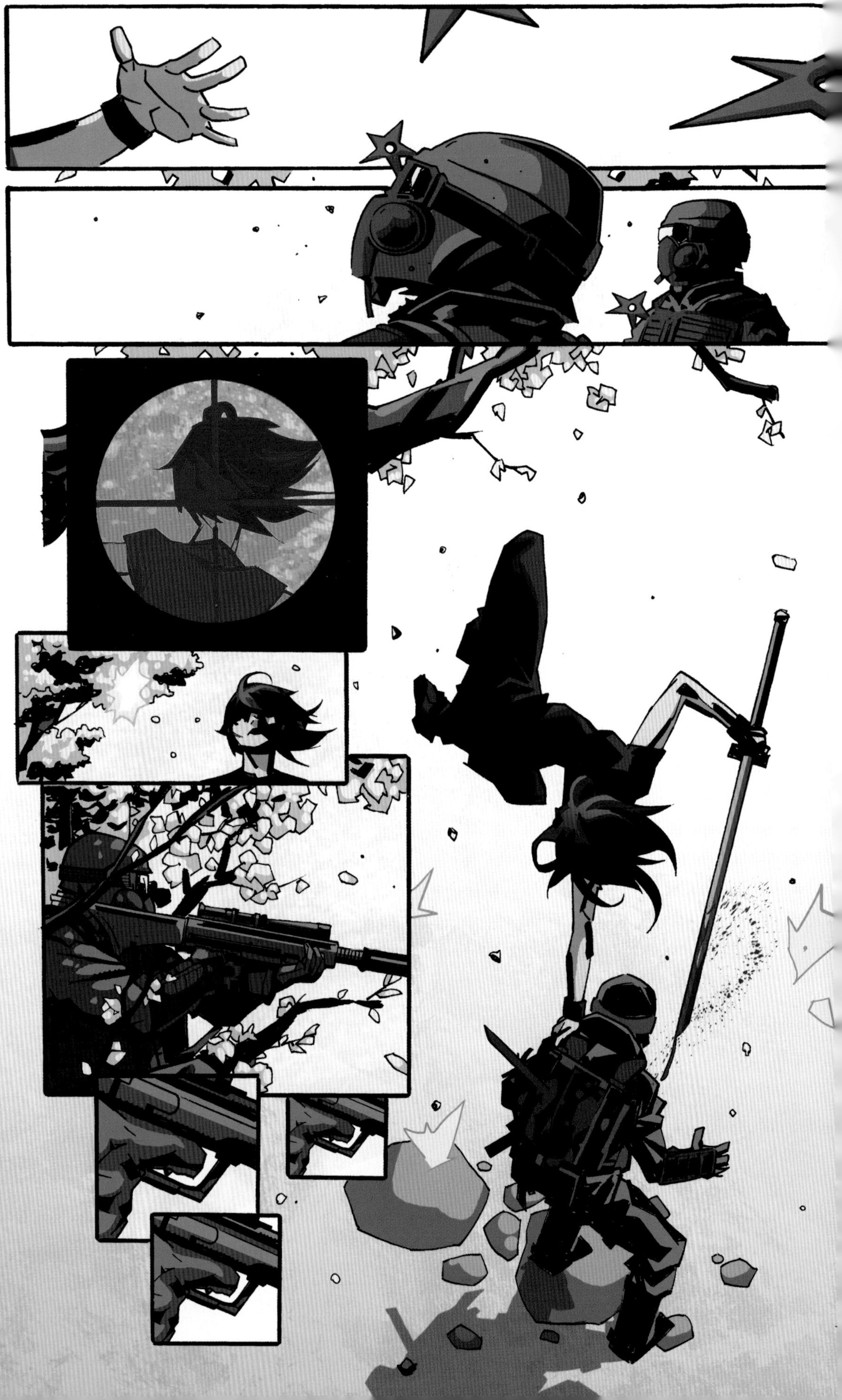

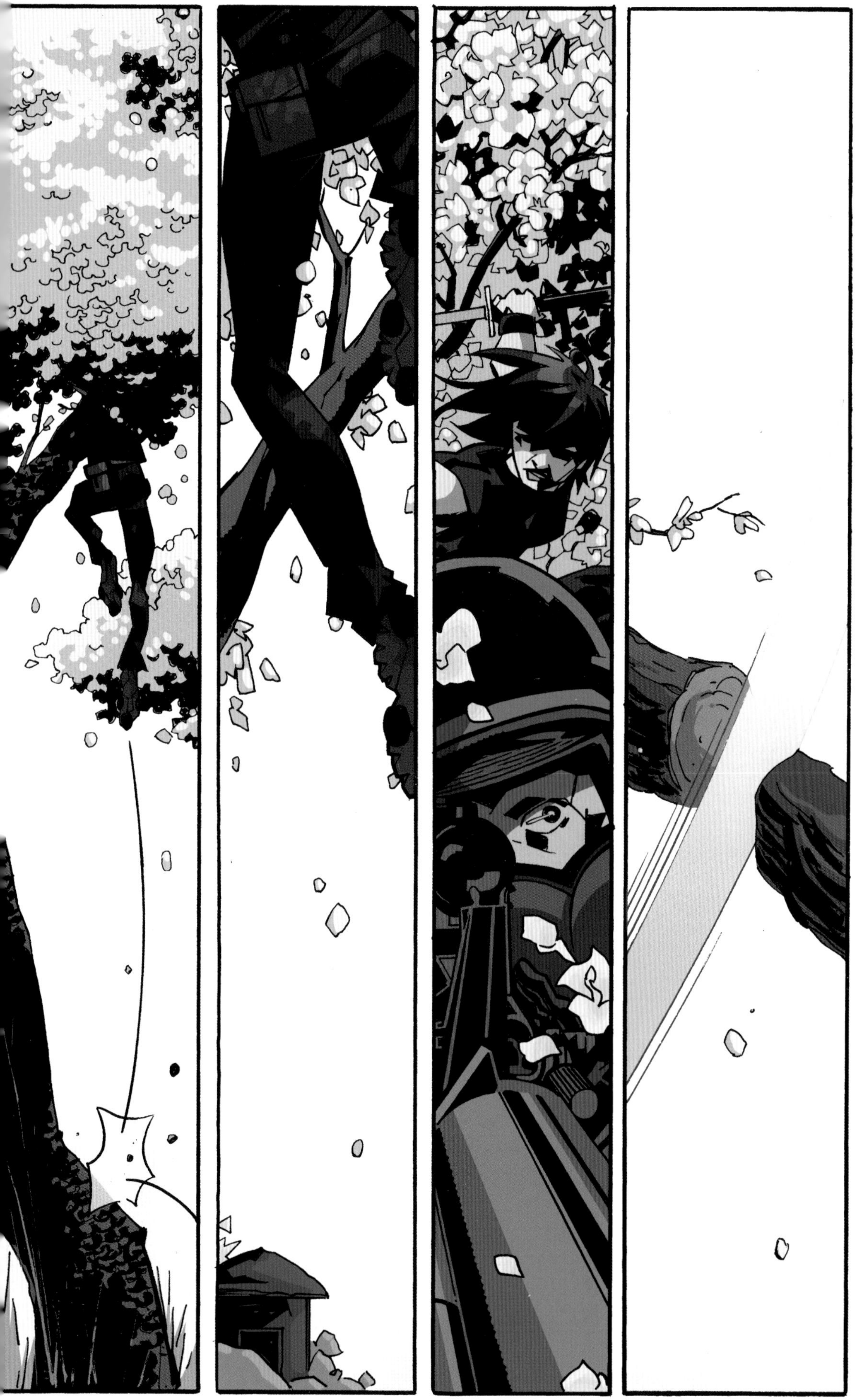

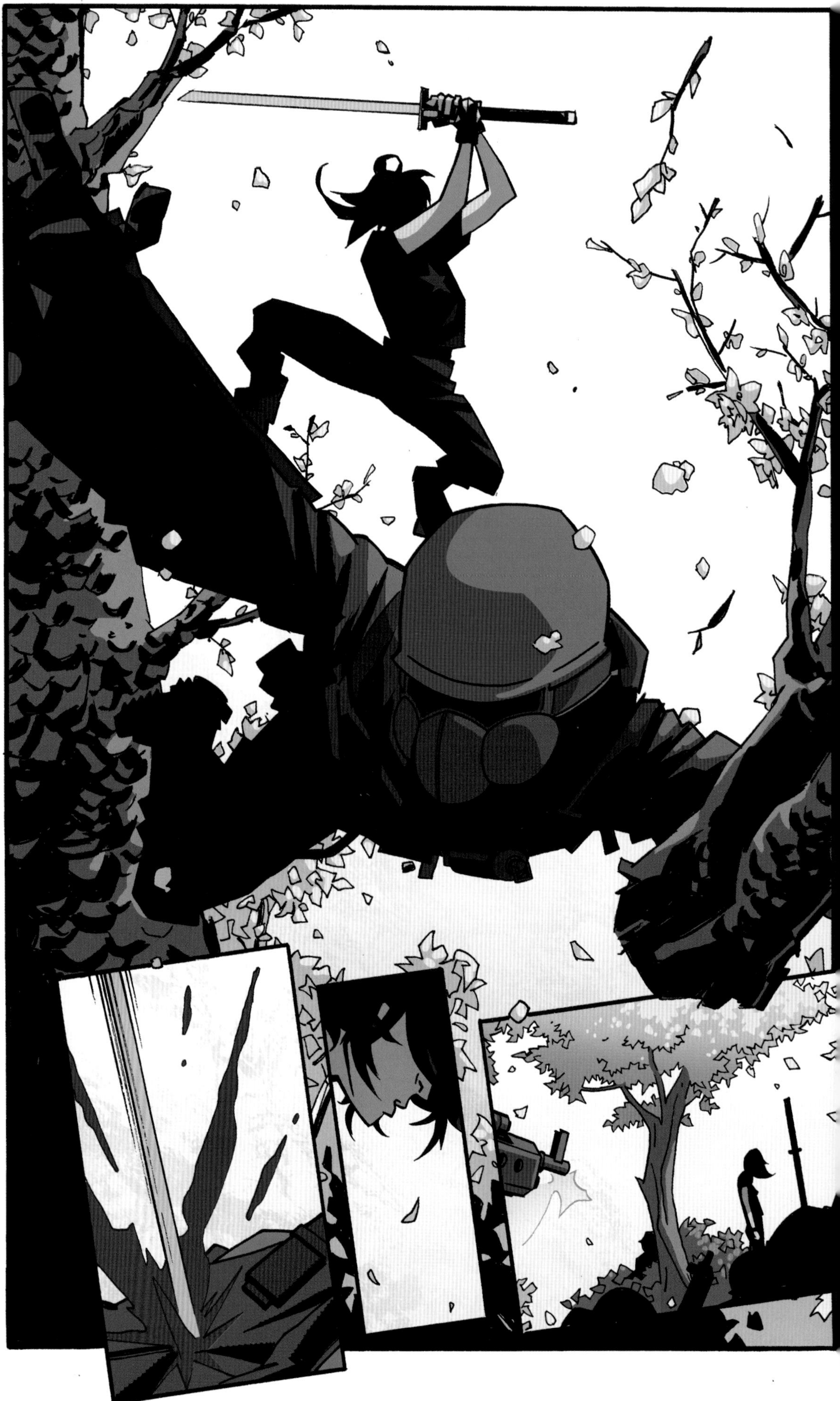

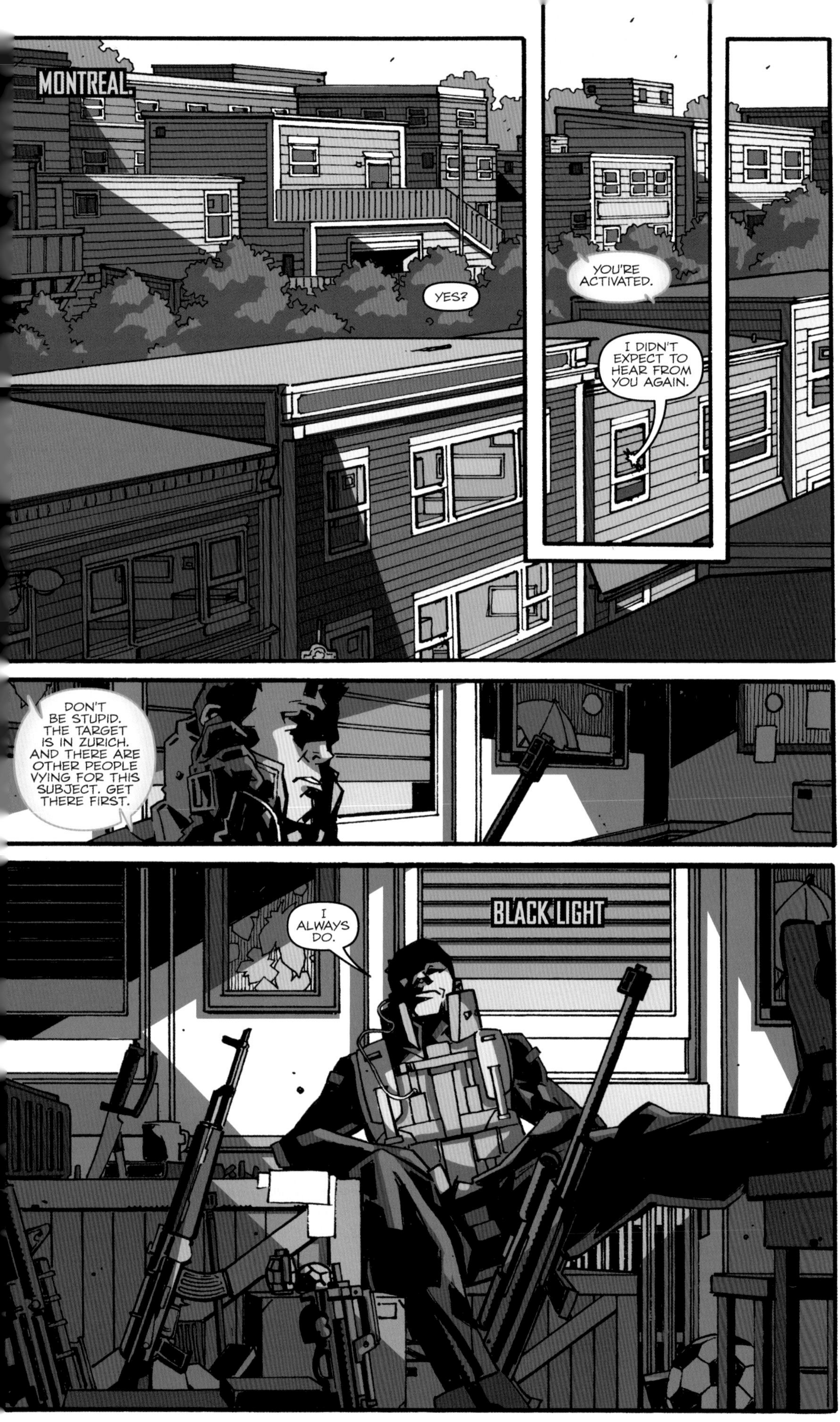
MONTREAL.
YES?
YOU'RE ACTIVATED.
I DIDN'T EXPECT TO HEAR FROM YOU AGAIN.
DON'T BE STUPID. THE TARGET IS IN ZURICH. AND THERE ARE OTHER PEOPLE VYING FOR THIS SUBJECT. GET THERE FIRST.
BLACK LIGHT
I ALWAYS DO.

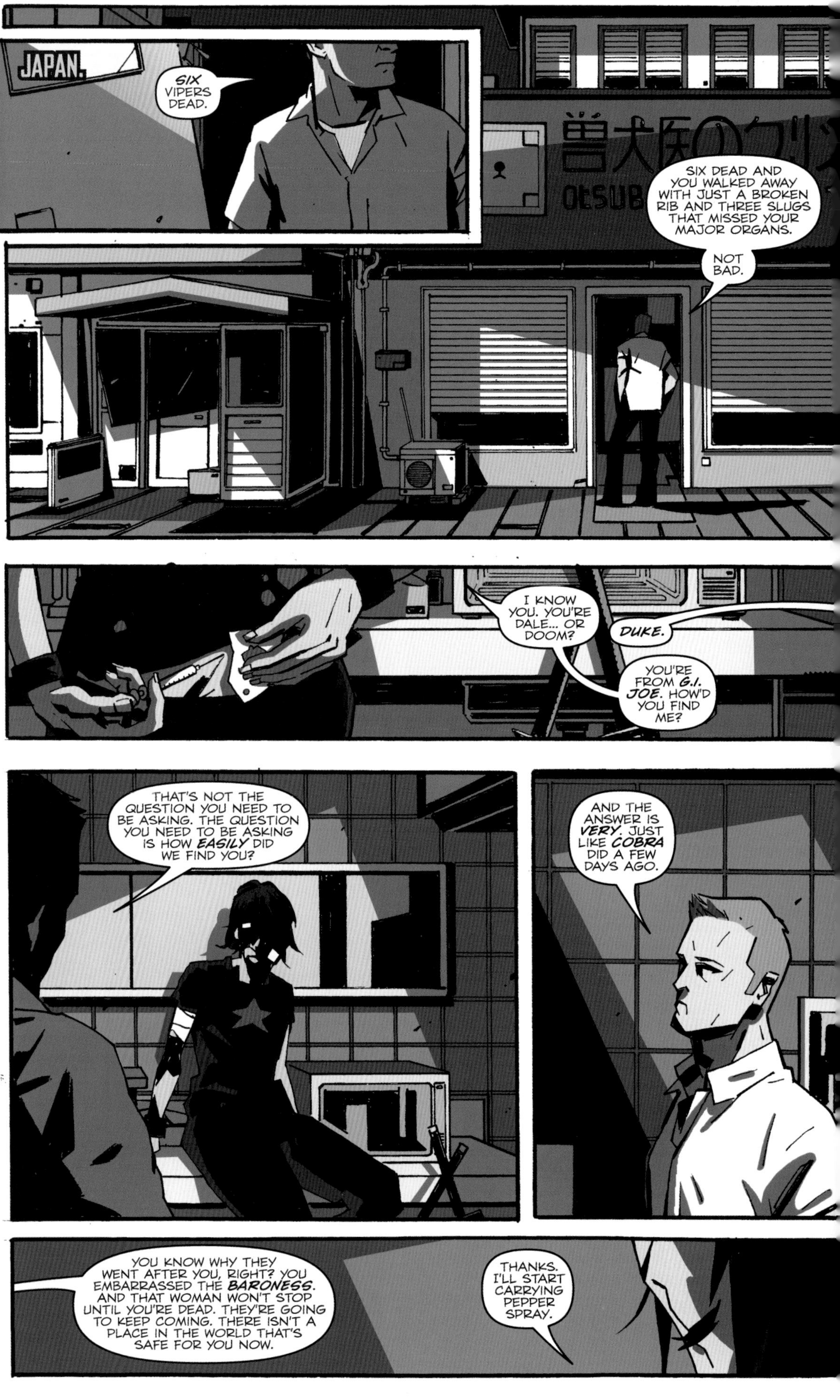
JAPAN.
SIX VIPERS DEAD.
SIX DEAD AND YOU WALKED AWAY WITH JUST A BROKEN RIB AND THREE SLUGS THAT MISSED YOUR MAJOR ORGANS.
NOT BAD.
I KNOW YOU. YOU'RE DALE... OR DOOM?
DUKE.
YOU'RE FROM G.I. JOE. HOW'D YOU FIND ME?
THAT'S NOT THE QUESTION YOU NEED TO BE ASKING. THE QUESTION YOU NEED TO BE ASKING IS HOW EASILY DID WE FIND YOU?
AND THE ANSWER IS VERY. JUST LIKE COBRA DID A FEW DAYS AGO.
YOU KNOW WHY THEY WENT AFTER YOU, RIGHT? YOU EMBARRASSED THE BARONESS. AND THAT WOMAN WON'T STOP UNTIL YOU'RE DEAD. THEY'RE GOING TO KEEP COMING. THERE ISN'T A PLACE IN THE WORLD THAT'S SAFE FOR YOU NOW.
THANKS. I'LL START CARRYING PEPPER SPRAY.

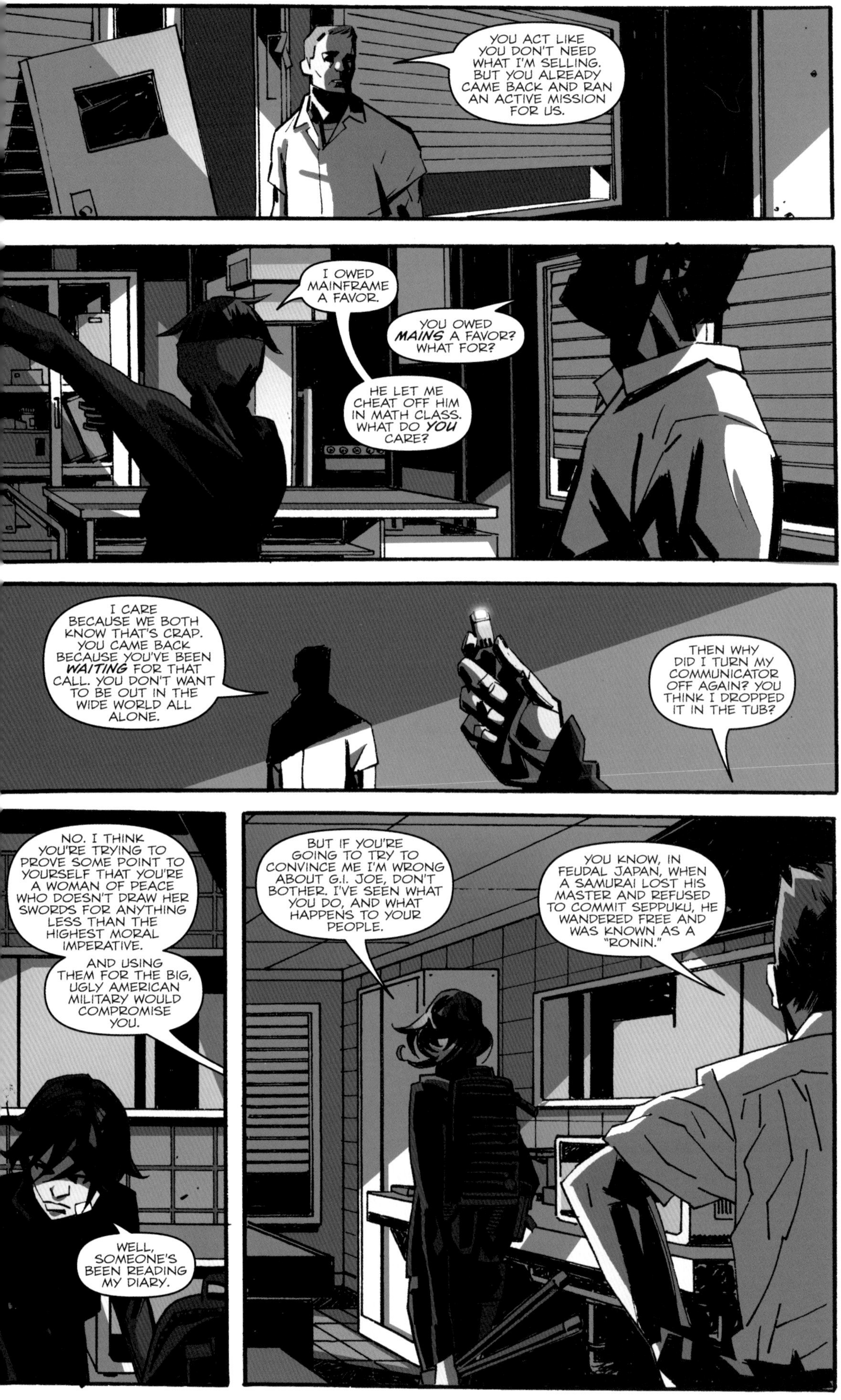
YOU ACT LIKE YOU DON'T NEED WHAT I'M SELLING. BUT YOU ALREADY CAME BACK AND RAN AN ACTIVE MISSION FOR US.
I OWED MAINFRAME A FAVOR.
YOU OWED MAINS A FAVOR? WHAT FOR?
HE LET ME CHEAT OFF HIM IN MATH CLASS. WHAT DO YOU CARE?
I CARE BECAUSE WE BOTH KNOW THAT'S CRAP. YOU CAME BACK BECAUSE YOU'VE BEEN WAITING FOR THAT CALL. YOU DON'T WANT TO BE OUT IN THE WIDE WORLD ALL ALONE.
THEN WHY DID I TURN MY COMMUNICATOR OFF AGAIN? YOU THINK I DROPPED IT IN THE TUB?
NO. I THINK YOU'RE TRYING TO PROVE SOME POINT TO YOURSELF THAT YOU'RE A WOMAN OF PEACE WHO DOESN'T DRAW HER SWORDS FOR ANYTHING LESS THAN THE HIGHEST MORAL IMPERATIVE.
AND USING THEM FOR THE BIG, UGLY AMERICAN MILITARY WOULD COMPROMISE YOU.
WELL, SOMEONE'S BEEN READING MY DIARY.
BUT IF YOU'RE GOING TO TRY TO CONVINCE ME I'M WRONG ABOUT G.I. JOE, DON'T BOTHER. I'VE SEEN WHAT YOU DO, AND WHAT HAPPENS TO YOUR PEOPLE.
YOU KNOW, IN FEUDAL JAPAN, WHEN A SAMURAI LOST HIS MASTER AND REFUSED TO COMMIT SEPPUKU, HE WANDERED FREE AND WAS KNOWN AS A "RONIN."

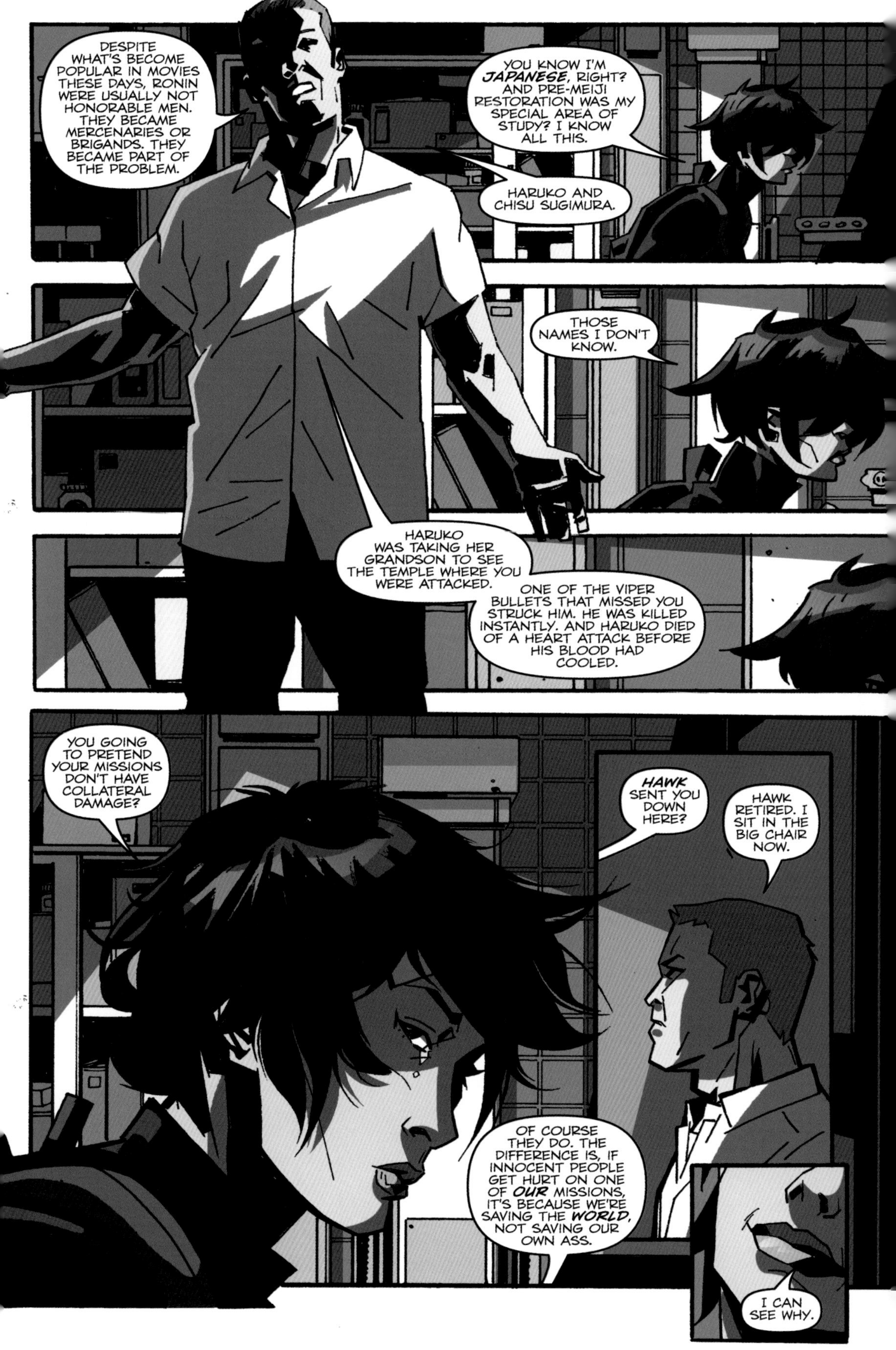
DESPITE WHAT'S BECOME POPULAR IN MOVIES THESE DAYS, RONIN WERE USUALLY NOT HONORABLE MEN. THEY BECAME MERCENARIES OR BRIGANDS. THEY BECAME PART OF THE PROBLEM.
YOU KNOW I'M JAPANESE, RIGHT? AND PRE-MEIJI RESTORATION WAS MY SPECIAL AREA OF STUDY? I KNOW ALL THIS.
HARUKO AND CHISU SUGIMURA.
THOSE NAMES I DON'T KNOW.
HARUKO WAS TAKING HER GRANDSON TO SEE THE TEMPLE WHERE YOU WERE ATTACKED.
ONE OF THE VIPER BULLETS THAT MISSED YOU STRUCK HIM. HE WAS KILLED INSTANTLY. AND HARUKO DIED OF A HEART ATTACK BEFORE HIS BLOOD HAD COOLED.
YOU GOING TO PRETEND YOUR MISSIONS DON'T HAVE COLLATERAL DAMAGE?
HAWK SENT YOU DOWN HERE?
HAWK RETIRED. I SIT IN THE BIG CHAIR NOW.
OF COURSE THEY DO. THE DIFFERENCE IS, IF INNOCENT PEOPLE GET HURT ON ONE OF OUR MISSIONS, IT'S BECAUSE WE'RE SAVING THE WORLD, NOT SAVING OUR OWN ASS.
I CAN SEE WHY.

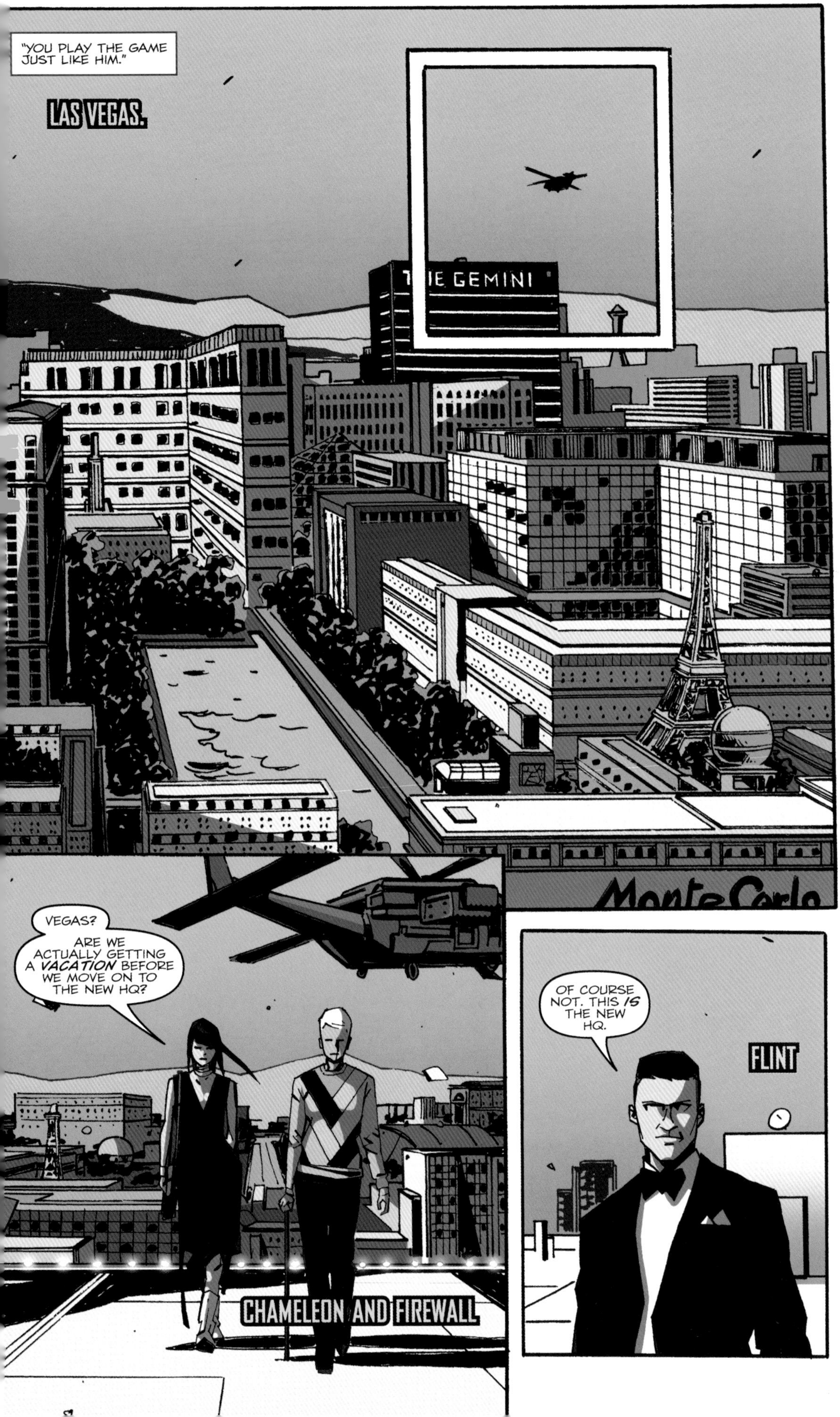
"YOU PLAY THE GAME JUST LIKE HIM."
LAS VEGAS.
THE GEMINI
Monte Carlo
VEGAS?
ARE WE ACTUALLY GETTING A *VACATION* BEFORE WE MOVE ON TO THE NEW HQ?
CHAMELEON AND FIREWALL
OF COURSE NOT. THIS *IS* THE NEW HQ.
FLINT

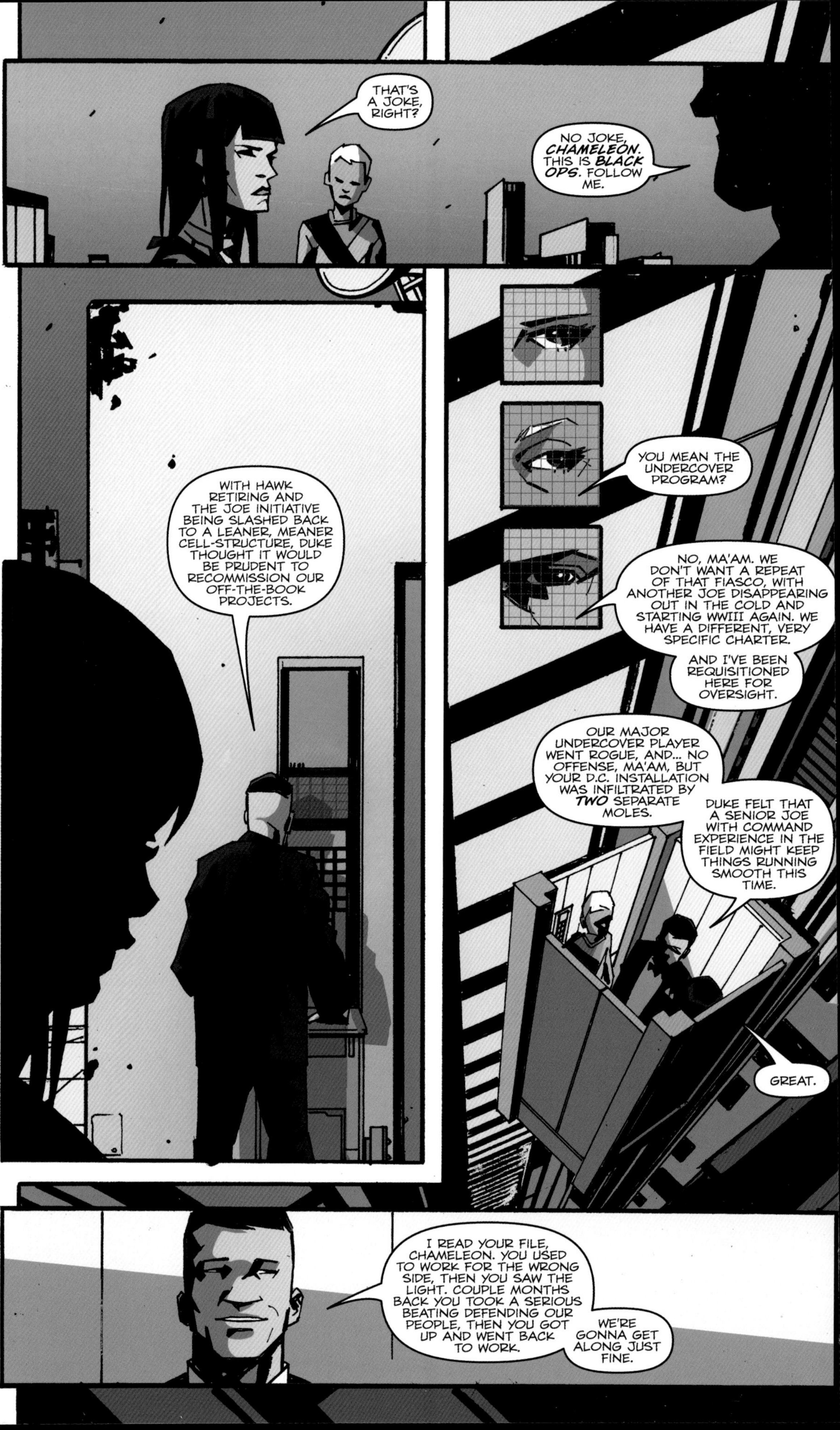
THAT'S A JOKE, RIGHT?
NO JOKE, CHAMELEON. THIS IS BLACK OPS. FOLLOW ME.
WITH HAWK RETIRING AND THE JOE INITIATIVE BEING SLASHED BACK TO A LEANER, MEANER CELL-STRUCTURE, DUKE THOUGHT IT WOULD BE PRUDENT TO RECOMMISSION OUR OFF-THE-BOOK PROJECTS.
YOU MEAN THE UNDERCOVER PROGRAM?
NO, MA'AM. WE DON'T WANT A REPEAT OF THAT FIASCO, WITH ANOTHER JOE DISAPPEARING OUT IN THE COLD AND STARTING WWIII AGAIN. WE HAVE A DIFFERENT, VERY SPECIFIC CHARTER.
AND I'VE BEEN REQUISITIONED HERE FOR OVERSIGHT.
OUR MAJOR UNDERCOVER PLAYER WENT ROGUE, AND... NO OFFENSE, MA'AM, BUT YOUR D.C. INSTALLATION WAS INFILTRATED BY TWO SEPARATE MOLES.
DUKE FELT THAT A SENIOR JOE WITH COMMAND EXPERIENCE IN THE FIELD MIGHT KEEP THINGS RUNNING SMOOTH THIS TIME.
GREAT.
I READ YOUR FILE, CHAMELEON. YOU USED TO WORK FOR THE WRONG SIDE, THEN YOU SAW THE LIGHT. COUPLE MONTHS BACK YOU TOOK A SERIOUS BEATING DEFENDING OUR PEOPLE, THEN YOU GOT UP AND WENT BACK TO WORK.
WE'RE GONNA GET ALONG JUST FINE.

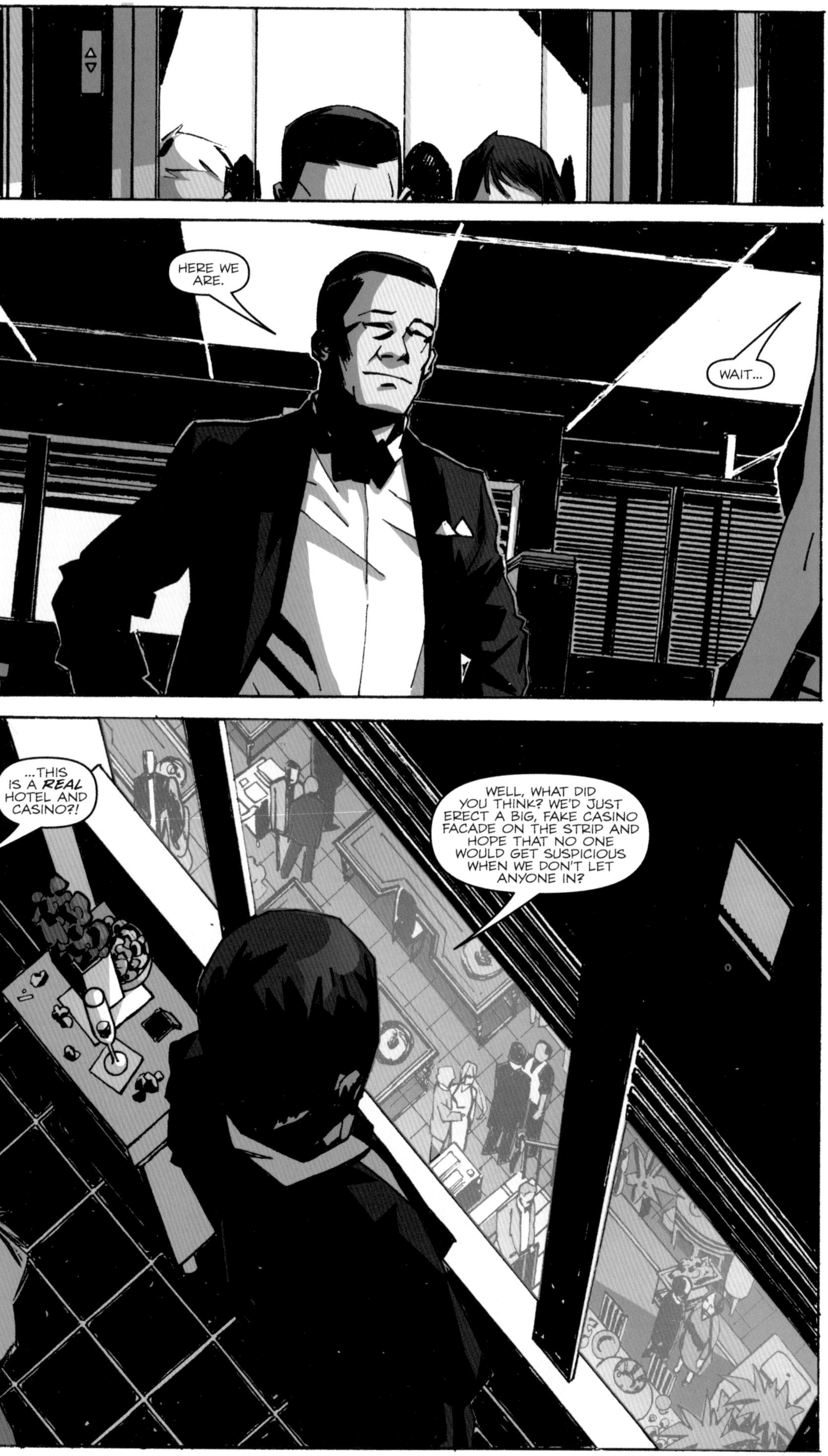
HERE WE ARE.
WAIT...
...THIS IS A ***REAL*** HOTEL AND CASINO?!
WELL, WHAT DID YOU THINK? WE'D JUST ERECT A BIG, FAKE CASINO FACADE ON THE STRIP AND HOPE THAT NO ONE WOULD GET SUSPICIOUS WHEN WE DON'T LET ANYONE IN?

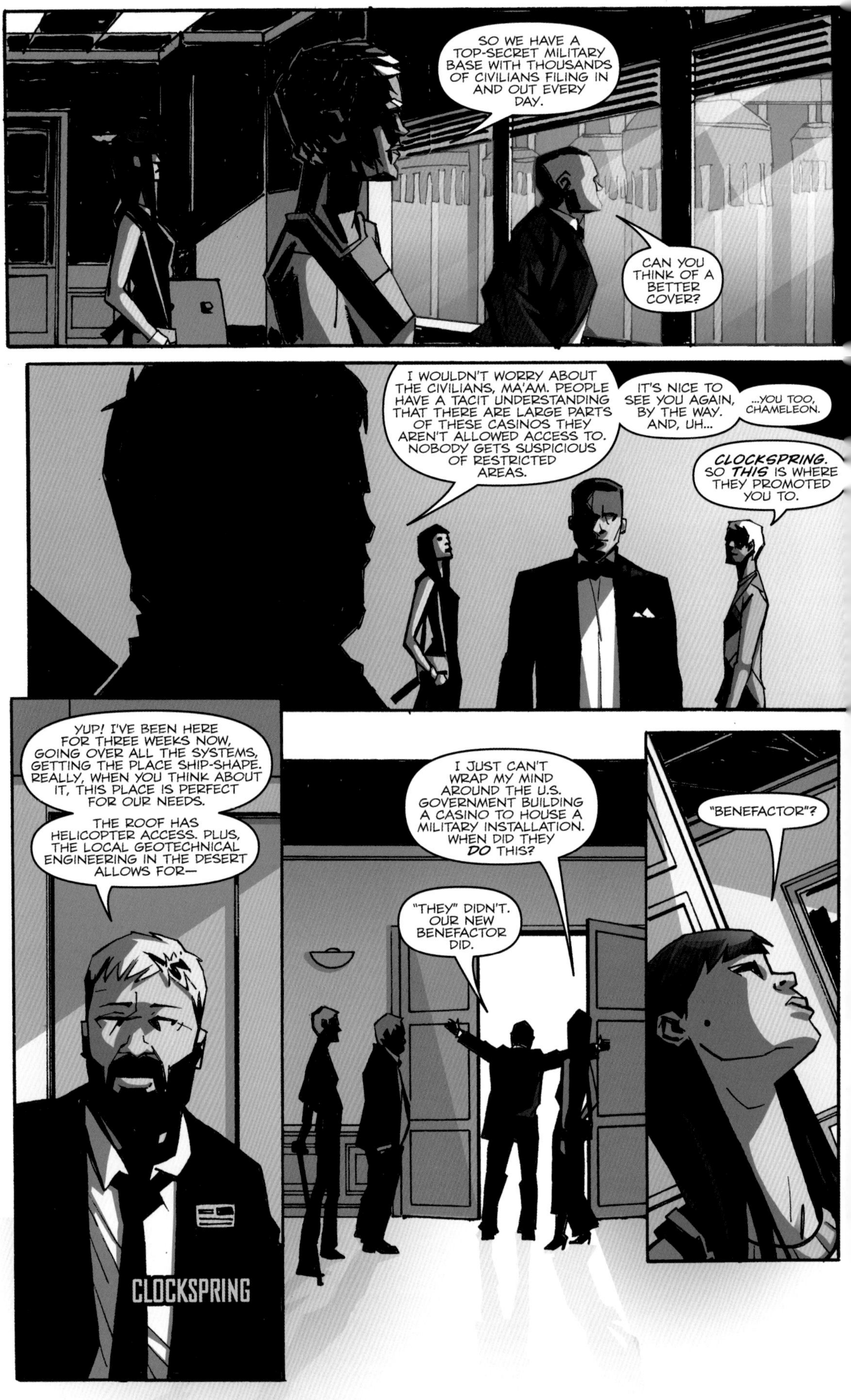

SO WE HAVE A TOP-SECRET MILITARY BASE WITH THOUSANDS OF CIVILIANS FILING IN AND OUT EVERY DAY.
CAN YOU THINK OF A BETTER COVER?
I WOULDN'T WORRY ABOUT THE CIVILIANS, MA'AM. PEOPLE HAVE A TACIT UNDERSTANDING THAT THERE ARE LARGE PARTS OF THESE CASINOS THEY AREN'T ALLOWED ACCESS TO. NOBODY GETS SUSPICIOUS OF RESTRICTED AREAS.
IT'S NICE TO SEE YOU AGAIN, BY THE WAY. AND, UH...
...YOU TOO, CHAMELEON.
CLOCKSPRING. SO THIS IS WHERE THEY PROMOTED YOU TO.
YUP! I'VE BEEN HERE FOR THREE WEEKS NOW, GOING OVER ALL THE SYSTEMS, GETTING THE PLACE SHIP-SHAPE. REALLY, WHEN YOU THINK ABOUT IT, THIS PLACE IS PERFECT FOR OUR NEEDS.
THE ROOF HAS HELICOPTER ACCESS. PLUS, THE LOCAL GEOTECHNICAL ENGINEERING IN THE DESERT ALLOWS FOR—
CLOCKSPRING
I JUST CAN'T WRAP MY MIND AROUND THE U.S. GOVERNMENT BUILDING A CASINO TO HOUSE A MILITARY INSTALLATION. WHEN DID THEY DO THIS?
"THEY" DIDN'T. OUR NEW BENEFACTOR DID.
"BENEFACTOR"?

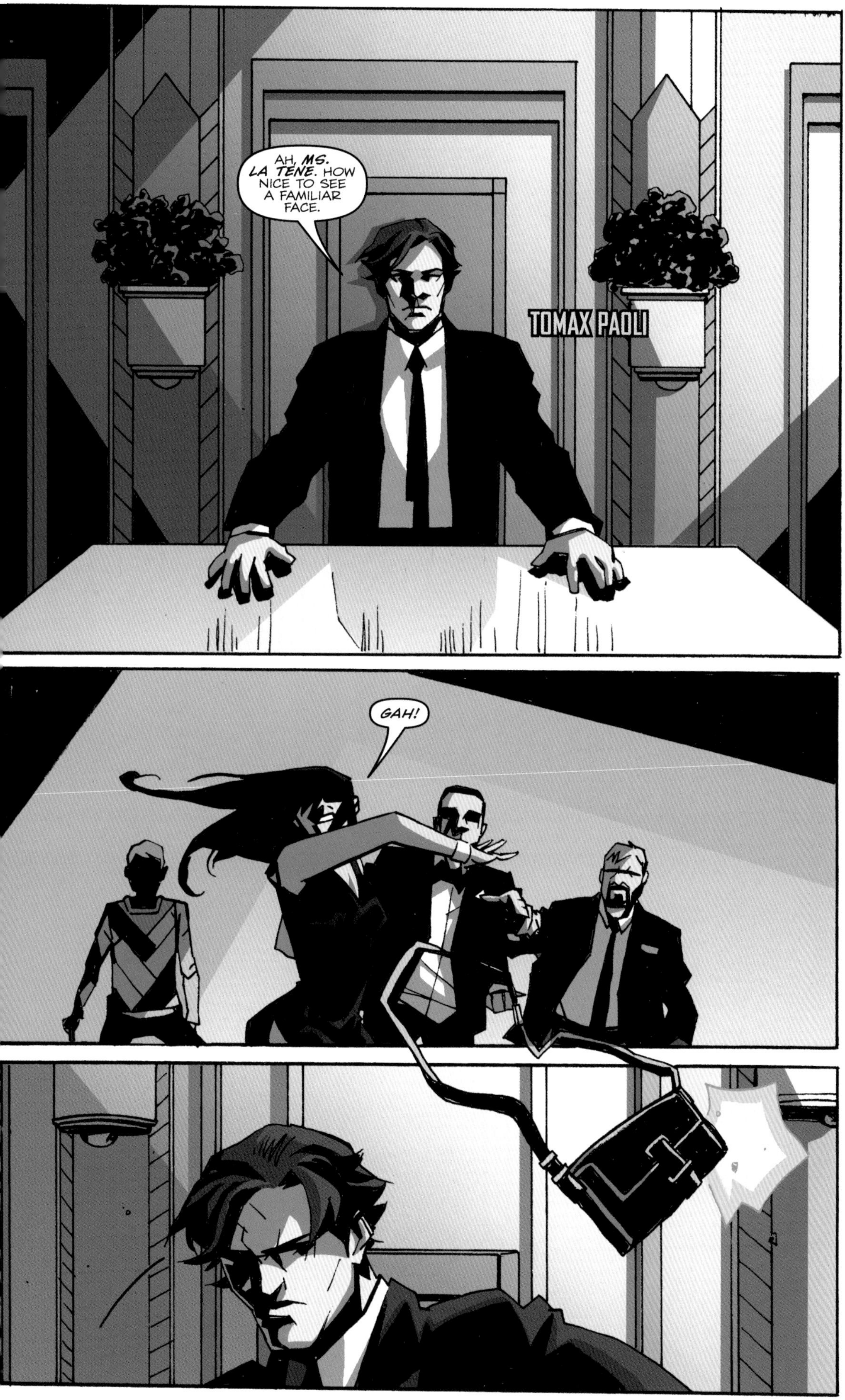
AH, MS. LA TENE. HOW NICE TO SEE A FAMILIAR FACE.
TOMAX PAOLI
GAH!

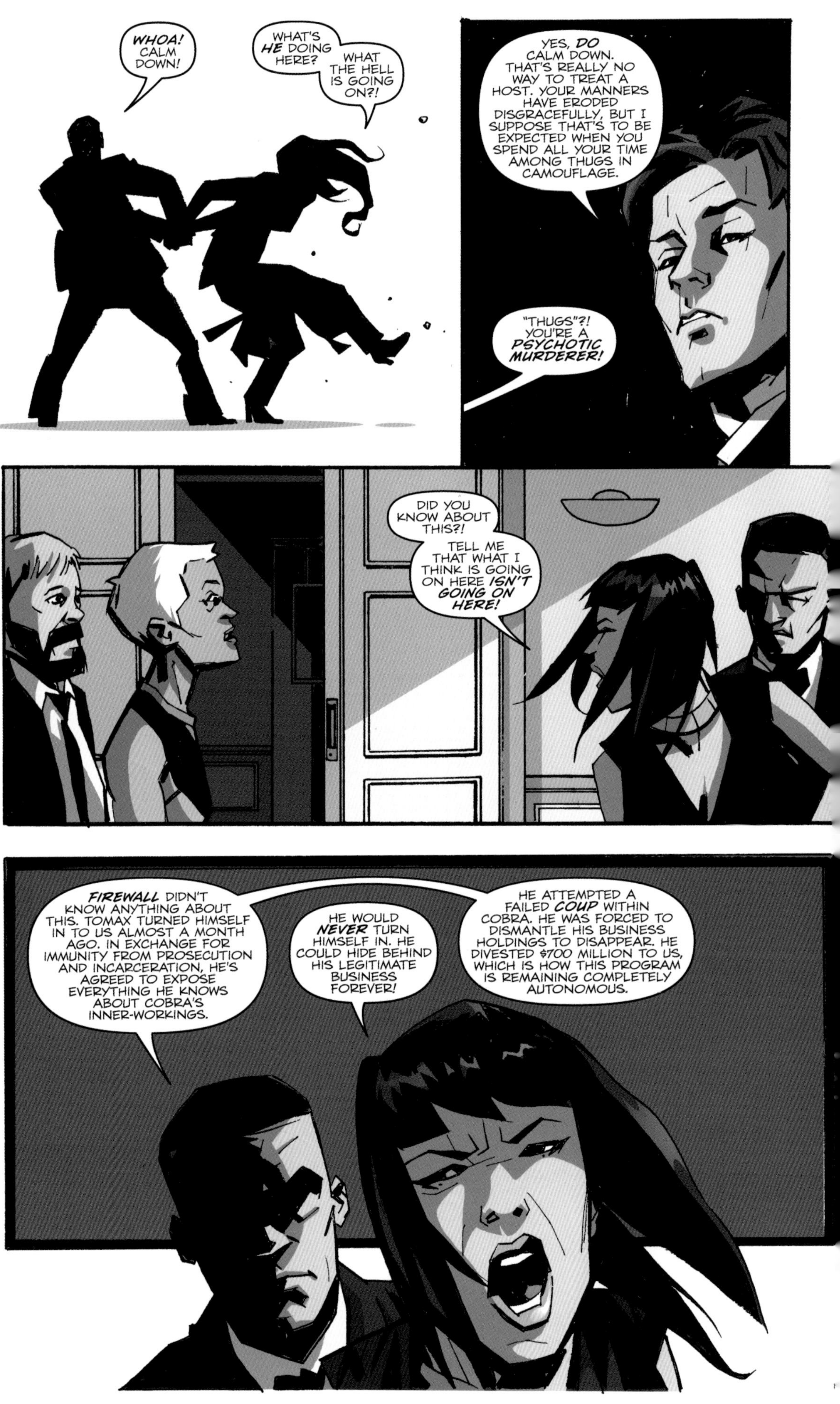
WHOA! CALM DOWN!
WHAT'S HE DOING HERE?
WHAT THE HELL IS GOING ON?!
YES, DO CALM DOWN. THAT'S REALLY NO WAY TO TREAT A HOST. YOUR MANNERS HAVE ERODED DISGRACEFULLY, BUT I SUPPOSE THAT'S TO BE EXPECTED WHEN YOU SPEND ALL YOUR TIME AMONG THUGS IN CAMOUFLAGE.
"THUGS"?! YOU'RE A PSYCHOTIC MURDERER!
DID YOU KNOW ABOUT THIS?!
TELL ME THAT WHAT I THINK IS GOING ON HERE ISN'T GOING ON HERE!
FIREWALL DIDN'T KNOW ANYTHING ABOUT THIS. TOMAX TURNED HIMSELF IN TO US ALMOST A MONTH AGO. IN EXCHANGE FOR IMMUNITY FROM PROSECUTION AND INCARCERATION, HE'S AGREED TO EXPOSE EVERYTHING HE KNOWS ABOUT COBRA'S INNER-WORKINGS.
HE WOULD NEVER TURN HIMSELF IN. HE COULD HIDE BEHIND HIS LEGITIMATE BUSINESS FOREVER!
HE ATTEMPTED A FAILED COUP WITHIN COBRA. HE WAS FORCED TO DISMANTLE HIS BUSINESS HOLDINGS TO DISAPPEAR. HE DIVESTED $700 MILLION TO US, WHICH IS HOW THIS PROGRAM IS REMAINING COMPLETELY AUTONOMOUS.

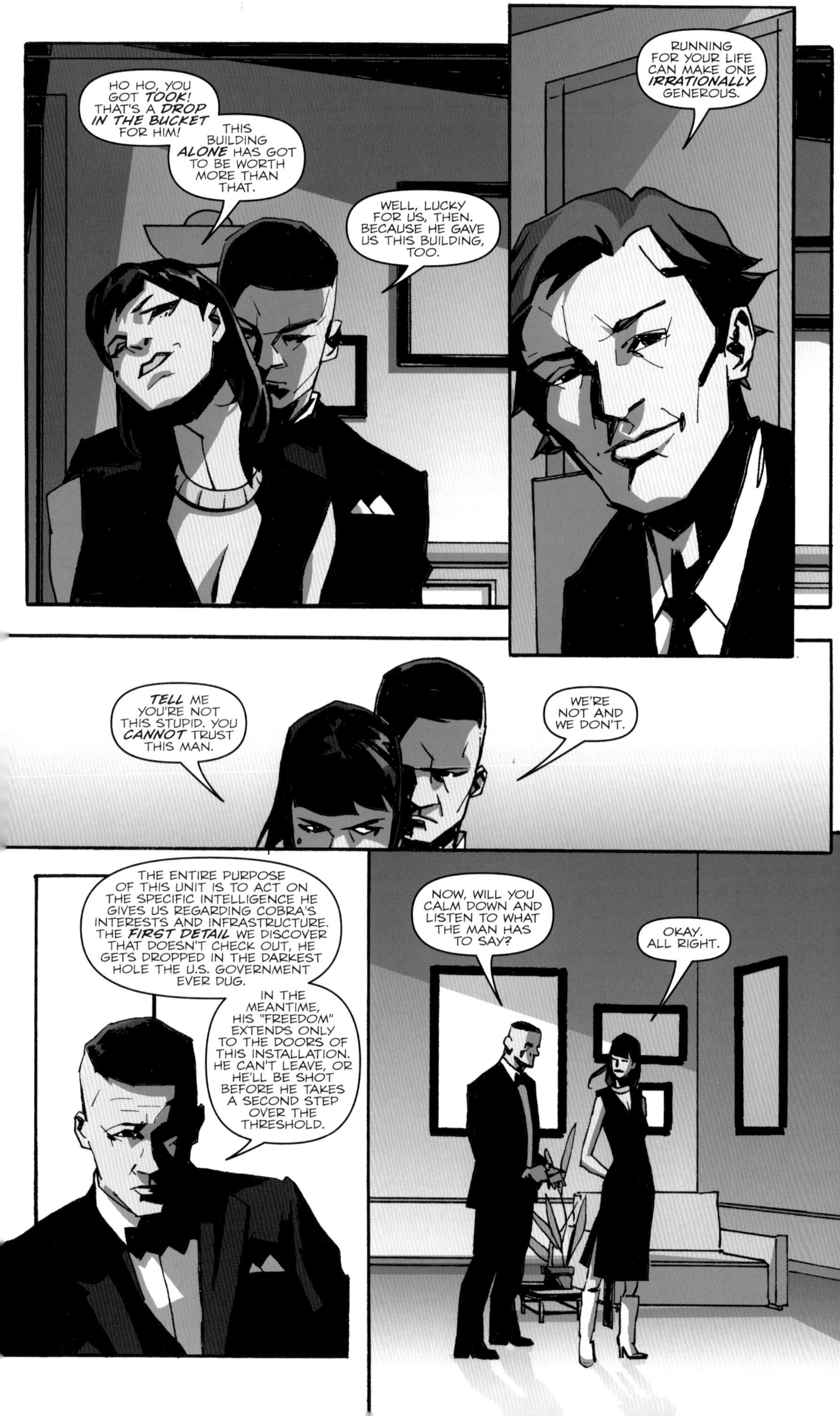
HO HO, YOU GOT TOOK! THAT'S A DROP IN THE BUCKET FOR HIM!
THIS BUILDING ALONE HAS GOT TO BE WORTH MORE THAN THAT.
WELL, LUCKY FOR US, THEN. BECAUSE HE GAVE US THIS BUILDING, TOO.
RUNNING FOR YOUR LIFE CAN MAKE ONE IRRATIONALLY GENEROUS.
TELL ME YOU'RE NOT THIS STUPID. YOU CANNOT TRUST THIS MAN.
WE'RE NOT AND WE DON'T.
THE ENTIRE PURPOSE OF THIS UNIT IS TO ACT ON THE SPECIFIC INTELLIGENCE HE GIVES US REGARDING COBRA'S INTERESTS AND INFRASTRUCTURE. THE FIRST DETAIL WE DISCOVER THAT DOESN'T CHECK OUT, HE GETS DROPPED IN THE DARKEST HOLE THE U.S. GOVERNMENT EVER DUG.
IN THE MEANTIME, HIS "FREEDOM" EXTENDS ONLY TO THE DOORS OF THIS INSTALLATION. HE CAN'T LEAVE, OR HE'LL BE SHOT BEFORE HE TAKES A SECOND STEP OVER THE THRESHOLD.
NOW, WILL YOU CALM DOWN AND LISTEN TO WHAT THE MAN HAS TO SAY?
OKAY. ALL RIGHT.

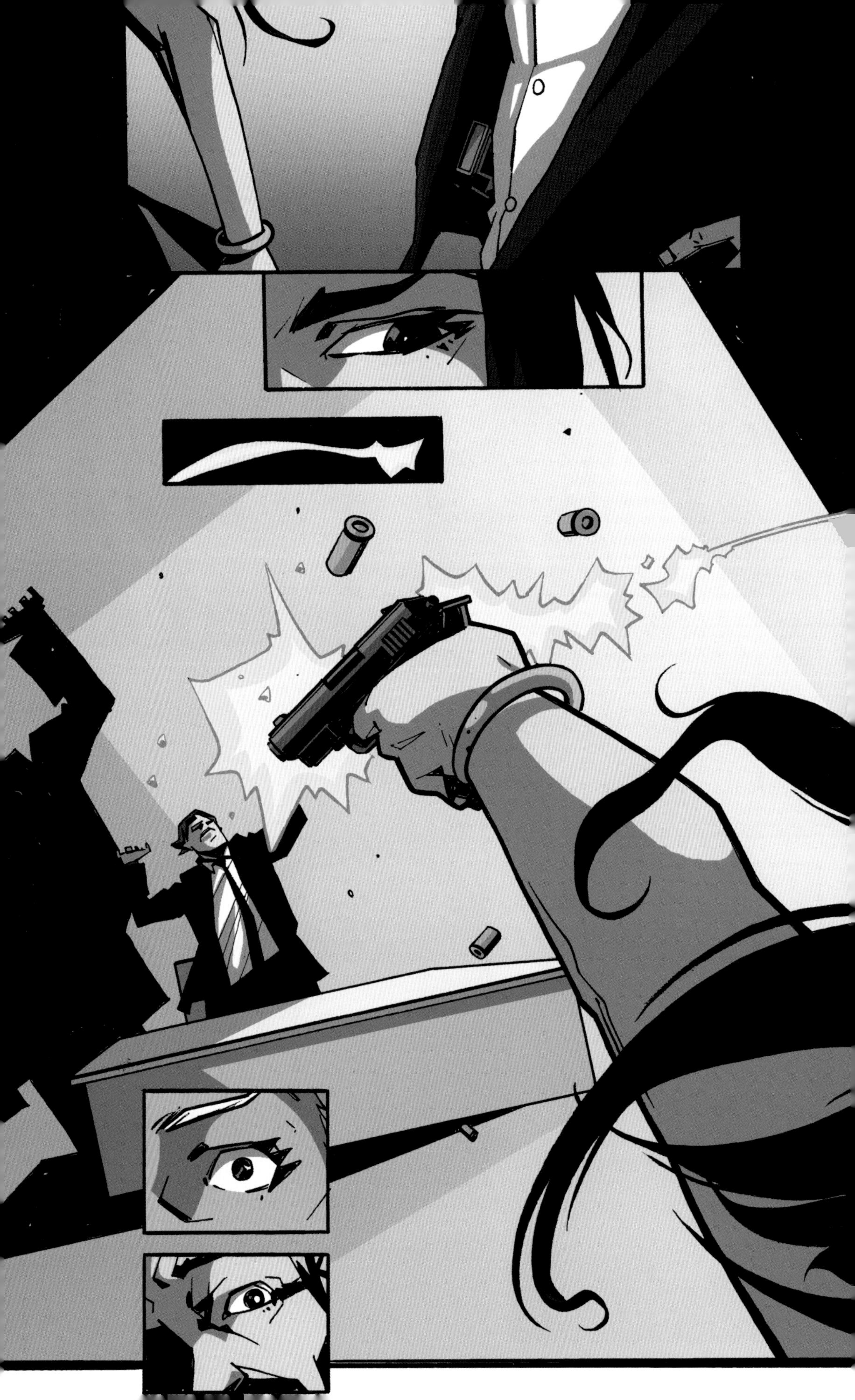

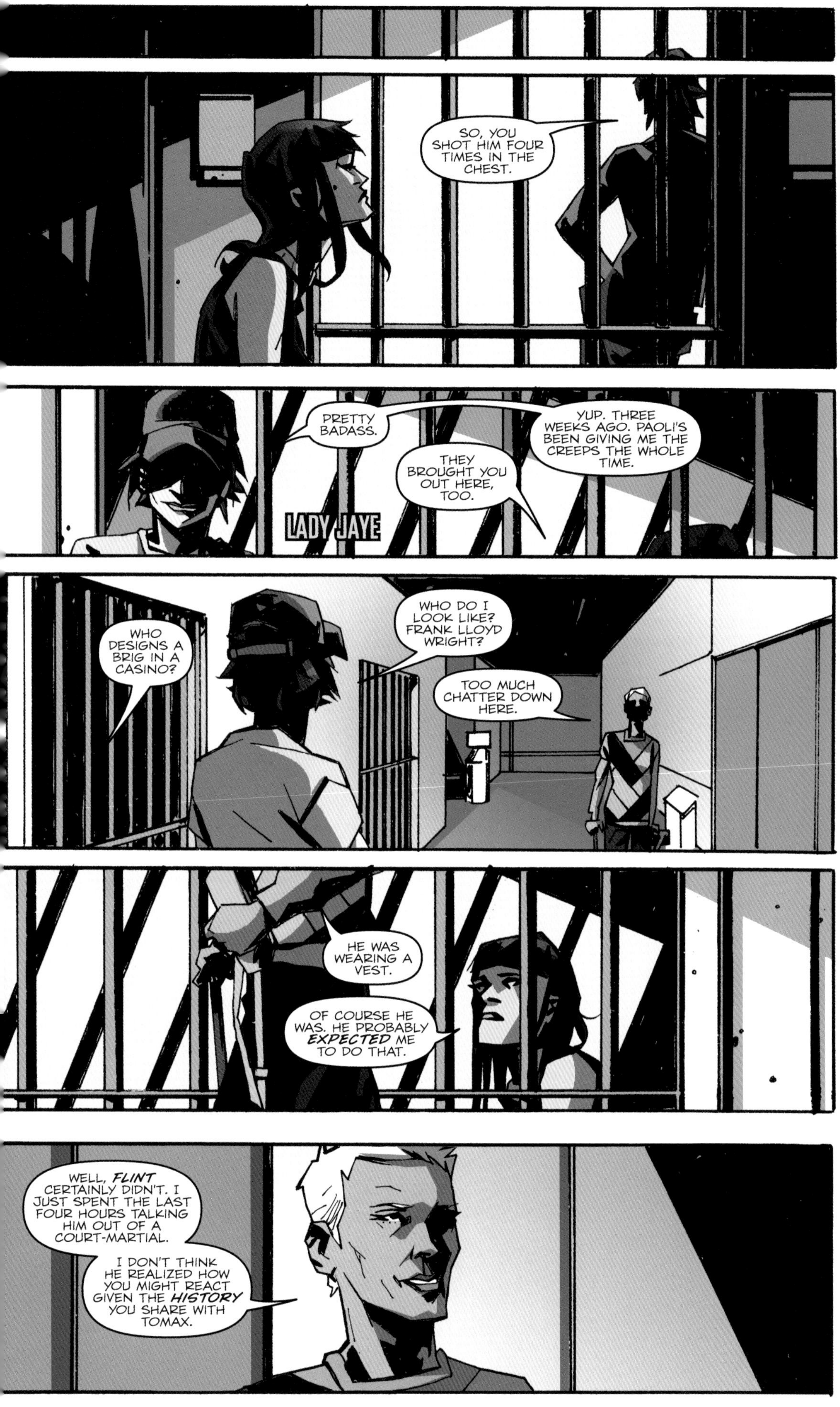
SO, YOU SHOT HIM FOUR TIMES IN THE CHEST.
PRETTY BADASS.
YUP. THREE WEEKS AGO. PAOLI'S BEEN GIVING ME THE CREEPS THE WHOLE TIME.
THEY BROUGHT YOU OUT HERE, TOO.
LADY JAYE
WHO DESIGNS A BRIG IN A CASINO?
WHO DO I LOOK LIKE? FRANK LLOYD WRIGHT?
TOO MUCH CHATTER DOWN HERE.
HE WAS WEARING A VEST.
OF COURSE HE WAS. HE PROBABLY EXPECTED ME TO DO THAT.
WELL, FLINT CERTAINLY DIDN'T. I JUST SPENT THE LAST FOUR HOURS TALKING HIM OUT OF A COURT-MARTIAL.
I DON'T THINK HE REALIZED HOW YOU MIGHT REACT GIVEN THE HISTORY YOU SHARE WITH TOMAX.

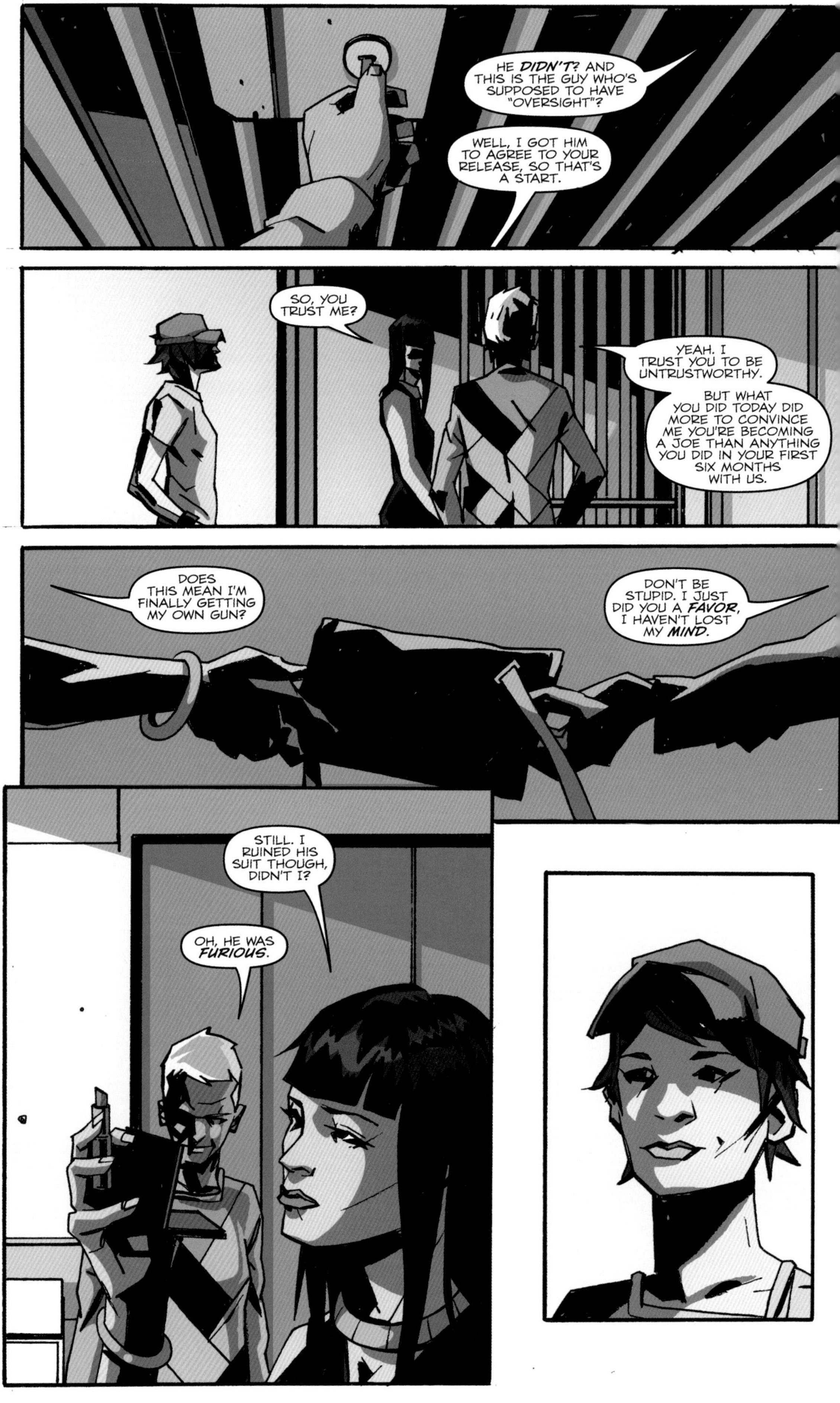
HE DIDN'T? AND THIS IS THE GUY WHO'S SUPPOSED TO HAVE "OVERSIGHT"?
WELL, I GOT HIM TO AGREE TO YOUR RELEASE, SO THAT'S A START.
SO, YOU TRUST ME?
YEAH. I TRUST YOU TO BE UNTRUSTWORTHY.
BUT WHAT YOU DID TODAY DID MORE TO CONVINCE ME YOU'RE BECOMING A JOE THAN ANYTHING YOU DID IN YOUR FIRST SIX MONTHS WITH US.
DOES THIS MEAN I'M FINALLY GETTING MY OWN GUN?
DON'T BE STUPID. I JUST DID YOU A FAVOR, I HAVEN'T LOST MY MIND.
STILL. I RUINED HIS SUIT THOUGH, DIDN'T I?
OH, HE WAS FURIOUS.

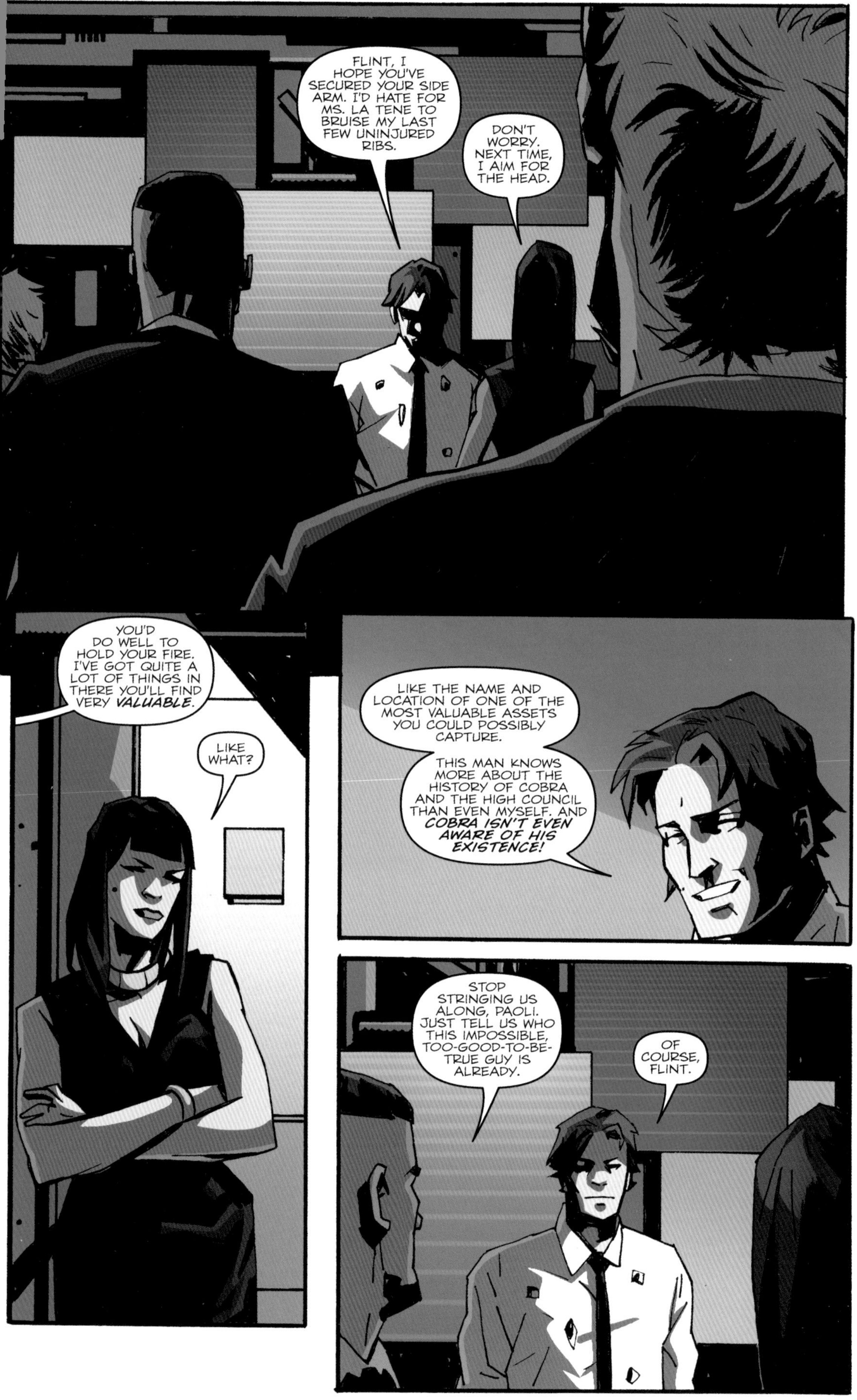
FLINT, I HOPE YOU'VE SECURED YOUR SIDE ARM. I'D HATE FOR MS. LA TENE TO BRUISE MY LAST FEW UNINJURED RIBS.
DON'T WORRY. NEXT TIME, I AIM FOR THE HEAD.
YOU'D DO WELL TO HOLD YOUR FIRE. I'VE GOT QUITE A LOT OF THINGS IN THERE YOU'LL FIND VERY VALUABLE.
LIKE WHAT?
LIKE THE NAME AND LOCATION OF ONE OF THE MOST VALUABLE ASSETS YOU COULD POSSIBLY CAPTURE.
THIS MAN KNOWS MORE ABOUT THE HISTORY OF COBRA AND THE HIGH COUNCIL THAN EVEN MYSELF. AND COBRA ISN'T EVEN AWARE OF HIS EXISTENCE!
STOP STRINGING US ALONG, PAOLI. JUST TELL US WHO THIS IMPOSSIBLE, TOO-GOOD-TO-BE-TRUE GUY IS ALREADY.
OF COURSE, FLINT.

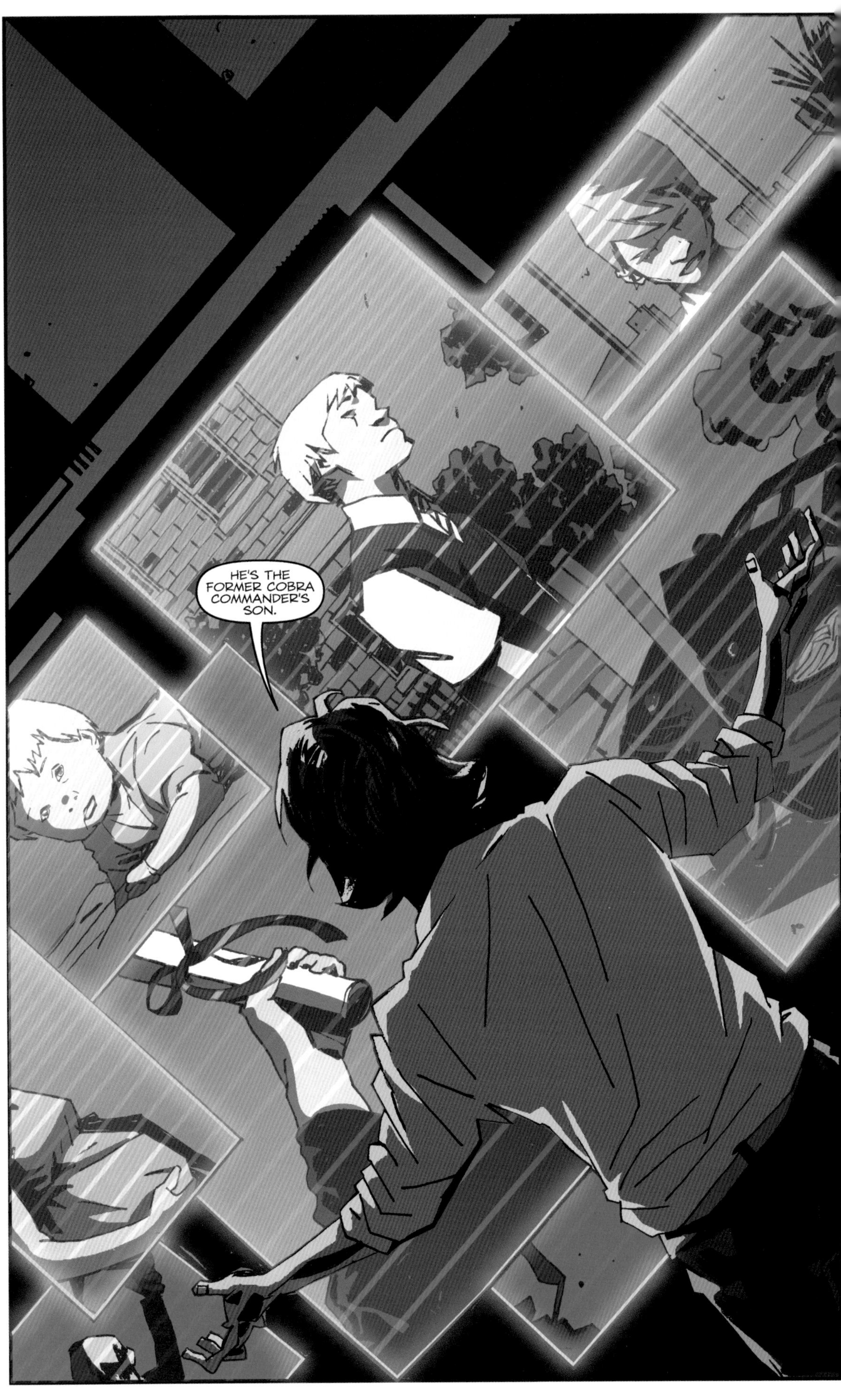
HE'S THE FORMER COBRA COMMANDER'S SON.

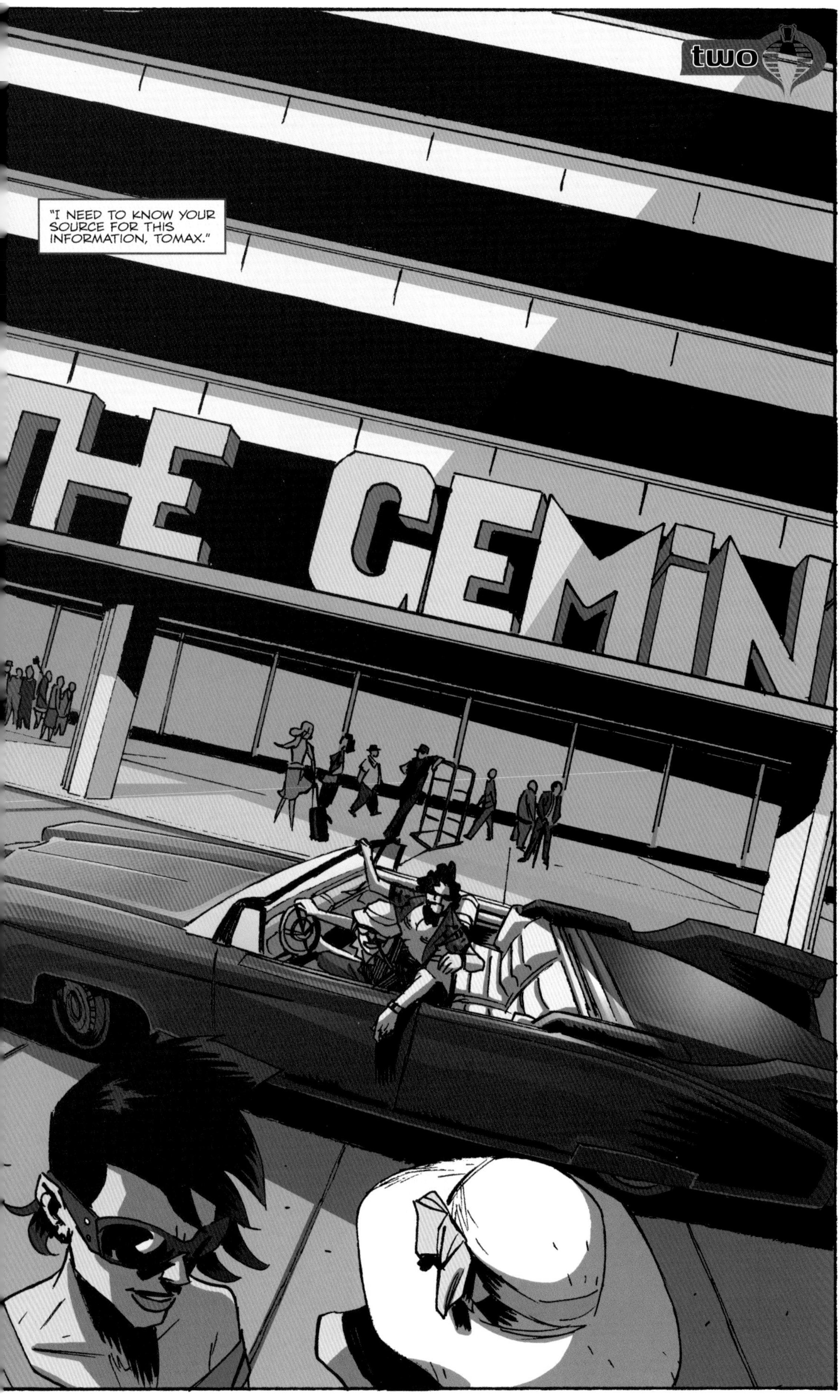
two
"I NEED TO KNOW YOUR SOURCE FOR THIS INFORMATION, TOMAX."

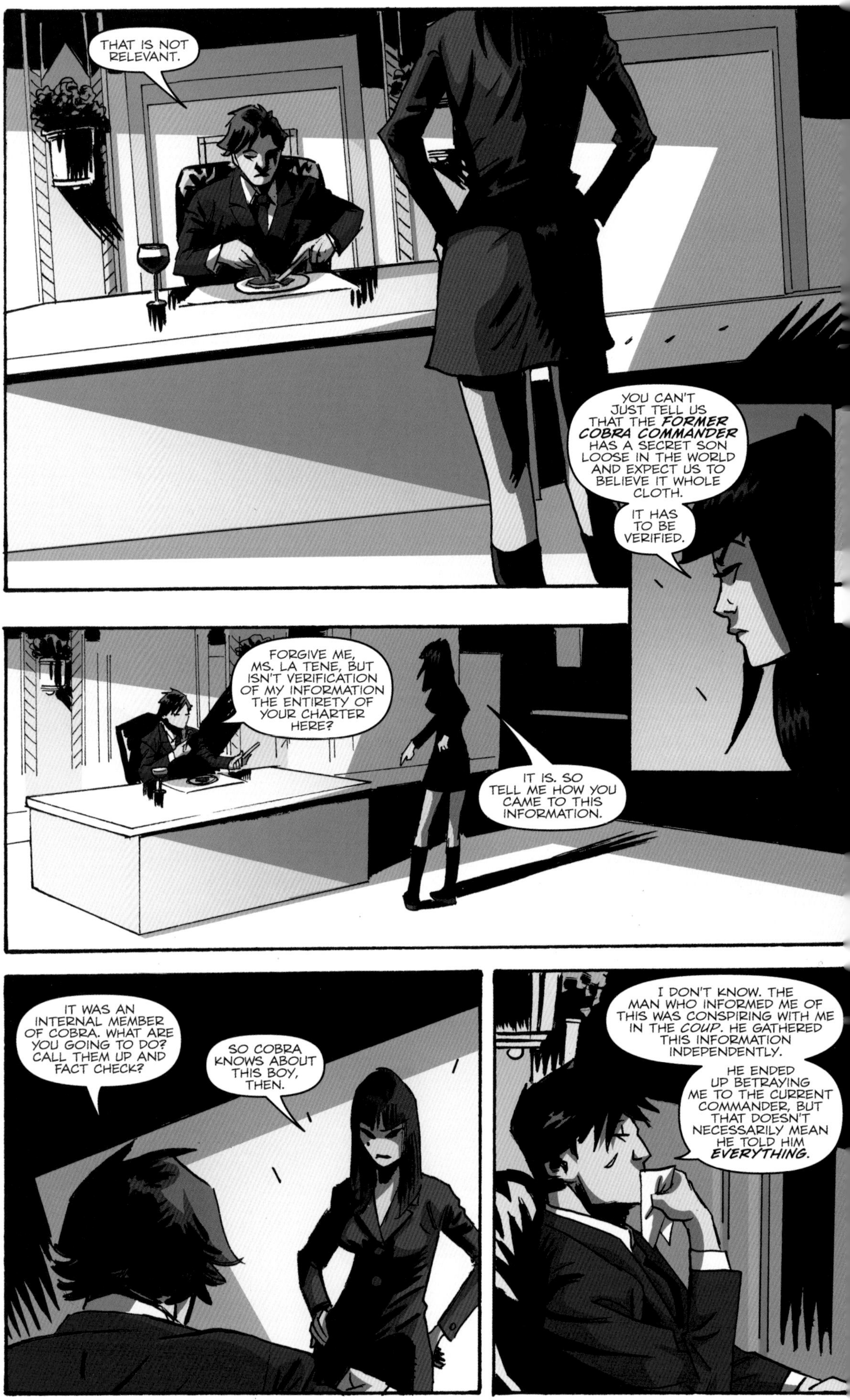
THAT IS NOT RELEVANT.
YOU CAN'T JUST TELL US THAT THE FORMER COBRA COMMANDER HAS A SECRET SON LOOSE IN THE WORLD AND EXPECT US TO BELIEVE IT WHOLE CLOTH.
IT HAS TO BE VERIFIED.
FORGIVE ME, MS. LA TENE, BUT ISN'T VERIFICATION OF MY INFORMATION THE ENTIRETY OF YOUR CHARTER HERE?
IT IS. SO TELL ME HOW YOU CAME TO THIS INFORMATION.
IT WAS AN INTERNAL MEMBER OF COBRA. WHAT ARE YOU GOING TO DO? CALL THEM UP AND FACT CHECK?
SO COBRA KNOWS ABOUT THIS BOY, THEN.
I DON'T KNOW. THE MAN WHO INFORMED ME OF THIS WAS CONSPIRING WITH ME IN THE COUP. HE GATHERED THIS INFORMATION INDEPENDENTLY.
HE ENDED UP BETRAYING ME TO THE CURRENT COMMANDER, BUT THAT DOESN'T NECESSARILY MEAN HE TOLD HIM EVERYTHING.

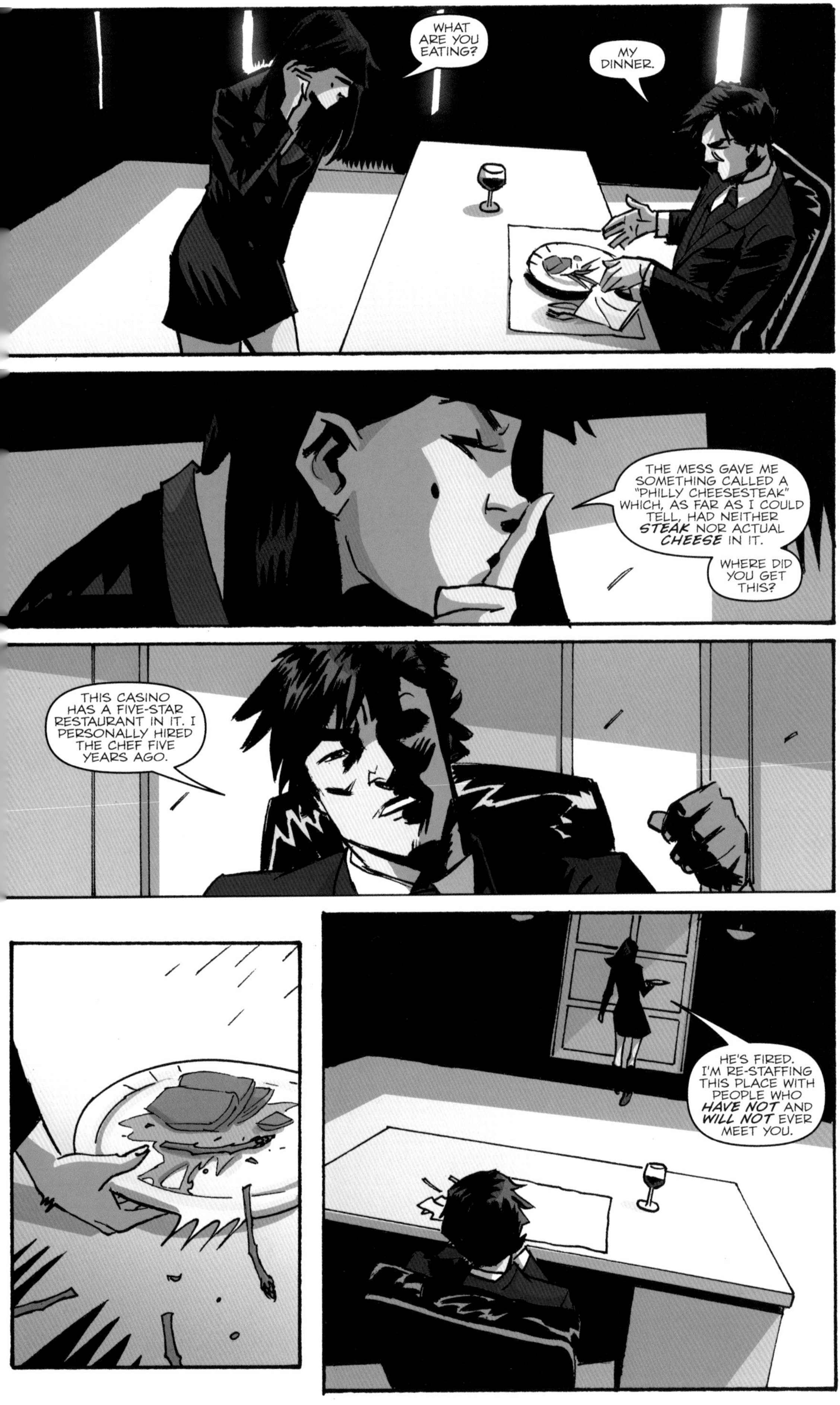
WHAT ARE YOU EATING?
MY DINNER.
THE MESS GAVE ME SOMETHING CALLED A "PHILLY CHEESESTEAK" WHICH, AS FAR AS I COULD TELL, HAD NEITHER ***STEAK*** NOR ACTUAL ***CHEESE*** IN IT.
WHERE DID YOU GET THIS?
THIS CASINO HAS A FIVE-STAR RESTAURANT IN IT. I PERSONALLY HIRED THE CHEF FIVE YEARS AGO.
HE'S FIRED. I'M RE-STAFFING THIS PLACE WITH PEOPLE WHO ***HAVE NOT*** AND ***WILL NOT*** EVER MEET YOU.

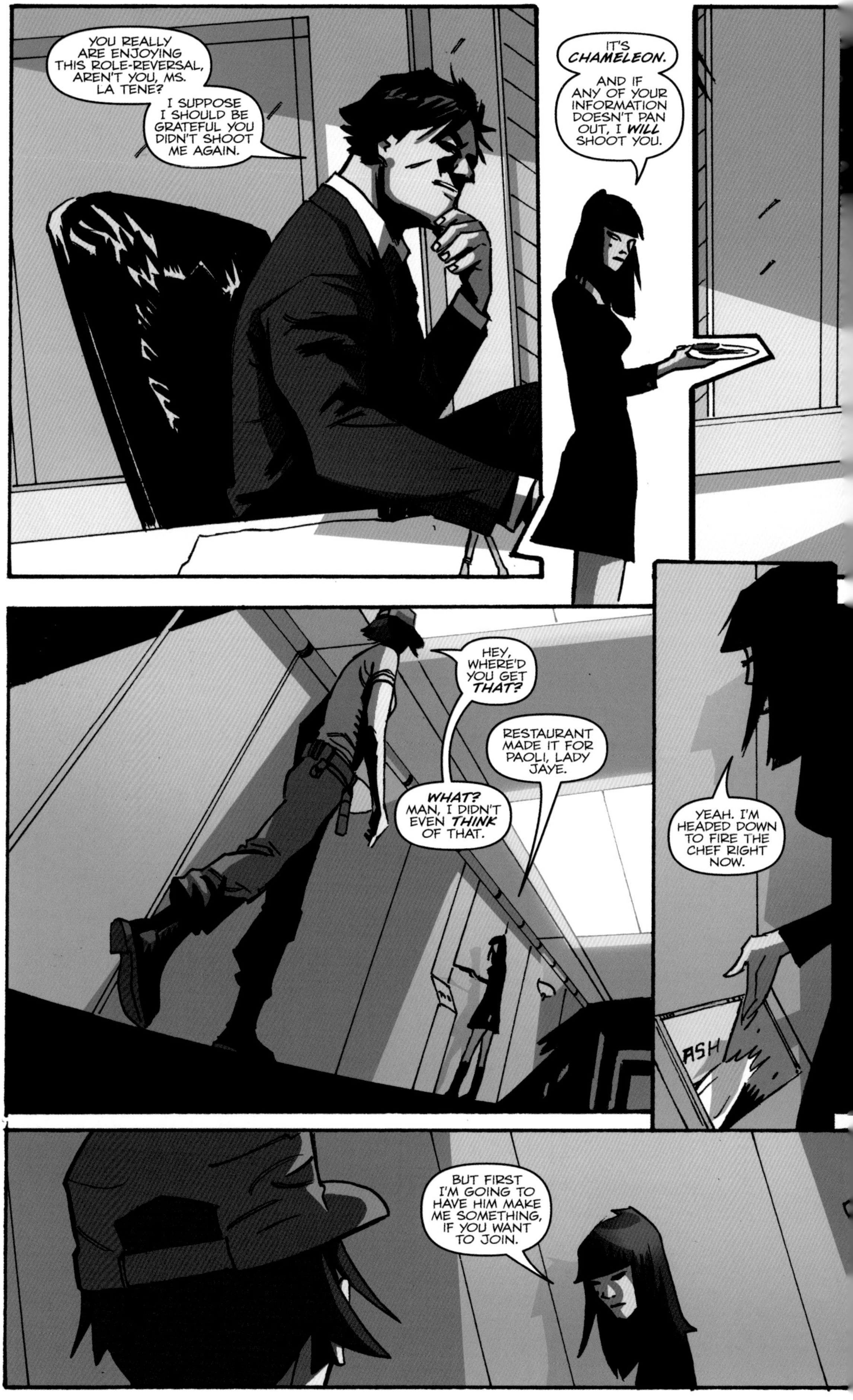
YOU REALLY ARE ENJOYING THIS ROLE-REVERSAL, AREN'T YOU, MS. LA TENE?
I SUPPOSE I SHOULD BE GRATEFUL YOU DIDN'T SHOOT ME AGAIN.
IT'S ***CHAMELEON.***
AND IF ANY OF YOUR INFORMATION DOESN'T PAN OUT, I ***WILL*** SHOOT YOU.
HEY, WHERE'D YOU GET ***THAT?***
RESTAURANT MADE IT FOR PAOLI, LADY JAYE.
WHAT? MAN, I DIDN'T EVEN ***THINK*** OF THAT.
ASH
YEAH. I'M HEADED DOWN TO FIRE THE CHEF RIGHT NOW.
BUT FIRST I'M GOING TO HAVE HIM MAKE ME SOMETHING, IF YOU WANT TO JOIN.

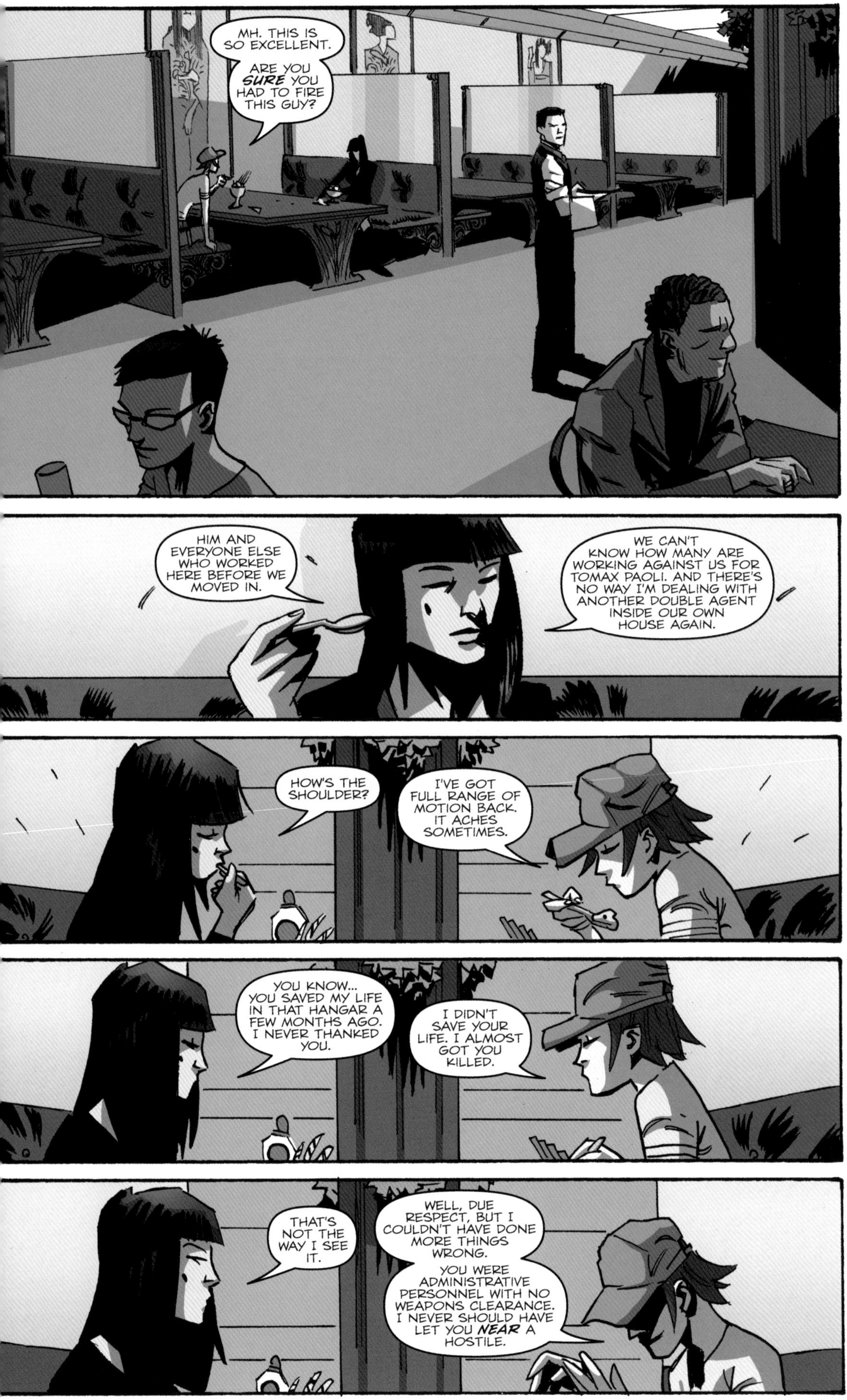
MH. THIS IS SO EXCELLENT.
ARE YOU *SURE* YOU HAD TO FIRE THIS GUY?
HIM AND EVERYONE ELSE WHO WORKED HERE BEFORE WE MOVED IN.
WE CAN'T KNOW HOW MANY ARE WORKING AGAINST US FOR TOMAX PAOLI. AND THERE'S NO WAY I'M DEALING WITH ANOTHER DOUBLE AGENT INSIDE OUR OWN HOUSE AGAIN.
HOW'S THE SHOULDER?
I'VE GOT FULL RANGE OF MOTION BACK. IT ACHES SOMETIMES.
YOU KNOW... YOU SAVED MY LIFE IN THAT HANGAR A FEW MONTHS AGO. I NEVER THANKED YOU.
I DIDN'T SAVE YOUR LIFE. I ALMOST GOT YOU KILLED.
THAT'S NOT THE WAY I SEE IT.
WELL, DUE RESPECT, BUT I COULDN'T HAVE DONE MORE THINGS WRONG.
YOU WERE ADMINISTRATIVE PERSONNEL WITH NO WEAPONS CLEARANCE. I NEVER SHOULD HAVE LET YOU *NEAR* A HOSTILE.

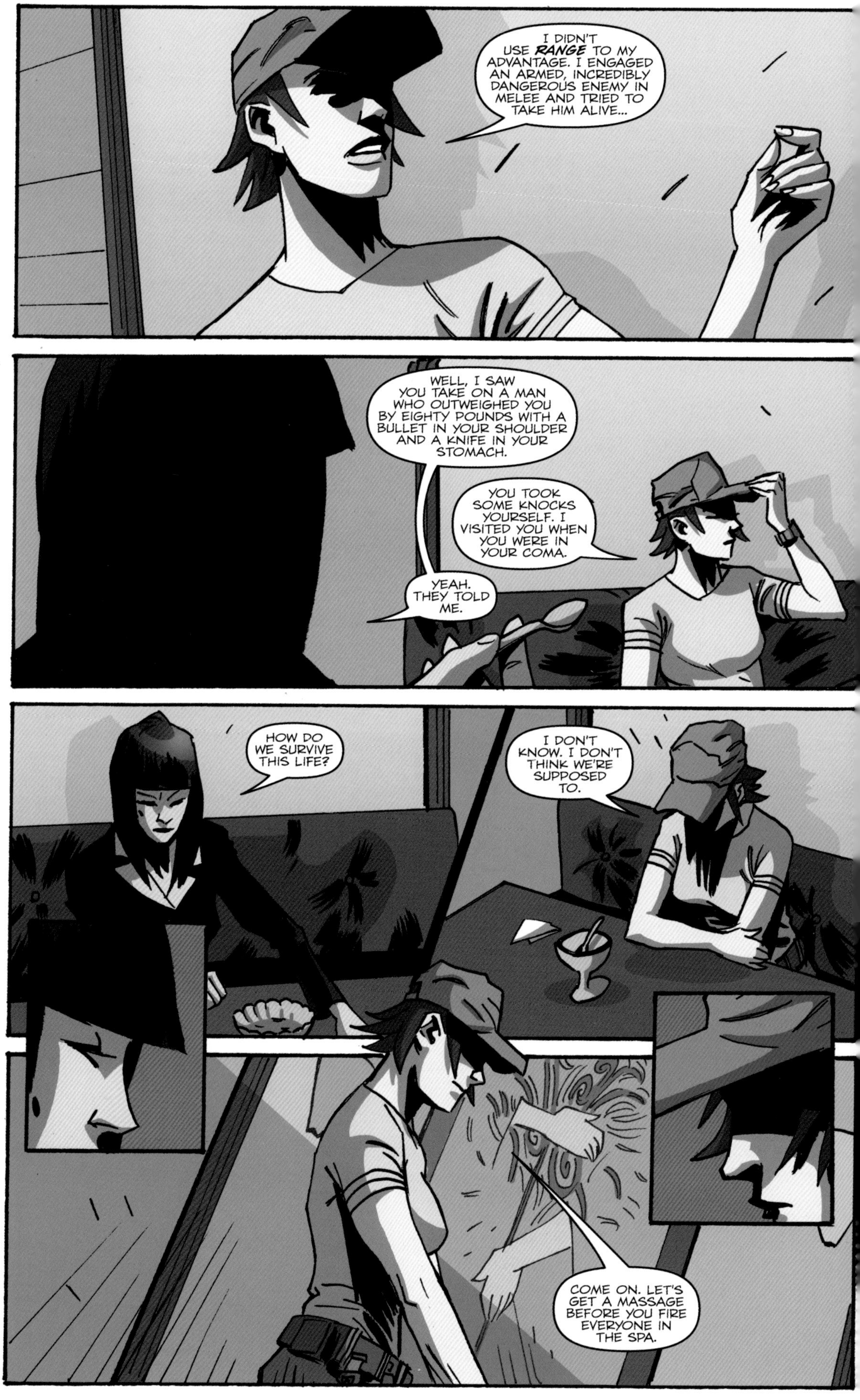
I DIDN'T USE *RANGE* TO MY ADVANTAGE. I ENGAGED AN ARMED, INCREDIBLY DANGEROUS ENEMY IN MELEE AND TRIED TO TAKE HIM ALIVE...
WELL, I SAW YOU TAKE ON A MAN WHO OUTWEIGHED YOU BY EIGHTY POUNDS WITH A BULLET IN YOUR SHOULDER AND A KNIFE IN YOUR STOMACH.
YOU TOOK SOME KNOCKS YOURSELF. I VISITED YOU WHEN YOU WERE IN YOUR COMA.
YEAH. THEY TOLD ME.
HOW DO WE SURVIVE THIS LIFE?
I DON'T KNOW. I DON'T THINK WE'RE SUPPOSED TO.
COME ON. LET'S GET A MASSAGE BEFORE YOU FIRE EVERYONE IN THE SPA.

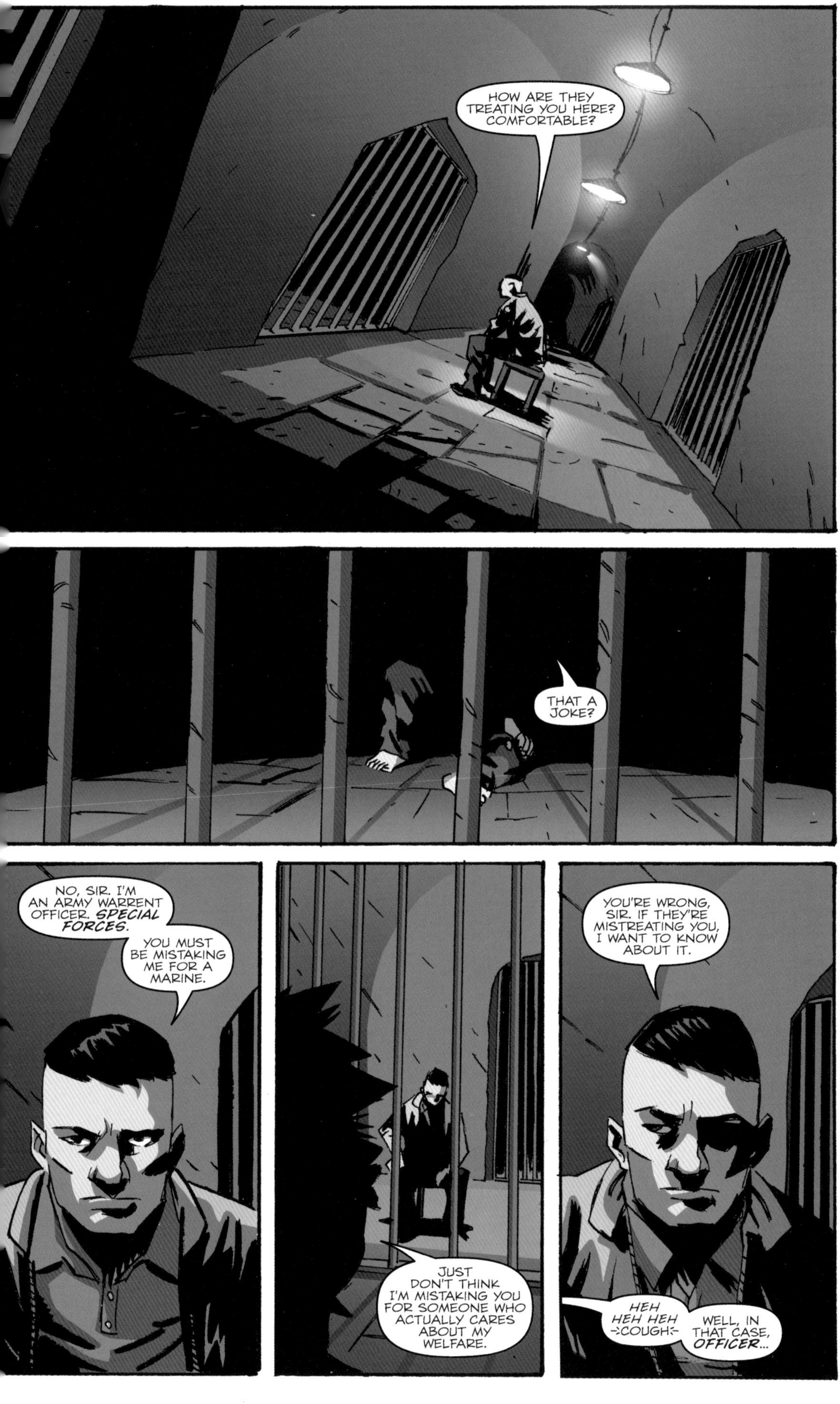
HOW ARE THEY TREATING YOU HERE? COMFORTABLE?
THAT A JOKE?
NO, SIR. I'M AN ARMY WARRENT OFFICER. *SPECIAL FORCES.*
YOU MUST BE MISTAKING ME FOR A MARINE.
JUST DON'T THINK I'M MISTAKING YOU FOR SOMEONE WHO ACTUALLY CARES ABOUT MY WELFARE.
YOU'RE WRONG, SIR. IF THEY'RE MISTREATING YOU, I WANT TO KNOW ABOUT IT.
HEH HEH HEH -:COUGH:-
WELL, IN THAT CASE, *OFFICER*...

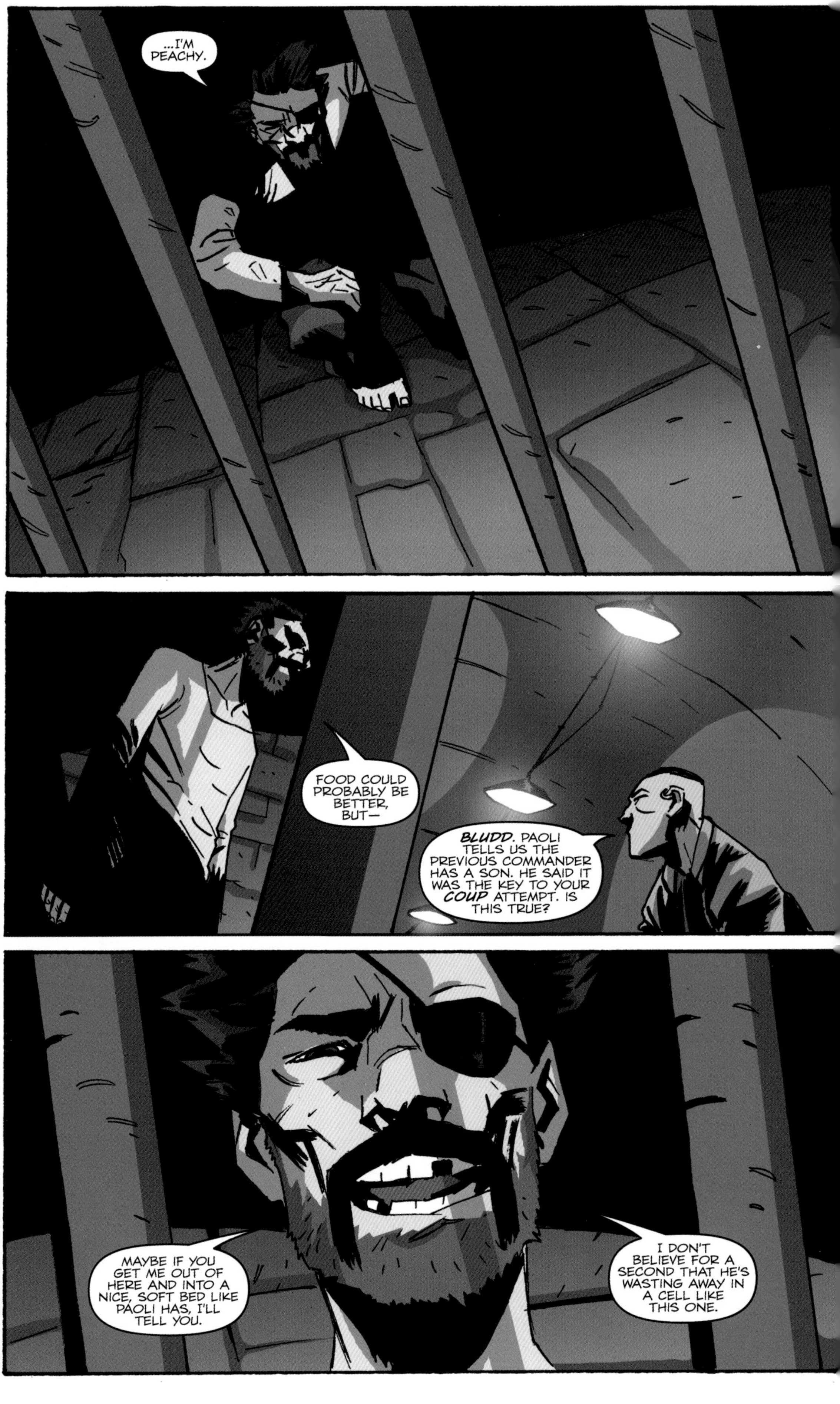
...I'M PEACHY.
FOOD COULD PROBABLY BE BETTER, BUT—
BLUDD. PAOLI TELLS US THE PREVIOUS COMMANDER HAS A SON. HE SAID IT WAS THE KEY TO YOUR COUP ATTEMPT. IS THIS TRUE?
MAYBE IF YOU GET ME OUT OF HERE AND INTO A NICE, SOFT BED LIKE PAOLI HAS, I'LL TELL YOU.
I DON'T BELIEVE FOR A SECOND THAT HE'S WASTING AWAY IN A CELL LIKE THIS ONE.

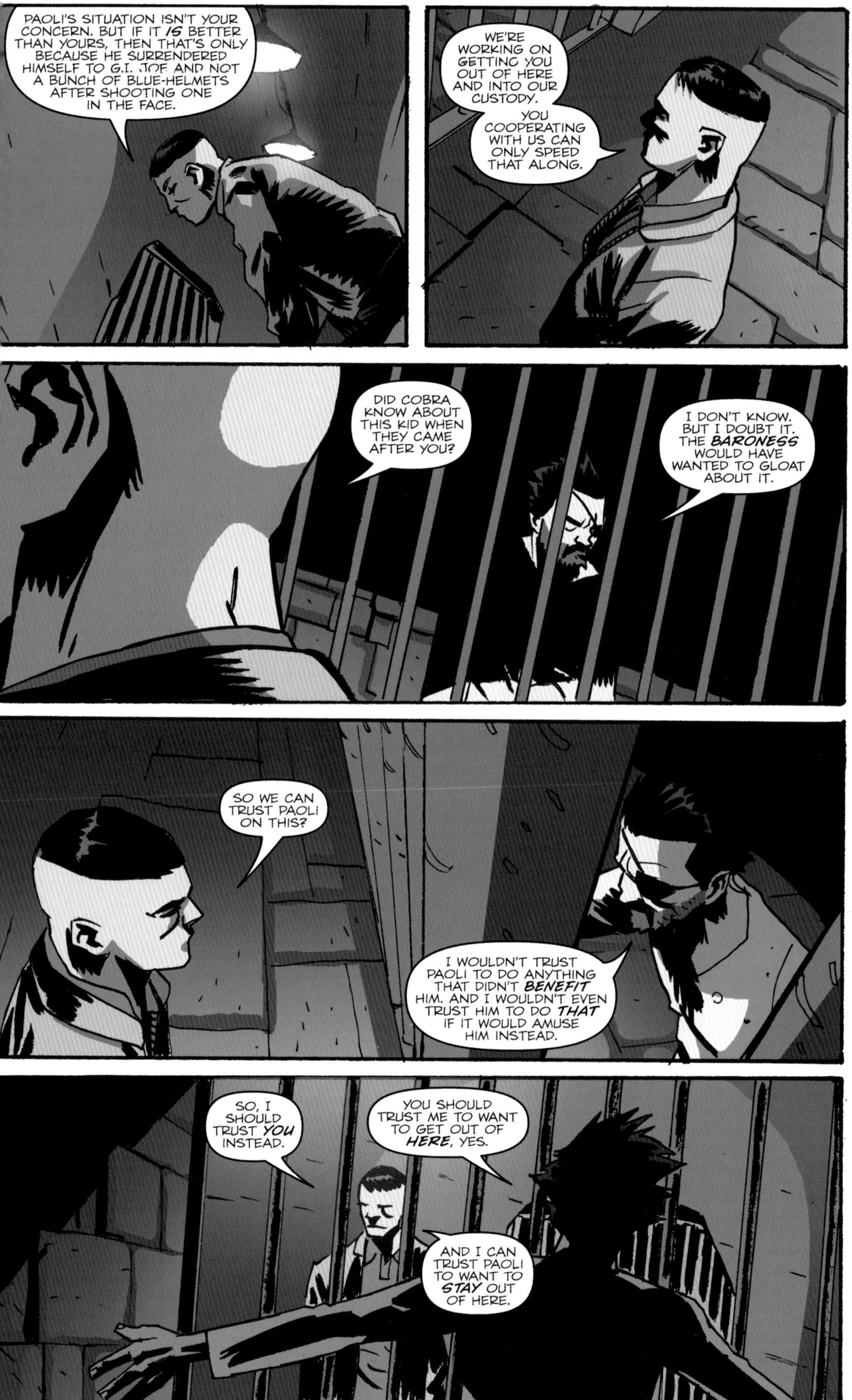
PAOLI'S SITUATION ISN'T YOUR CONCERN. BUT IF IT *IS* BETTER THAN YOURS, THEN THAT'S ONLY BECAUSE HE SURRENDERED HIMSELF TO G.I. JOE AND NOT A BUNCH OF BLUE-HELMETS AFTER SHOOTING ONE IN THE FACE.
WE'RE WORKING ON GETTING YOU OUT OF HERE AND INTO OUR CUSTODY.
YOU COOPERATING WITH US CAN ONLY SPEED THAT ALONG.
DID COBRA KNOW ABOUT THIS KID WHEN THEY CAME AFTER YOU?
I DON'T KNOW. BUT I DOUBT IT. THE *BARONESS* WOULD HAVE WANTED TO GLOAT ABOUT IT.
SO WE CAN TRUST PAOLI ON THIS?
I WOULDN'T TRUST PAOLI TO DO ANYTHING THAT DIDN'T *BENEFIT* HIM. AND I WOULDN'T EVEN TRUST HIM TO DO *THAT* IF IT WOULD AMUSE HIM INSTEAD.
SO, I SHOULD TRUST *YOU* INSTEAD.
YOU SHOULD TRUST ME TO WANT TO GET OUT OF *HERE*, YES.
AND I CAN TRUST PAOLI TO WANT TO *STAY* OUT OF HERE.

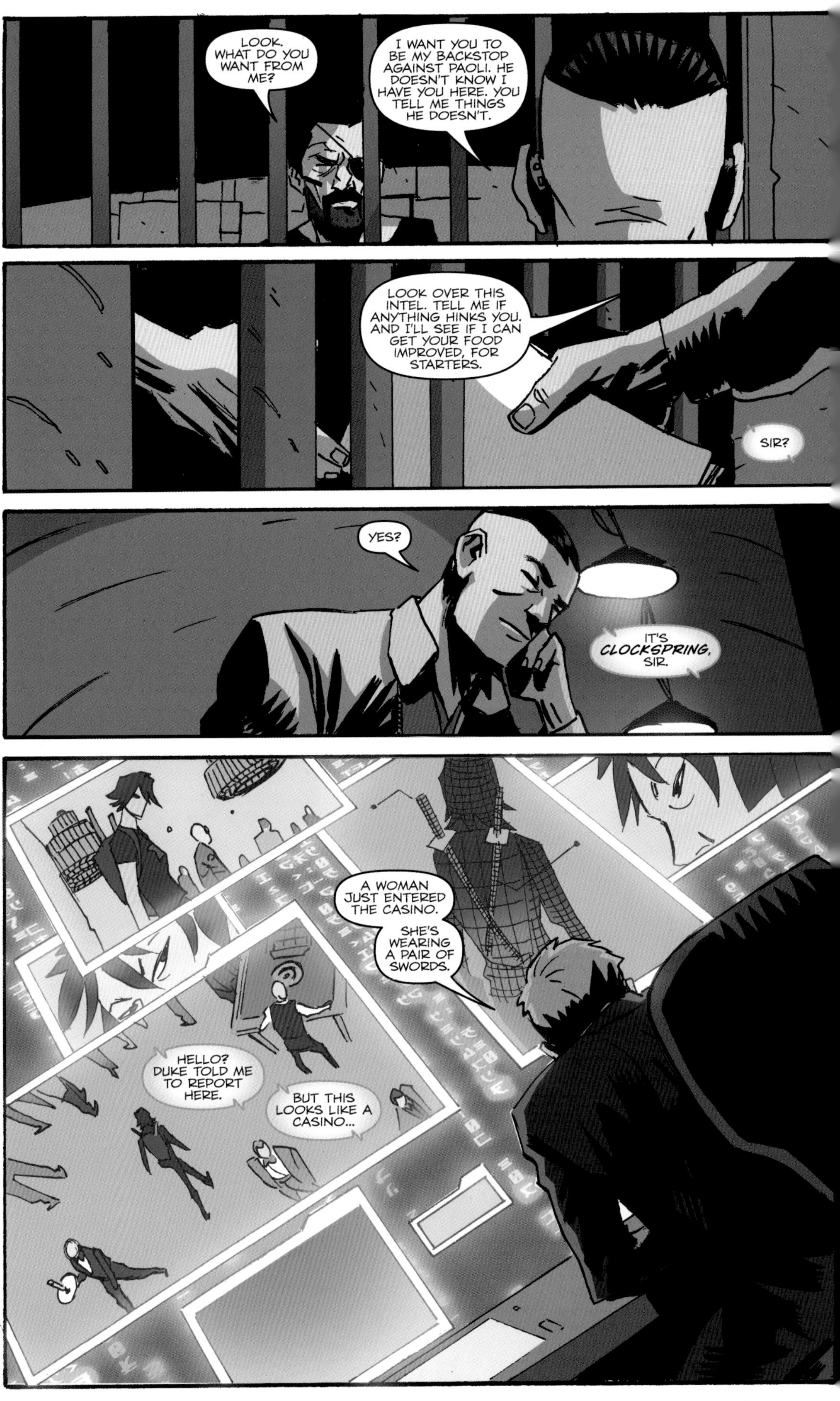
LOOK. WHAT DO YOU WANT FROM ME?
I WANT YOU TO BE MY BACKSTOP AGAINST PAOLI. HE DOESN'T KNOW I HAVE YOU HERE. YOU TELL ME THINGS HE DOESN'T.
LOOK OVER THIS INTEL. TELL ME IF ANYTHING HINKS YOU. AND I'LL SEE IF I CAN GET YOUR FOOD IMPROVED, FOR STARTERS.
SIR?
YES?
IT'S CLOCKSPRING, SIR.
A WOMAN JUST ENTERED THE CASINO.
SHE'S WEARING A PAIR OF SWORDS.
HELLO? DUKE TOLD ME TO REPORT HERE.
BUT THIS LOOKS LIKE A CASINO...

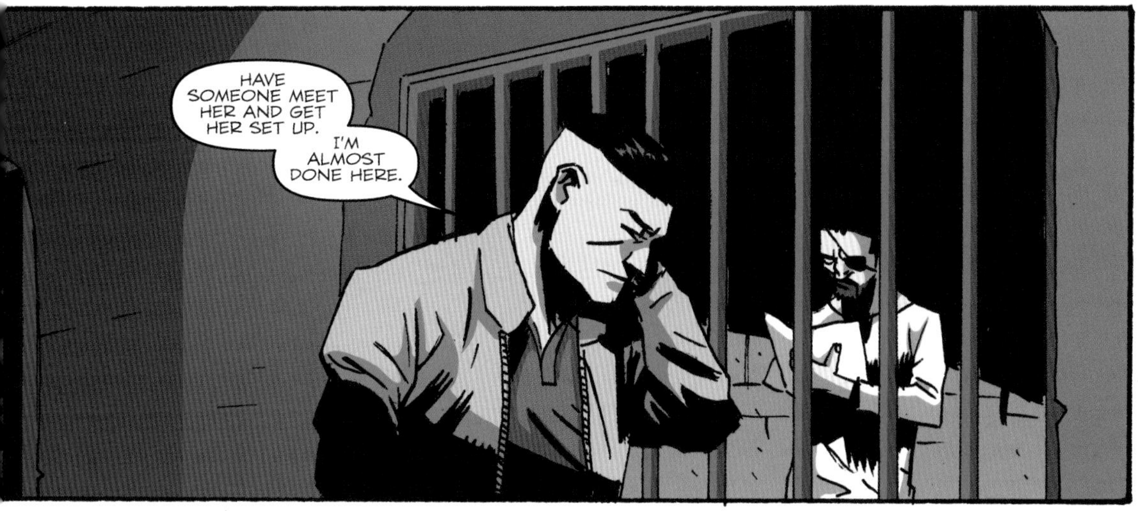
HAVE SOMEONE MEET HER AND GET HER SET UP.
I'M ALMOST DONE HERE.

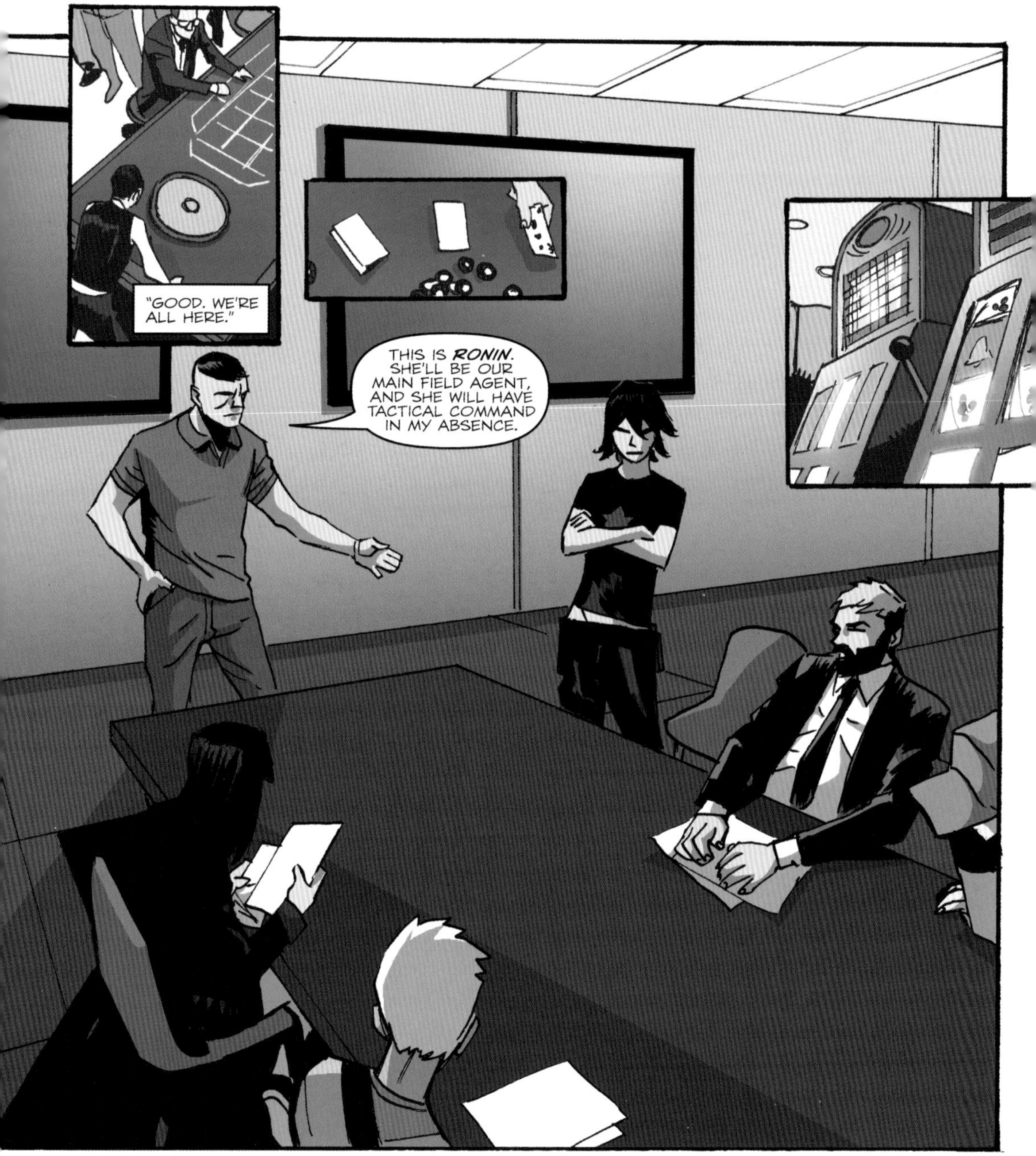
"GOOD. WE'RE ALL HERE."
THIS IS RONIN. SHE'LL BE OUR MAIN FIELD AGENT, AND SHE WILL HAVE TACTICAL COMMAND IN MY ABSENCE.

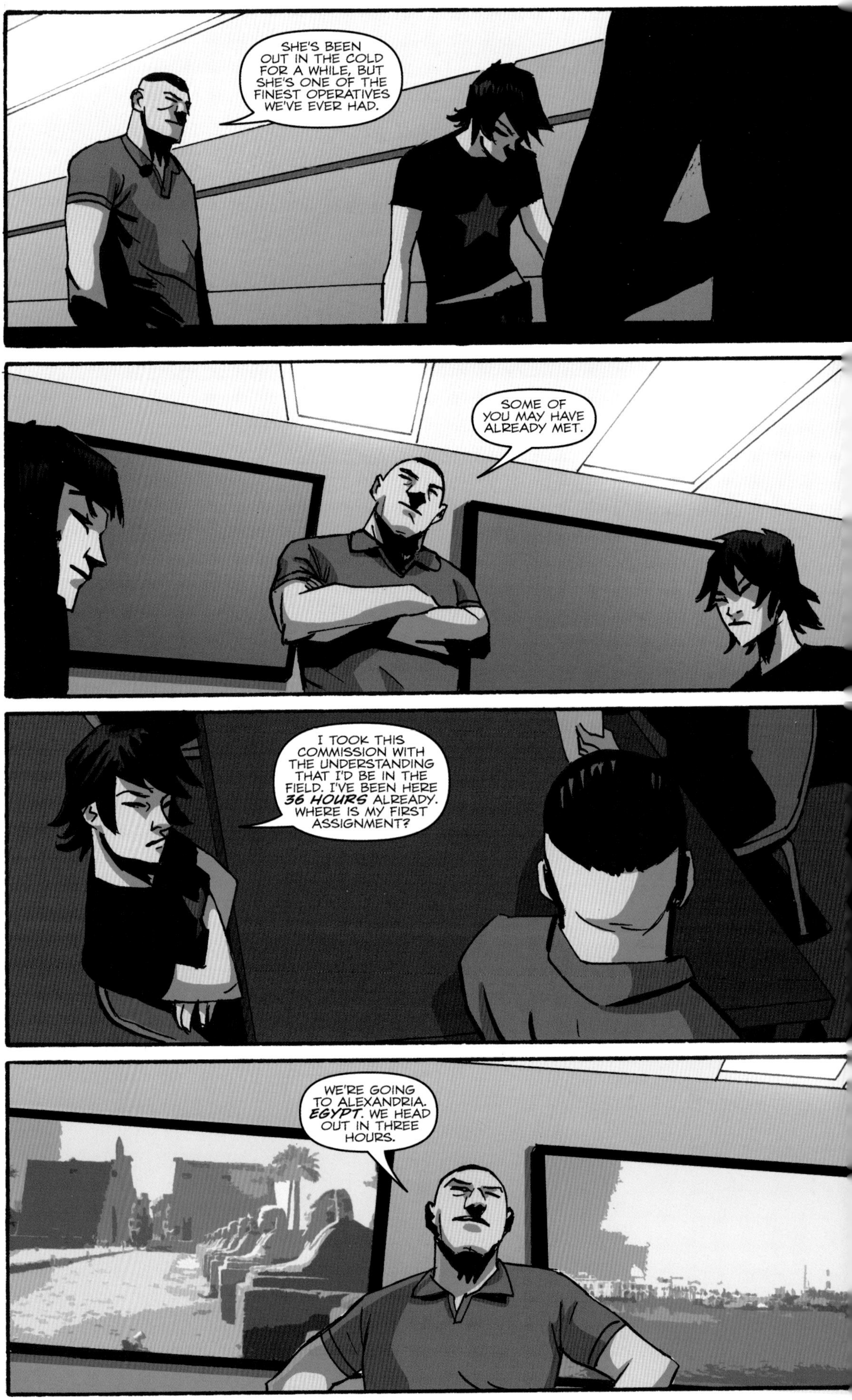
SHE'S BEEN OUT IN THE COLD FOR A WHILE, BUT SHE'S ONE OF THE FINEST OPERATIVES WE'VE EVER HAD.
SOME OF YOU MAY HAVE ALREADY MET.
I TOOK THIS COMMISSION WITH THE UNDERSTANDING THAT I'D BE IN THE FIELD. I'VE BEEN HERE ***36 HOURS*** ALREADY. WHERE IS MY FIRST ASSIGNMENT?
WE'RE GOING TO ALEXANDRIA. ***EGYPT***. WE HEAD OUT IN THREE HOURS.

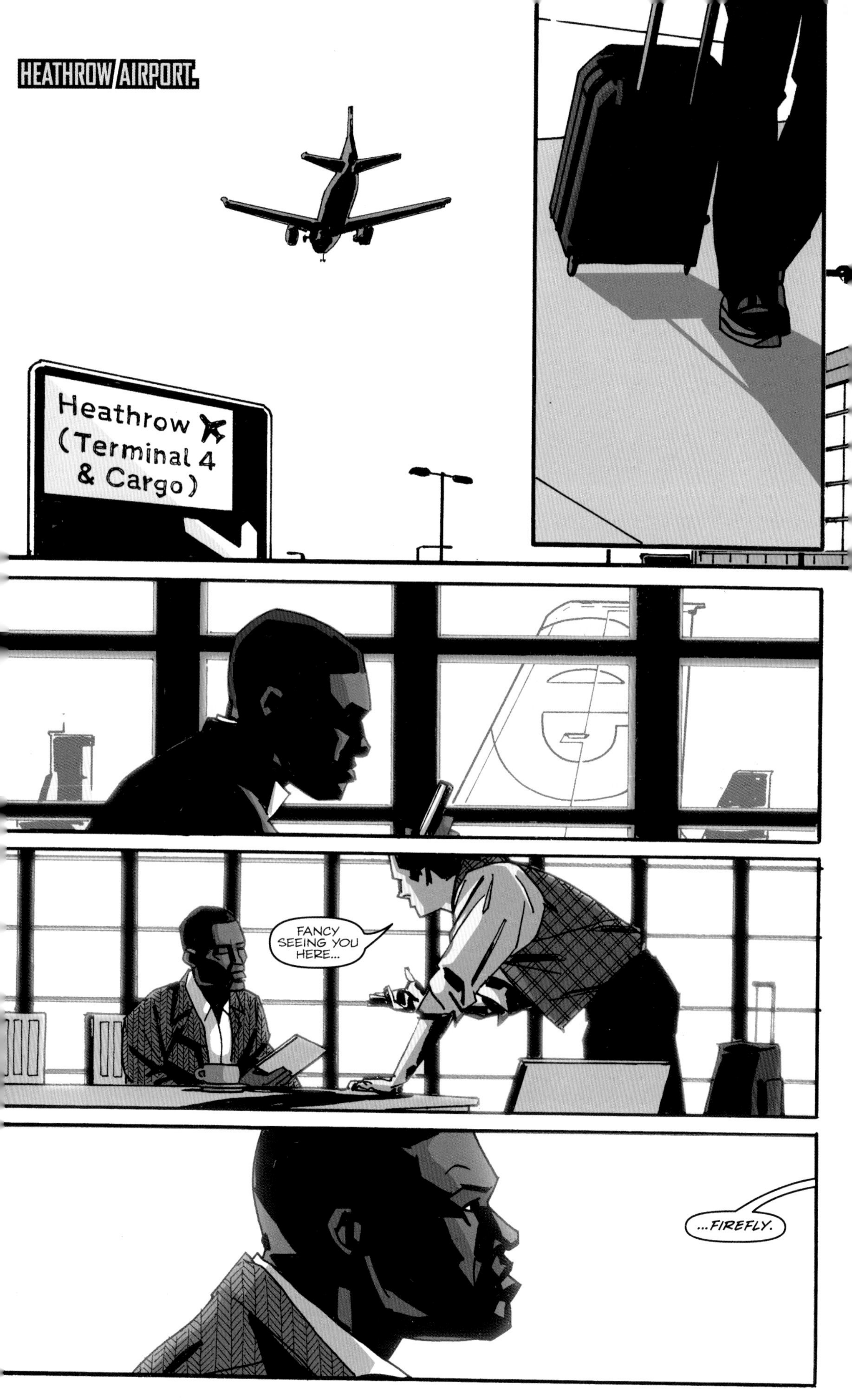
HEATHROW AIRPORT.
Heathrow (Terminal 4 & Cargo)
FANCY SEEING YOU HERE...
...FIREFLY.

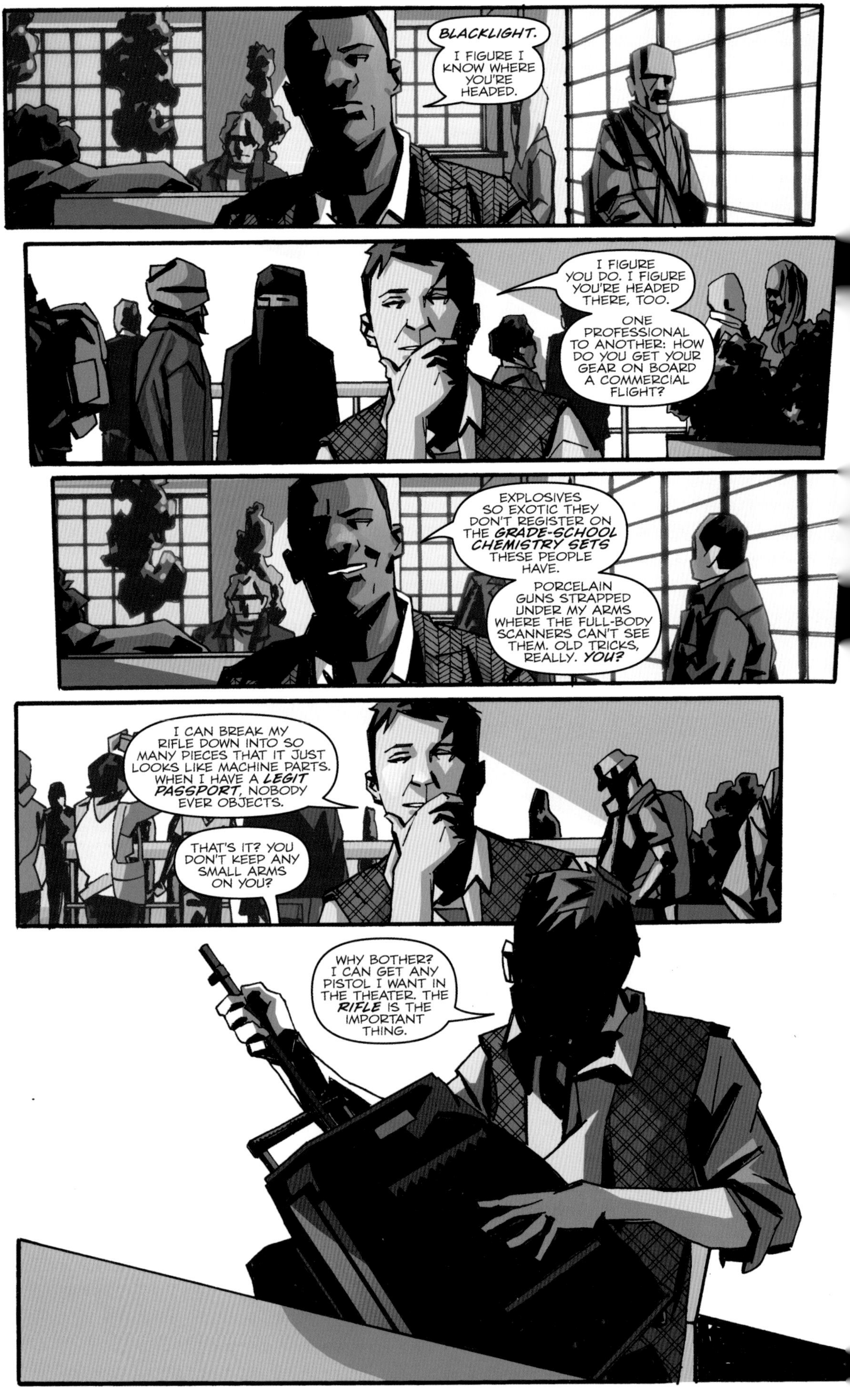
BLACKLIGHT.
I FIGURE I KNOW WHERE YOU'RE HEADED.
I FIGURE YOU DO. I FIGURE YOU'RE HEADED THERE, TOO.
ONE PROFESSIONAL TO ANOTHER: HOW DO YOU GET YOUR GEAR ON BOARD A COMMERCIAL FLIGHT?
EXPLOSIVES SO EXOTIC THEY DON'T REGISTER ON THE GRADE-SCHOOL CHEMISTRY SETS THESE PEOPLE HAVE.
PORCELAIN GUNS STRAPPED UNDER MY ARMS WHERE THE FULL-BODY SCANNERS CAN'T SEE THEM. OLD TRICKS, REALLY. YOU?
I CAN BREAK MY RIFLE DOWN INTO SO MANY PIECES THAT IT JUST LOOKS LIKE MACHINE PARTS. WHEN I HAVE A LEGIT PASSPORT, NOBODY EVER OBJECTS.
THAT'S IT? YOU DON'T KEEP ANY SMALL ARMS ON YOU?
WHY BOTHER? I CAN GET ANY PISTOL I WANT IN THE THEATER. THE RIFLE IS THE IMPORTANT THING.

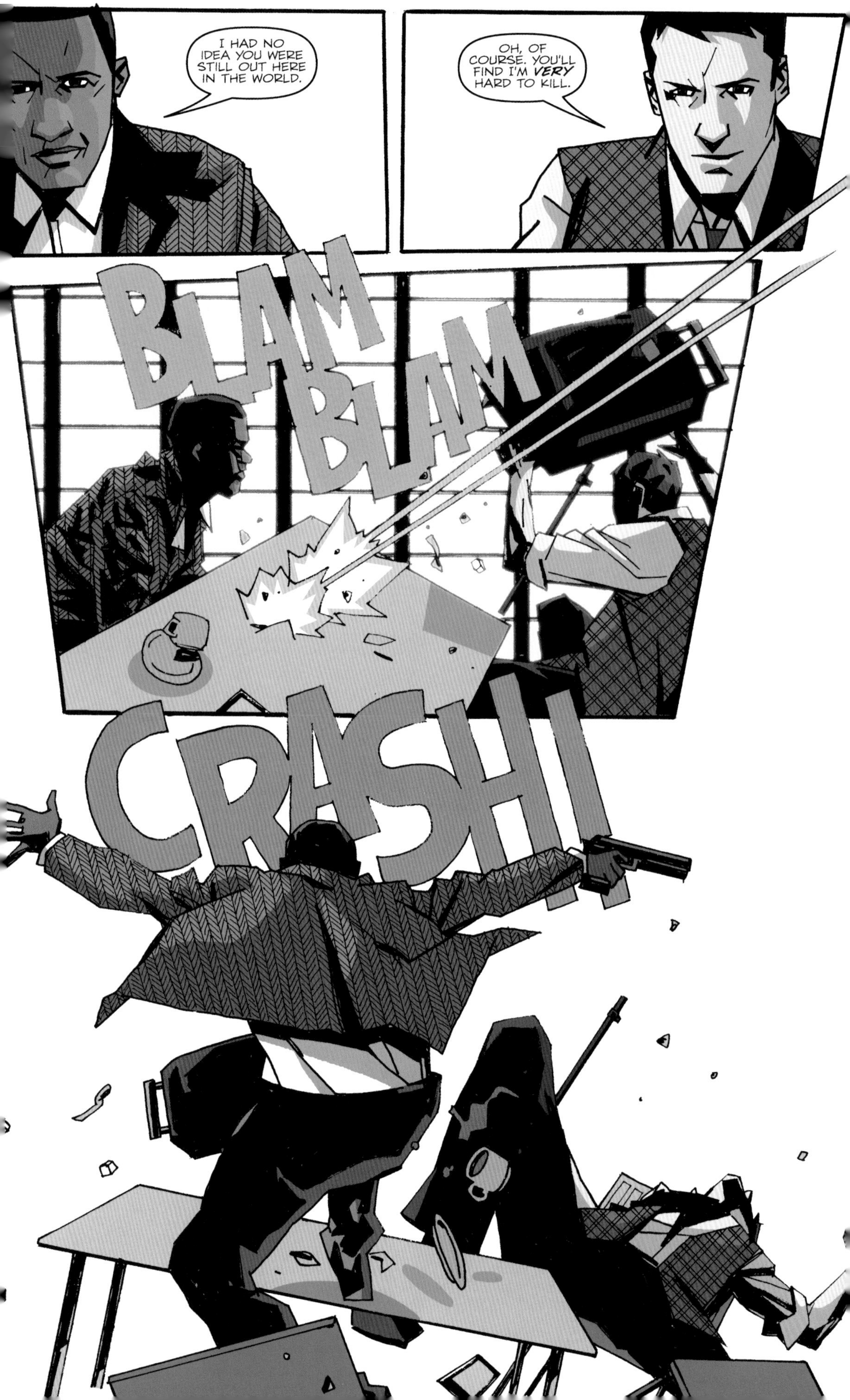

I HAD NO IDEA YOU WERE STILL OUT HERE IN THE WORLD.
OH, OF COURSE. YOU'LL FIND I'M *VERY* HARD TO KILL.
BLAM BLAM
CRASH!

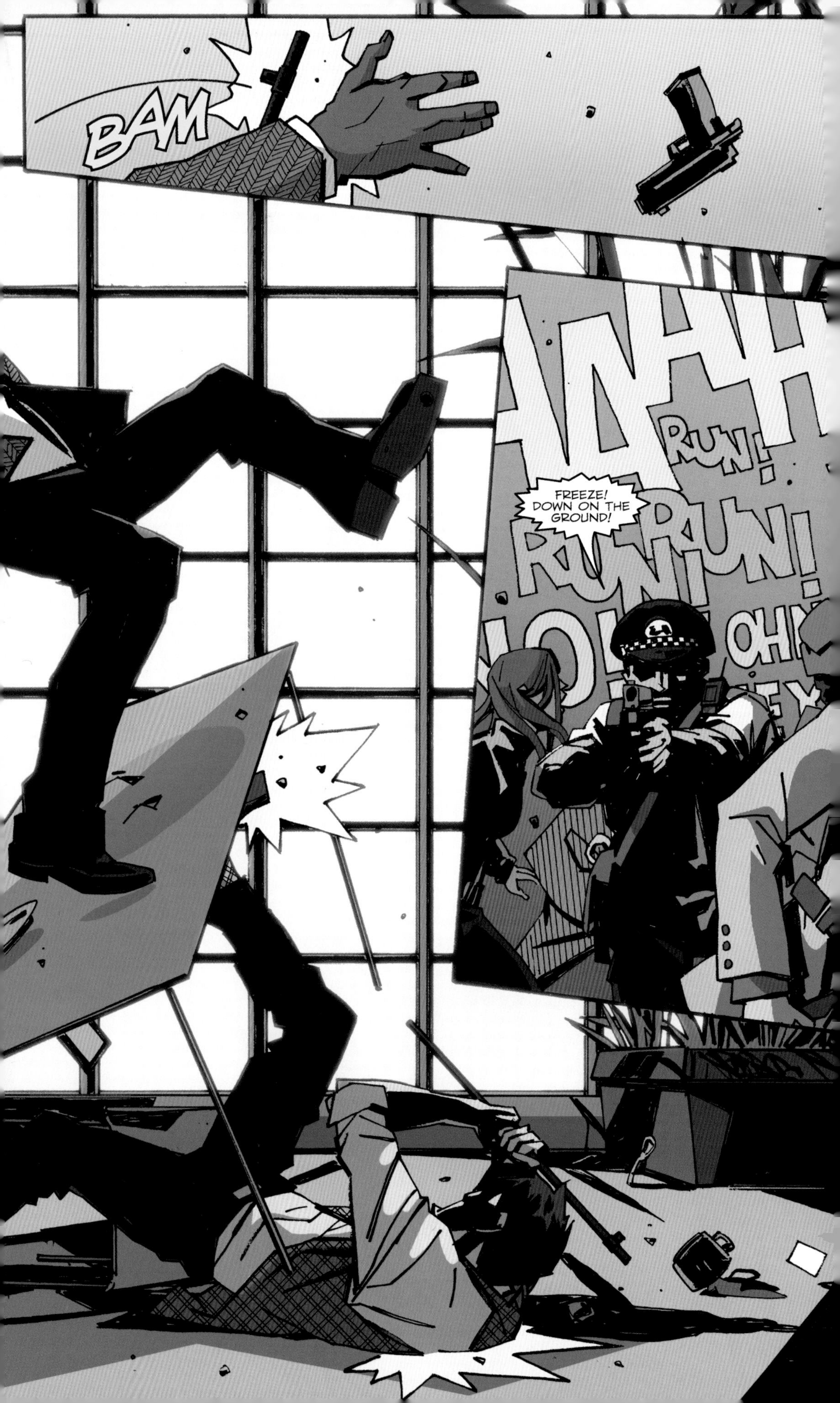
BAM
RUN!
FREEZE! DOWN ON THE GROUND!
RUN! RUN!

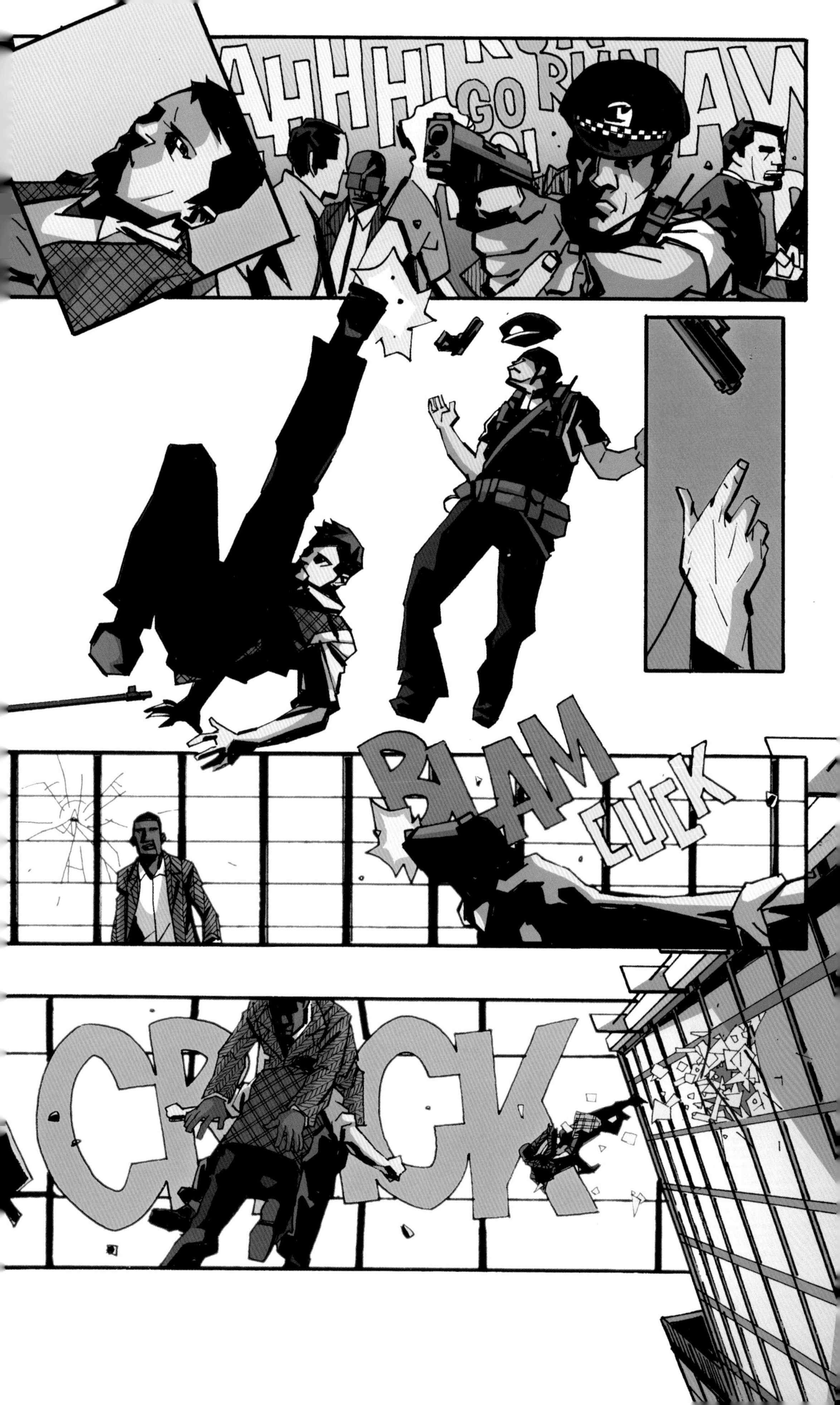
GO
BLAM
CLICK
CRACK

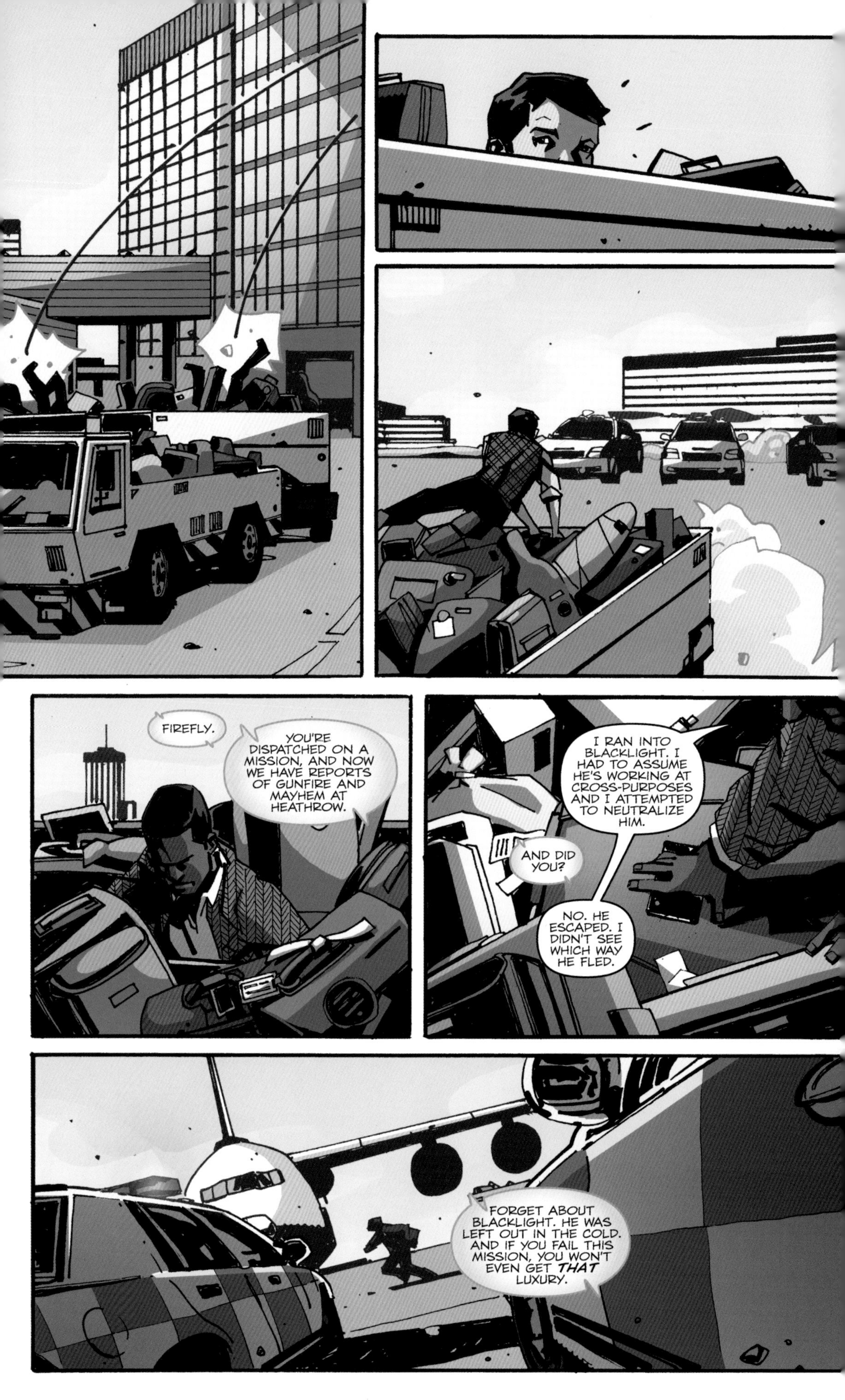
FIREFLY.
YOU'RE DISPATCHED ON A MISSION, AND NOW WE HAVE REPORTS OF GUNFIRE AND MAYHEM AT HEATHROW.
I RAN INTO BLACKLIGHT. I HAD TO ASSUME HE'S WORKING AT CROSS-PURPOSES AND I ATTEMPTED TO NEUTRALIZE HIM.
AND DID YOU?
NO. HE ESCAPED. I DIDN'T SEE WHICH WAY HE FLED.
FORGET ABOUT BLACKLIGHT. HE WAS LEFT OUT IN THE COLD. AND IF YOU FAIL THIS MISSION, YOU WON'T EVEN GET *THAT* LUXURY.

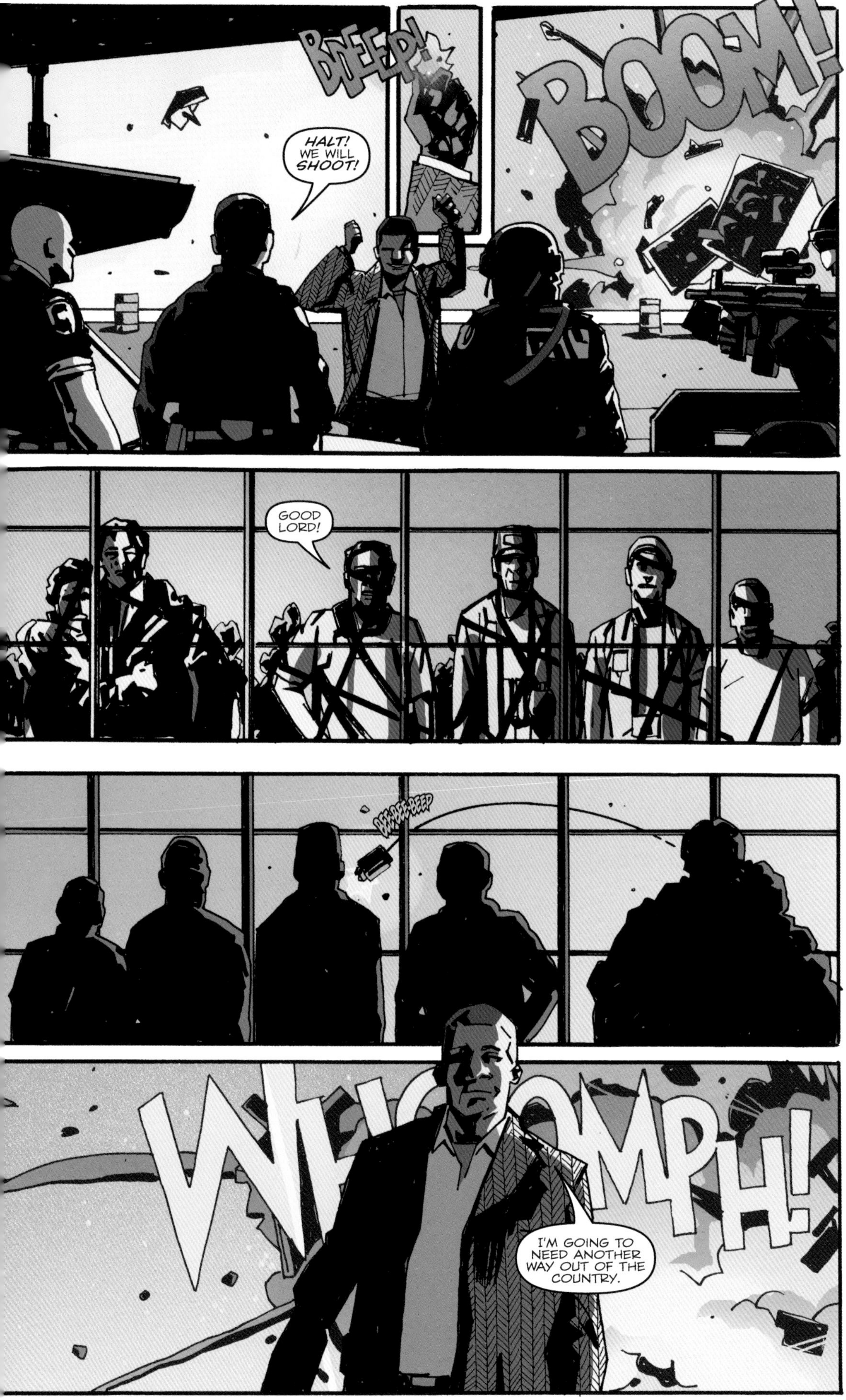
BEEEP!
HALT! WE WILL SHOOT!
BOOM!
GOOD LORD!
BEE-BEE-BEEP
WHOOMPH!
I'M GOING TO NEED ANOTHER WAY OUT OF THE COUNTRY.

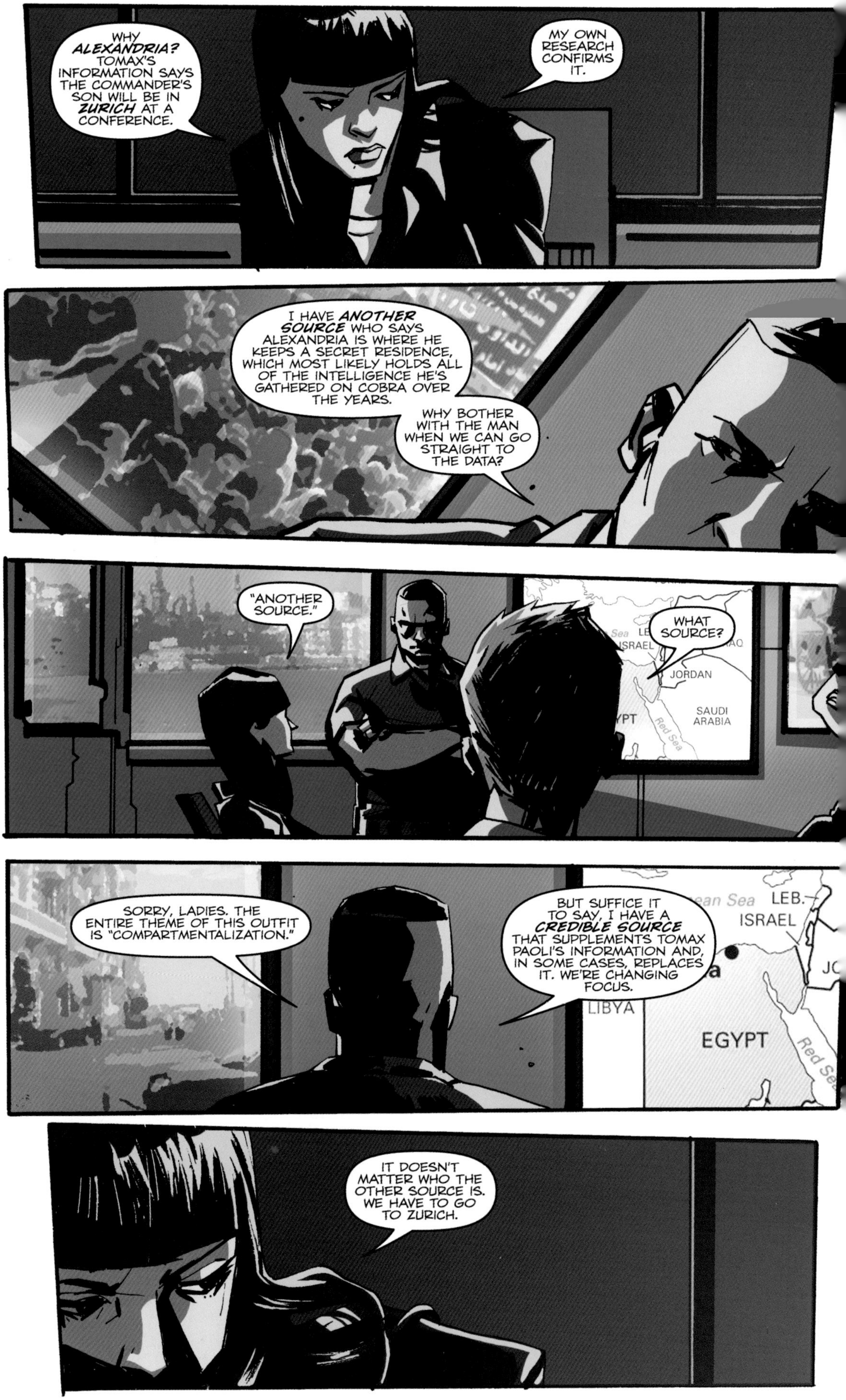

WHY *ALEXANDRIA?* TOMAX'S INFORMATION SAYS THE COMMANDER'S SON WILL BE IN *ZURICH* AT A CONFERENCE.
MY OWN RESEARCH CONFIRMS IT.
I HAVE *ANOTHER SOURCE* WHO SAYS ALEXANDRIA IS WHERE HE KEEPS A SECRET RESIDENCE, WHICH MOST LIKELY HOLDS ALL OF THE INTELLIGENCE HE'S GATHERED ON COBRA OVER THE YEARS.
WHY BOTHER WITH THE MAN WHEN WE CAN GO STRAIGHT TO THE DATA?
"ANOTHER SOURCE."
WHAT SOURCE?
ISRAEL
JORDAN
SAUDI ARABIA
Red Sea
SORRY, LADIES. THE ENTIRE THEME OF THIS OUTFIT IS "COMPARTMENTALIZATION."
BUT SUFFICE IT TO SAY, I HAVE A *CREDIBLE SOURCE* THAT SUPPLEMENTS TOMAX PAOLI'S INFORMATION AND, IN SOME CASES, REPLACES IT. WE'RE CHANGING FOCUS.
LEB.
ISRAEL
LIBYA
EGYPT
IT DOESN'T MATTER WHO THE OTHER SOURCE IS. WE HAVE TO GO TO ZURICH.

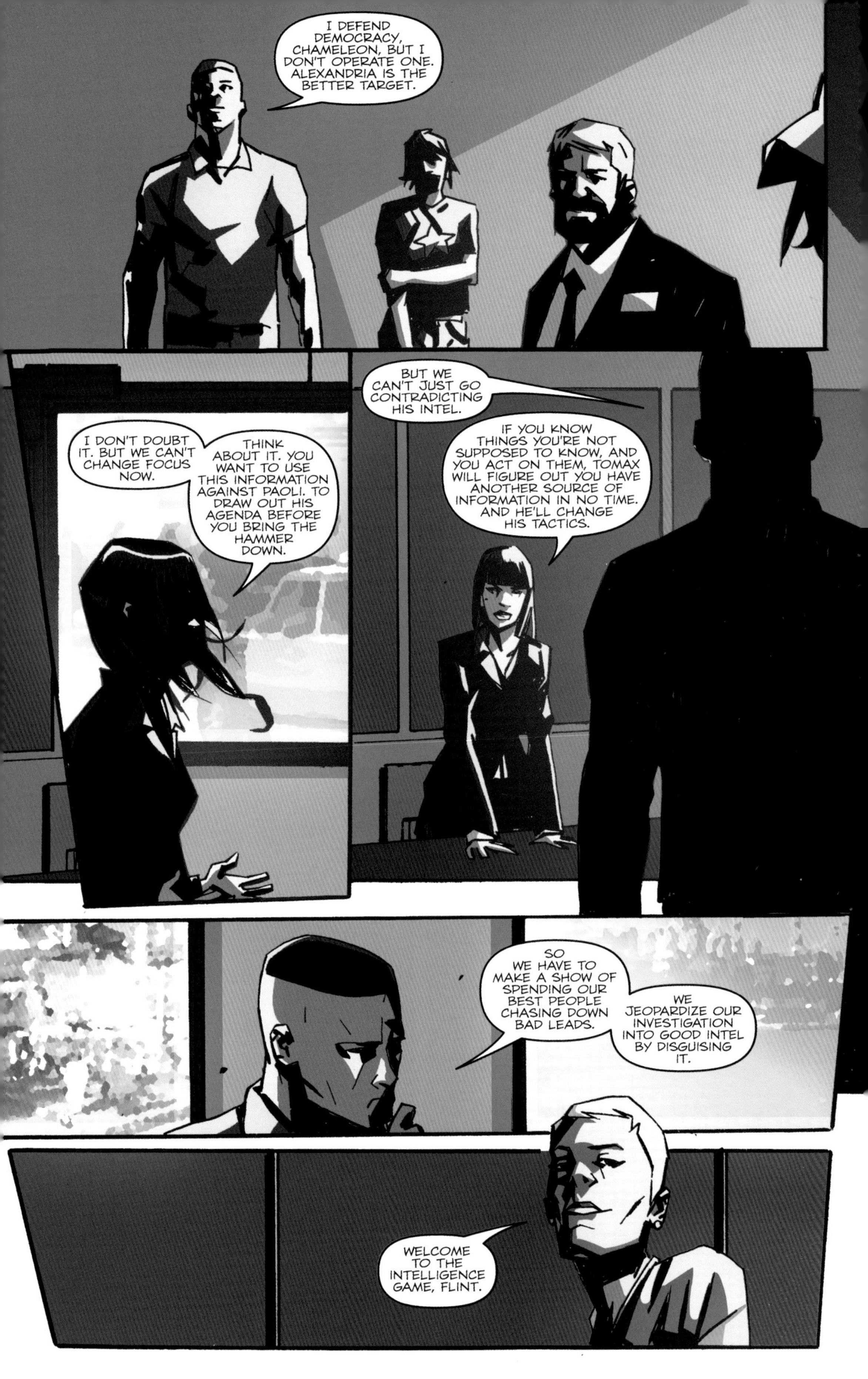
I DEFEND DEMOCRACY, CHAMELEON, BUT I DON'T OPERATE ONE. ALEXANDRIA IS THE BETTER TARGET.
I DON'T DOUBT IT. BUT WE CAN'T CHANGE FOCUS NOW.
THINK ABOUT IT. YOU WANT TO USE THIS INFORMATION AGAINST PAOLI. TO DRAW OUT HIS AGENDA BEFORE YOU BRING THE HAMMER DOWN.
BUT WE CAN'T JUST GO CONTRADICTING HIS INTEL.
IF YOU KNOW THINGS YOU'RE NOT SUPPOSED TO KNOW, AND YOU ACT ON THEM, TOMAX WILL FIGURE OUT YOU HAVE ANOTHER SOURCE OF INFORMATION IN NO TIME. AND HE'LL CHANGE HIS TACTICS.
SO WE HAVE TO MAKE A SHOW OF SPENDING OUR BEST PEOPLE CHASING DOWN BAD LEADS.
WE JEOPARDIZE OUR INVESTIGATION INTO GOOD INTEL BY DISGUISING IT.
WELCOME TO THE INTELLIGENCE GAME, FLINT.

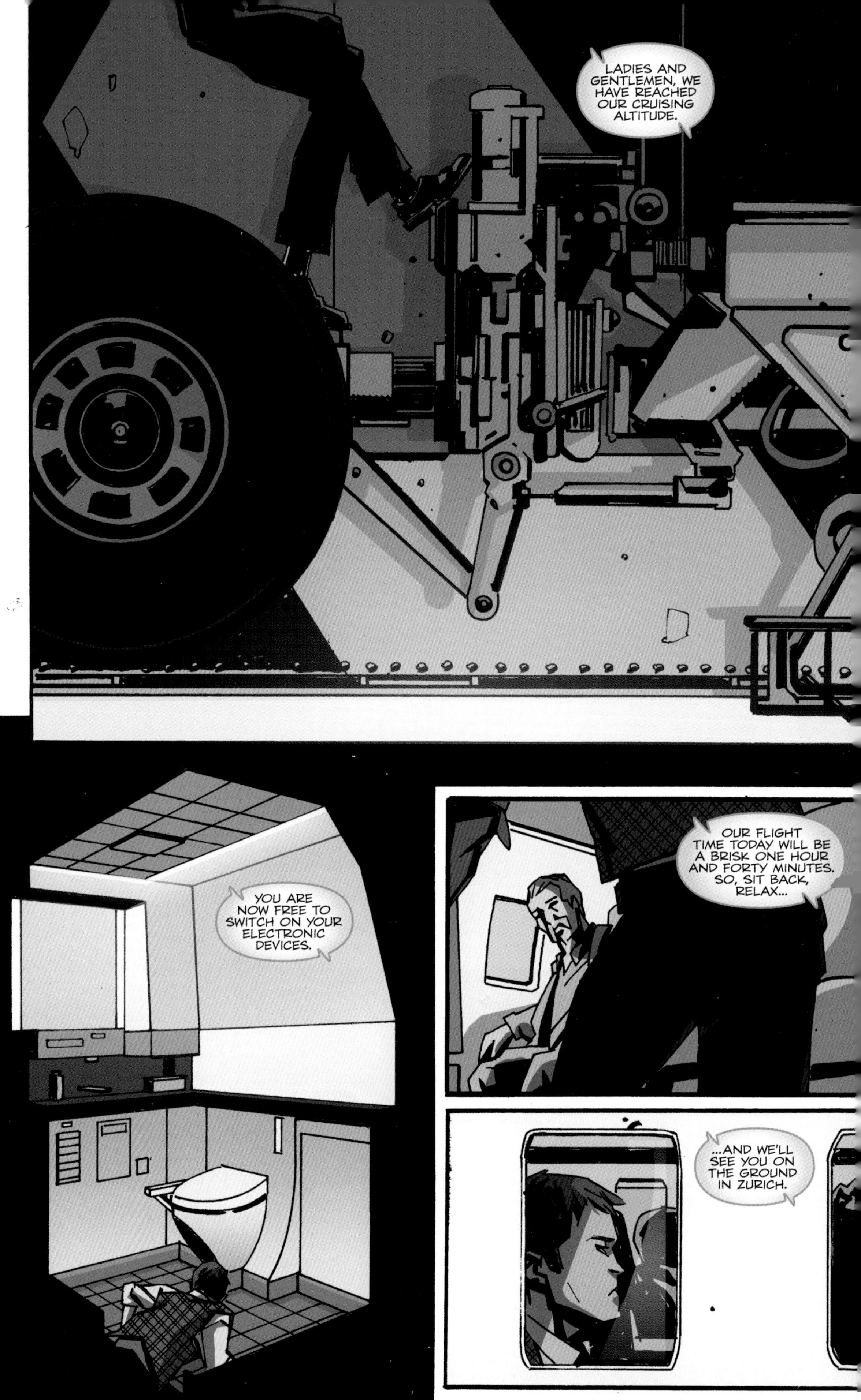
LADIES AND GENTLEMEN, WE HAVE REACHED OUR CRUISING ALTITUDE.
YOU ARE NOW FREE TO SWITCH ON YOUR ELECTRONIC DEVICES.
OUR FLIGHT TIME TODAY WILL BE A BRISK ONE HOUR AND FORTY MINUTES. SO, SIT BACK, RELAX...
...AND WE'LL SEE YOU ON THE GROUND IN ZURICH.

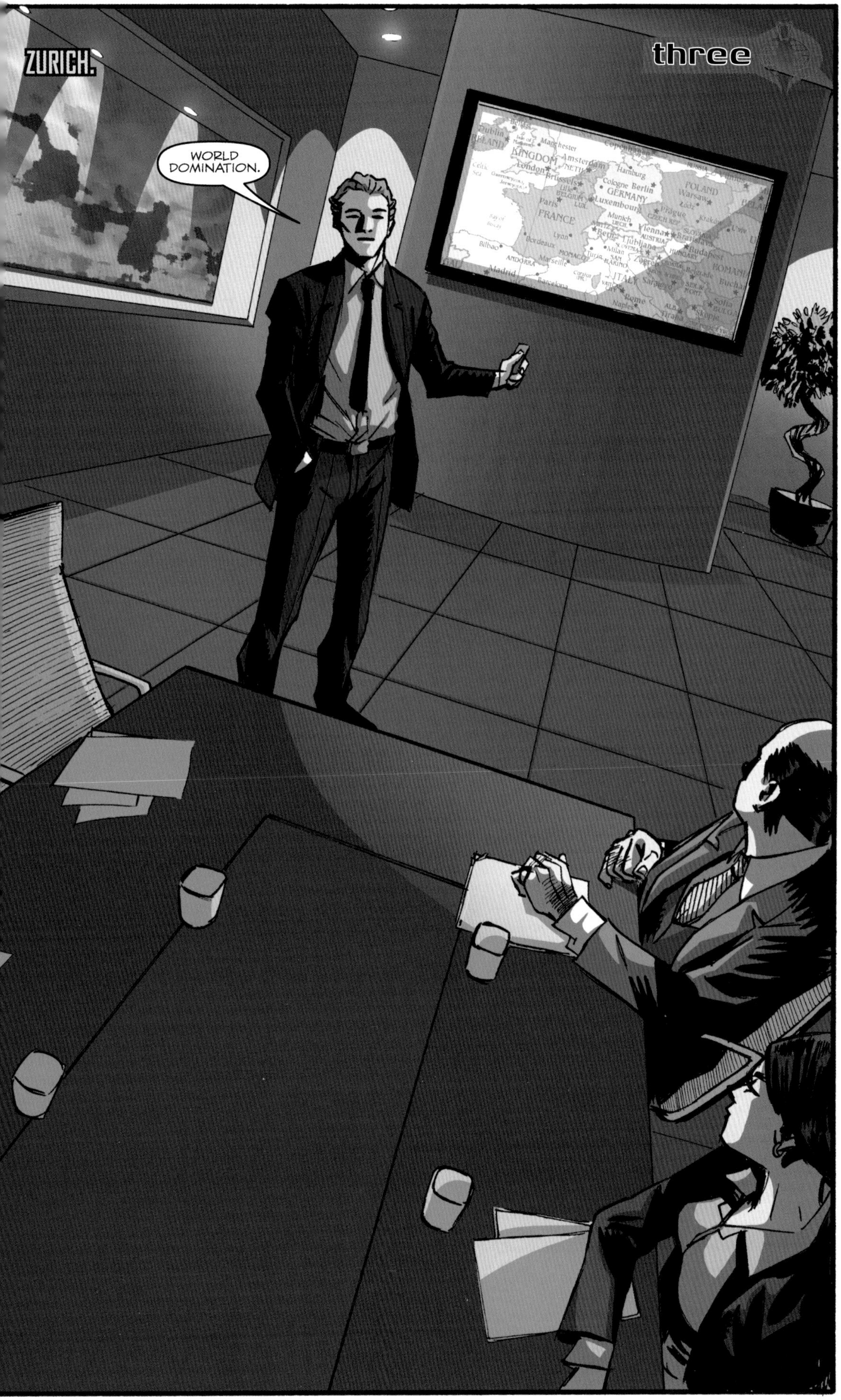
ZURICH.
three
WORLD DOMINATION.

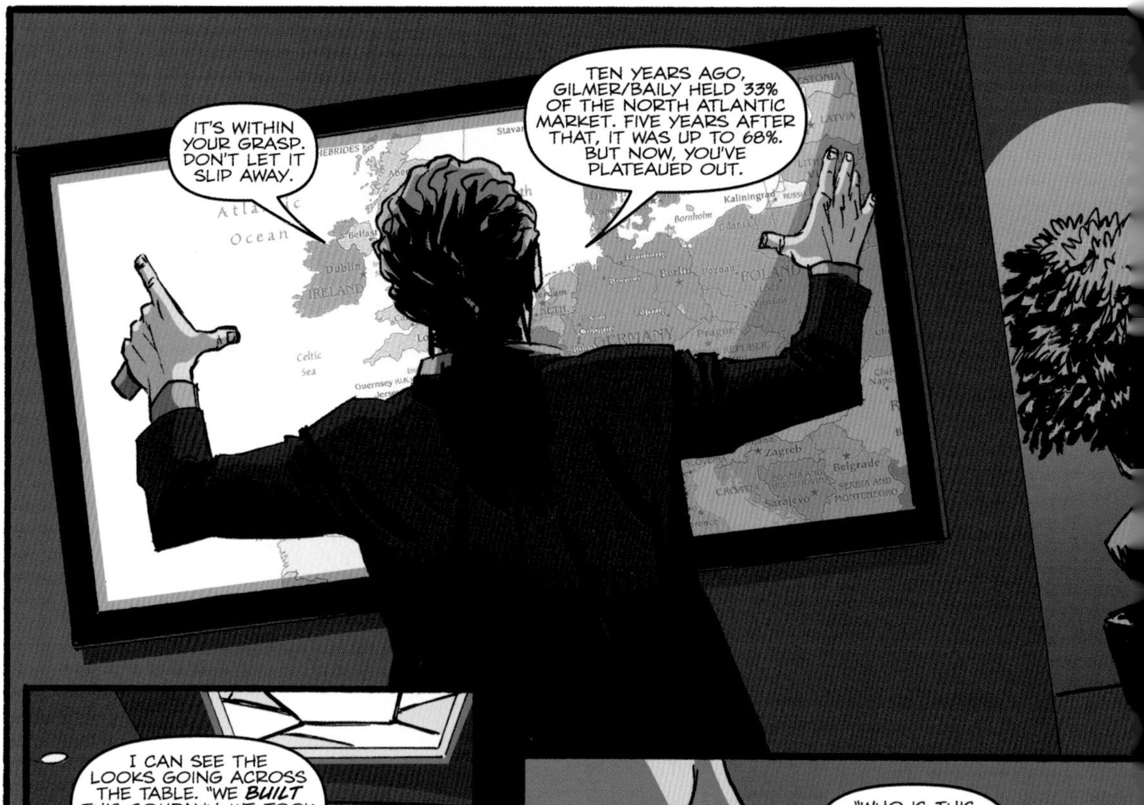
TEN YEARS AGO, GILMER/BAILY HELD 33% OF THE NORTH ATLANTIC MARKET. FIVE YEARS AFTER THAT, IT WAS UP TO 68%. BUT NOW, YOU'VE PLATEAUED OUT.
IT'S WITHIN YOUR GRASP. DON'T LET IT SLIP AWAY.

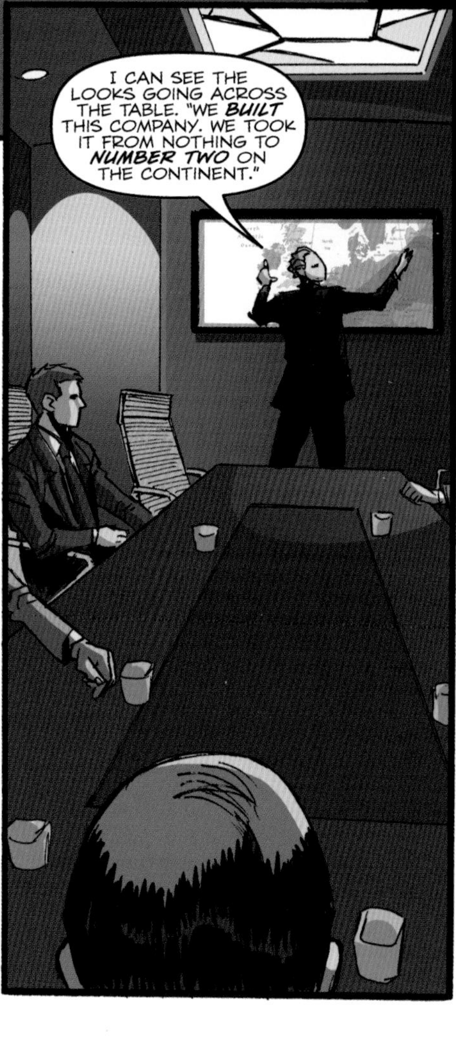
I CAN SEE THE LOOKS GOING ACROSS THE TABLE. "WE BUILT THIS COMPANY. WE TOOK IT FROM NOTHING TO NUMBER TWO ON THE CONTINENT."

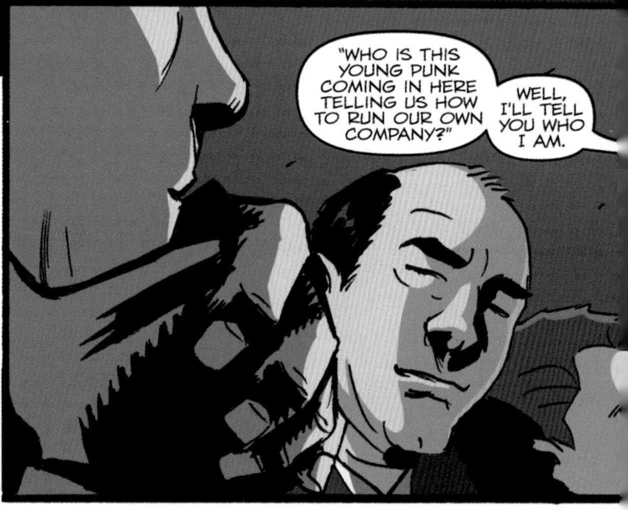
"WHO IS THIS YOUNG PUNK COMING IN HERE TELLING US HOW TO RUN OUR OWN COMPANY?"
WELL, I'LL TELL YOU WHO I AM.

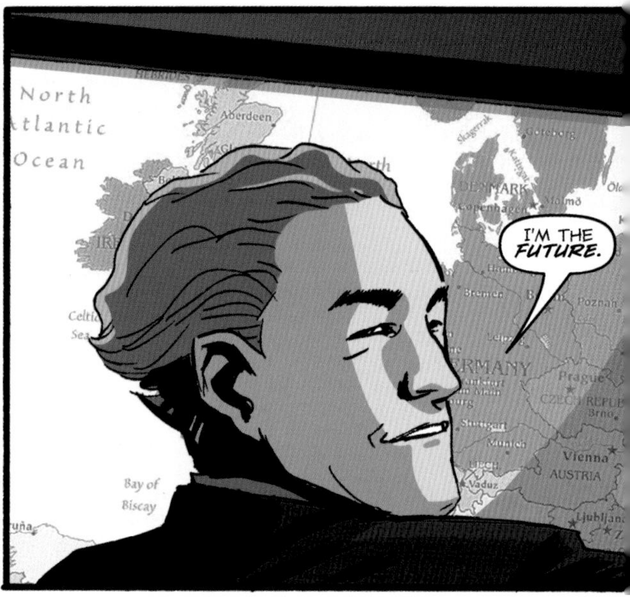
I'M THE FUTURE.

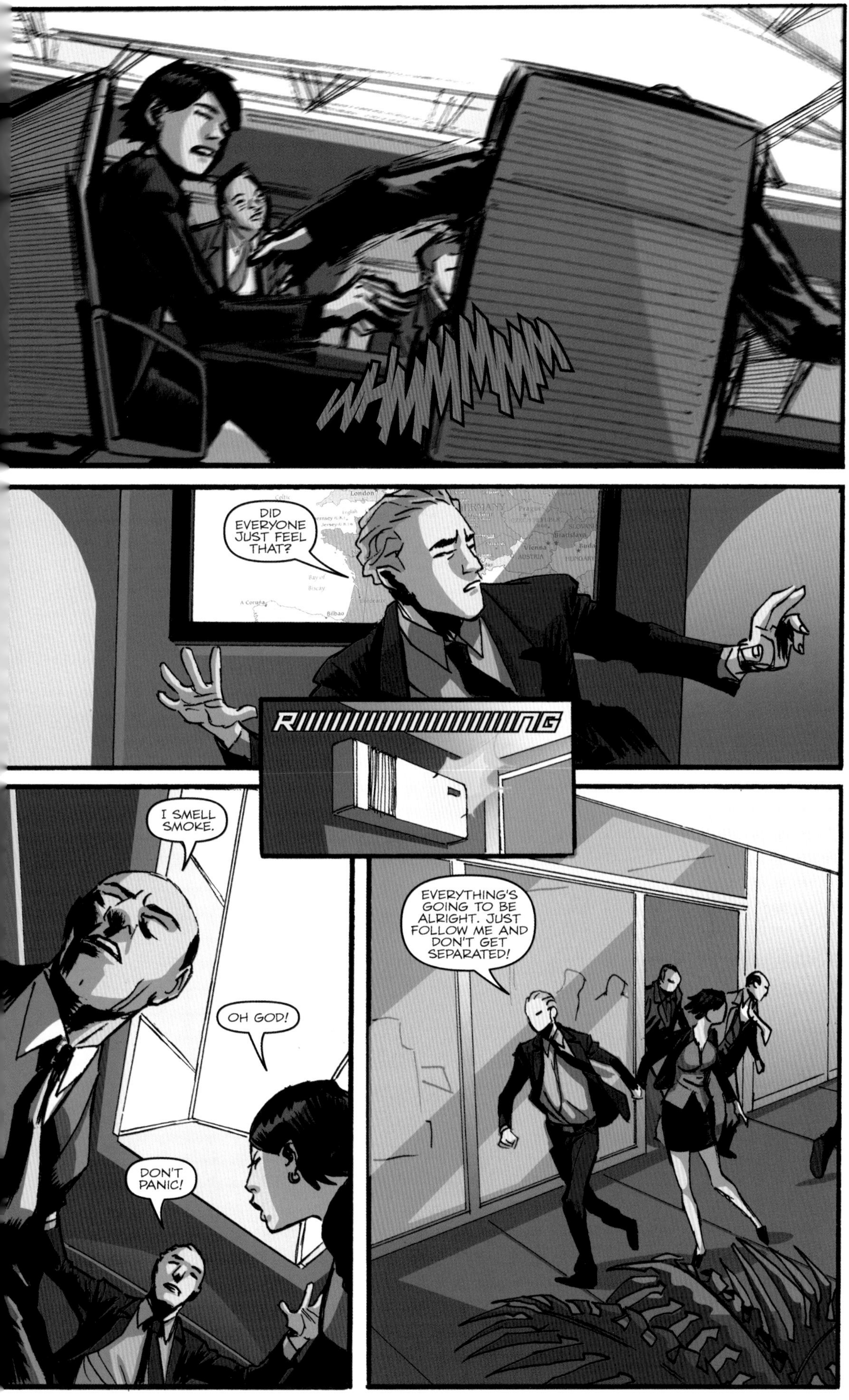
WHMMMMMM
DID EVERYONE JUST FEEL THAT?
RIIIIIIIIIIIIIIIIIIIIIING
I SMELL SMOKE.
OH GOD!
DON'T PANIC!
EVERYTHING'S GOING TO BE ALRIGHT. JUST FOLLOW ME AND DON'T GET SEPARATED!

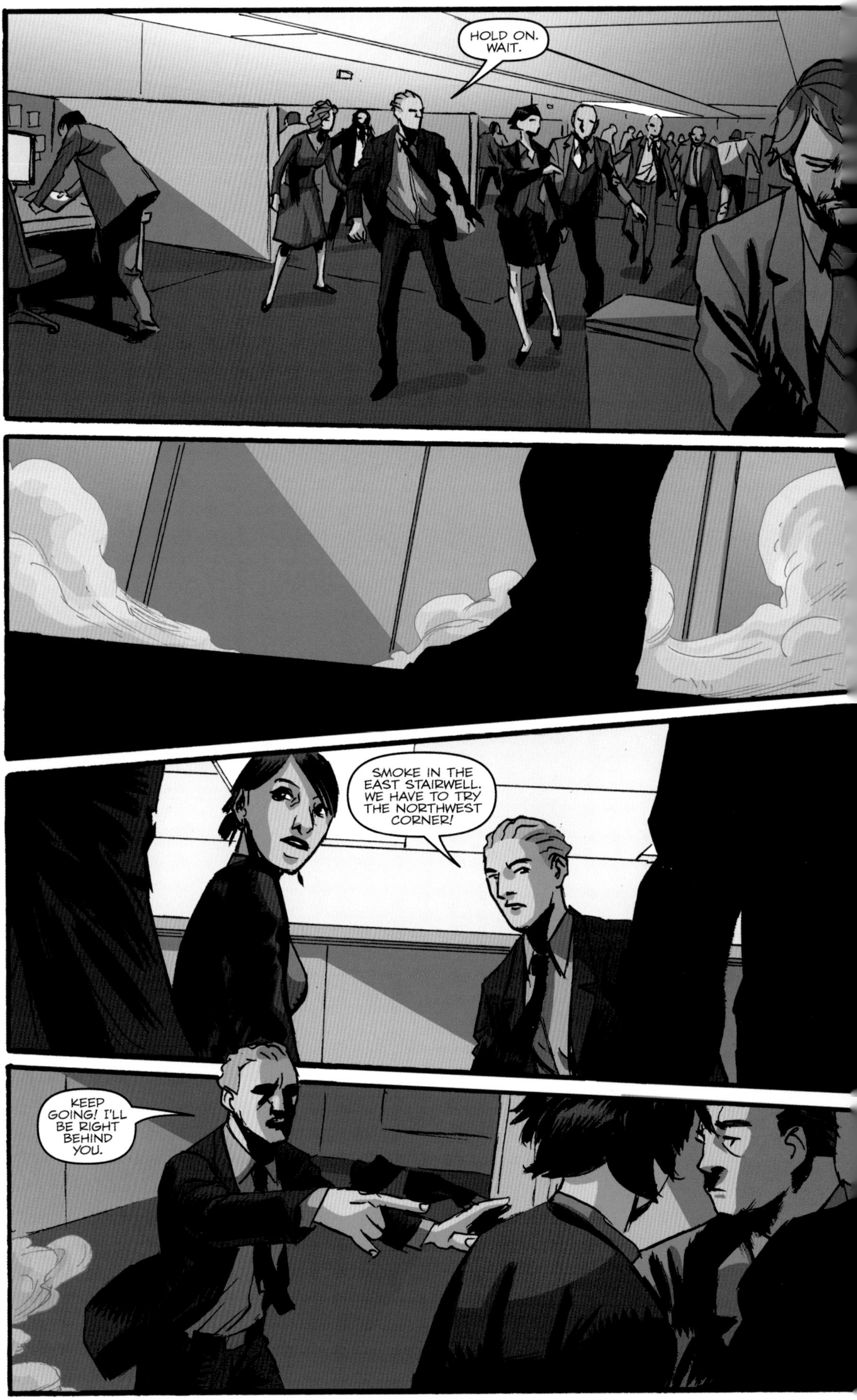
HOLD ON. WAIT.
SMOKE IN THE EAST STAIRWELL. WE HAVE TO TRY THE NORTHWEST CORNER!
KEEP GOING! I'LL BE RIGHT BEHIND YOU.

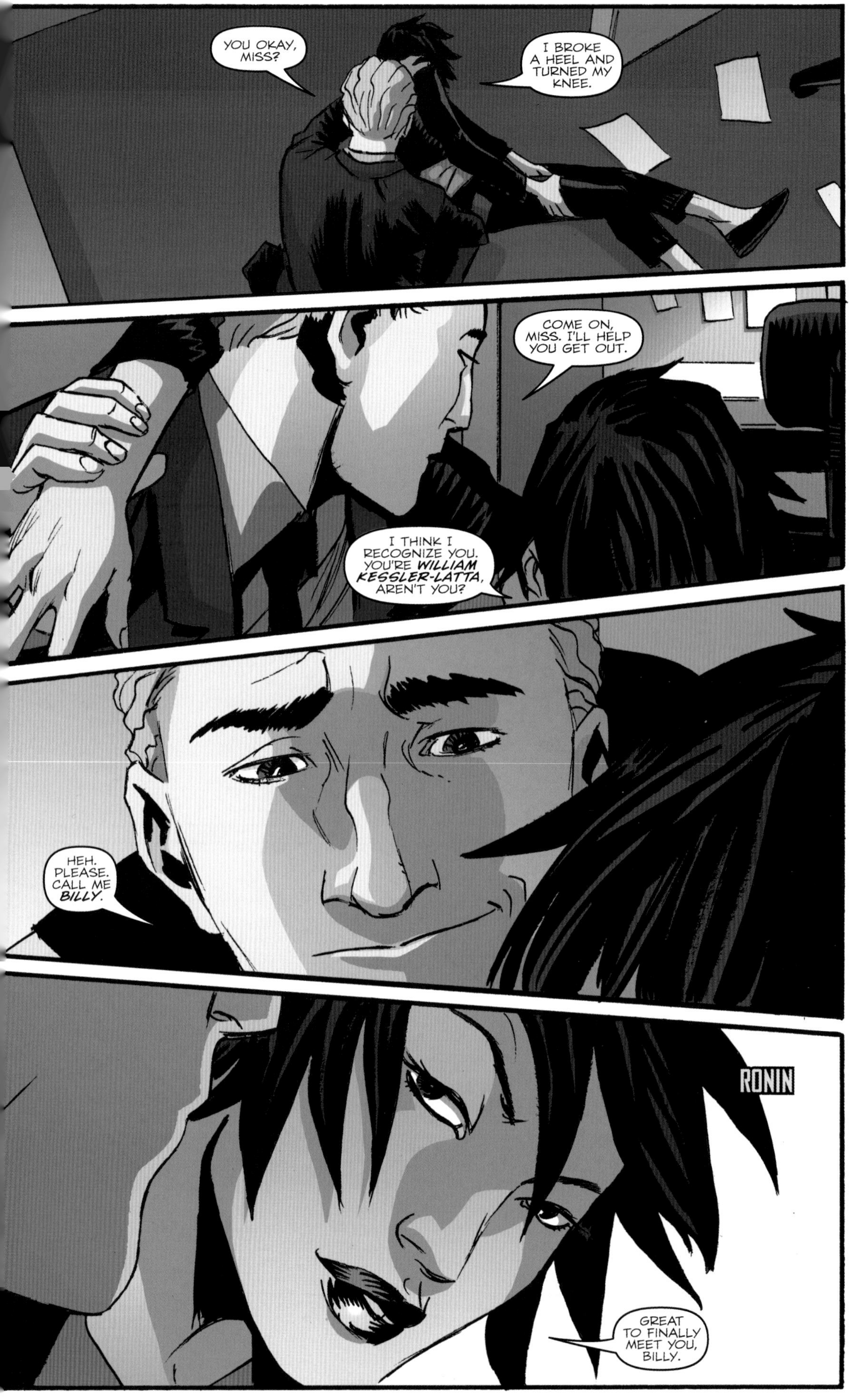
YOU OKAY, MISS?
I BROKE A HEEL AND TURNED MY KNEE.
COME ON, MISS. I'LL HELP YOU GET OUT.
I THINK I RECOGNIZE YOU. YOU'RE **WILLIAM KESSLER-LATTA**, AREN'T YOU?
HEH. PLEASE. CALL ME **BILLY**.
RONIN
GREAT TO FINALLY MEET YOU, BILLY.

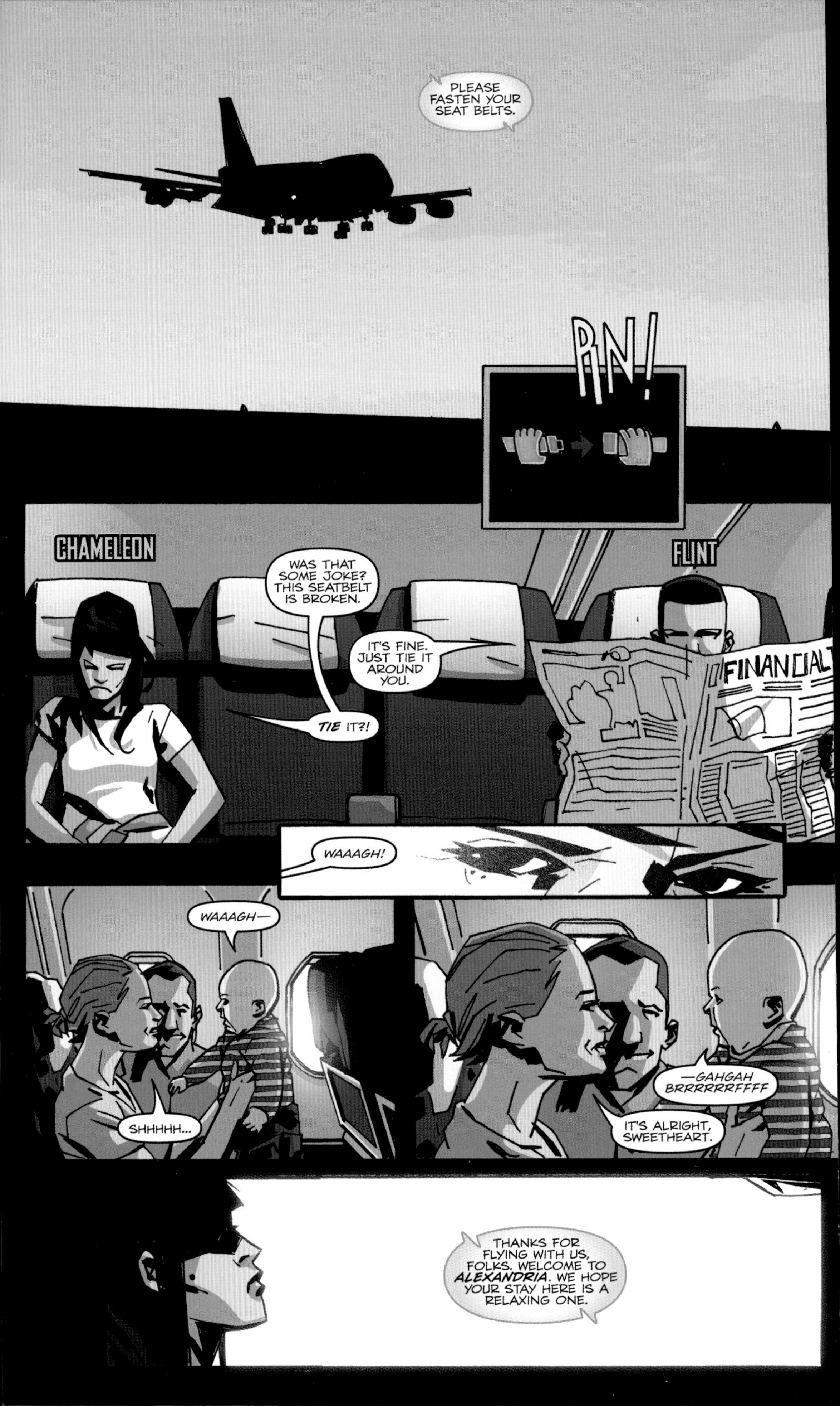
PLEASE FASTEN YOUR SEAT BELTS.
RN!
CHAMELEON
FLINT
WAS THAT SOME JOKE? THIS SEATBELT IS BROKEN.
IT'S FINE. JUST TIE IT AROUND YOU.
TIE IT?!
FINANCIAL
WAAAGH!
WAAAGH—
SHHHHH...
—GAHGAH BRRRRRRFFFF
IT'S ALRIGHT, SWEETHEART.
THANKS FOR FLYING WITH US, FOLKS. WELCOME TO ALEXANDRIA. WE HOPE YOUR STAY HERE IS A RELAXING ONE.

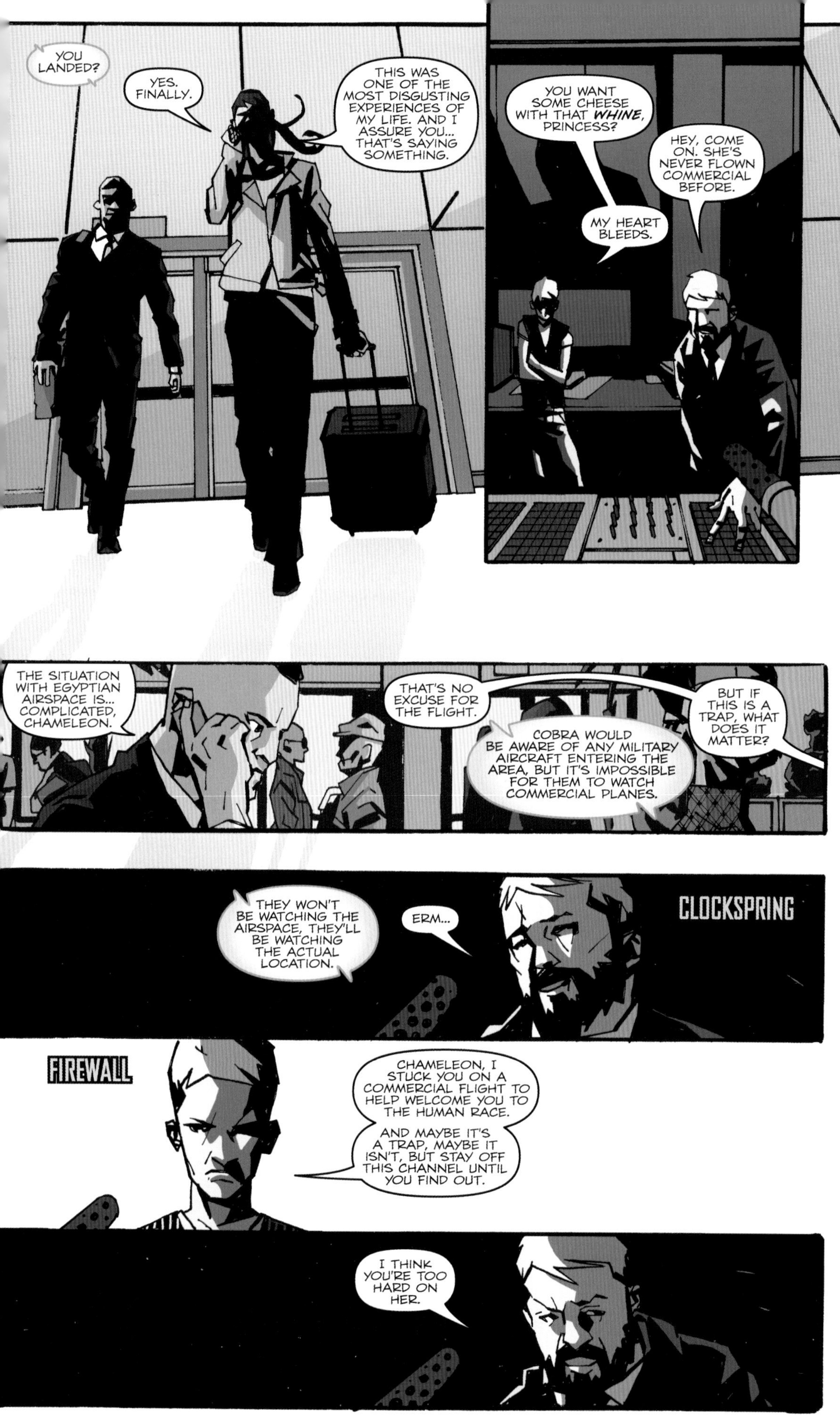

YOU LANDED?
YES. FINALLY.
THIS WAS ONE OF THE MOST DISGUSTING EXPERIENCES OF MY LIFE. AND I ASSURE YOU... THAT'S SAYING SOMETHING.
YOU WANT SOME CHEESE WITH THAT *WHINE*, PRINCESS?
HEY, COME ON. SHE'S NEVER FLOWN COMMERCIAL BEFORE.
MY HEART BLEEDS.
THE SITUATION WITH EGYPTIAN AIRSPACE IS... COMPLICATED, CHAMELEON.
THAT'S NO EXCUSE FOR THE FLIGHT.
COBRA WOULD BE AWARE OF ANY MILITARY AIRCRAFT ENTERING THE AREA, BUT IT'S IMPOSSIBLE FOR THEM TO WATCH COMMERCIAL PLANES.
BUT IF THIS IS A TRAP, WHAT DOES IT MATTER?
THEY WON'T BE WATCHING THE AIRSPACE, THEY'LL BE WATCHING THE ACTUAL LOCATION.
ERM...
CLOCKSPRING
FIREWALL
CHAMELEON, I STUCK YOU ON A COMMERCIAL FLIGHT TO HELP WELCOME YOU TO THE HUMAN RACE.
AND MAYBE IT'S A TRAP, MAYBE IT ISN'T, BUT STAY OFF THIS CHANNEL UNTIL YOU FIND OUT.
I THINK YOU'RE TOO HARD ON HER.

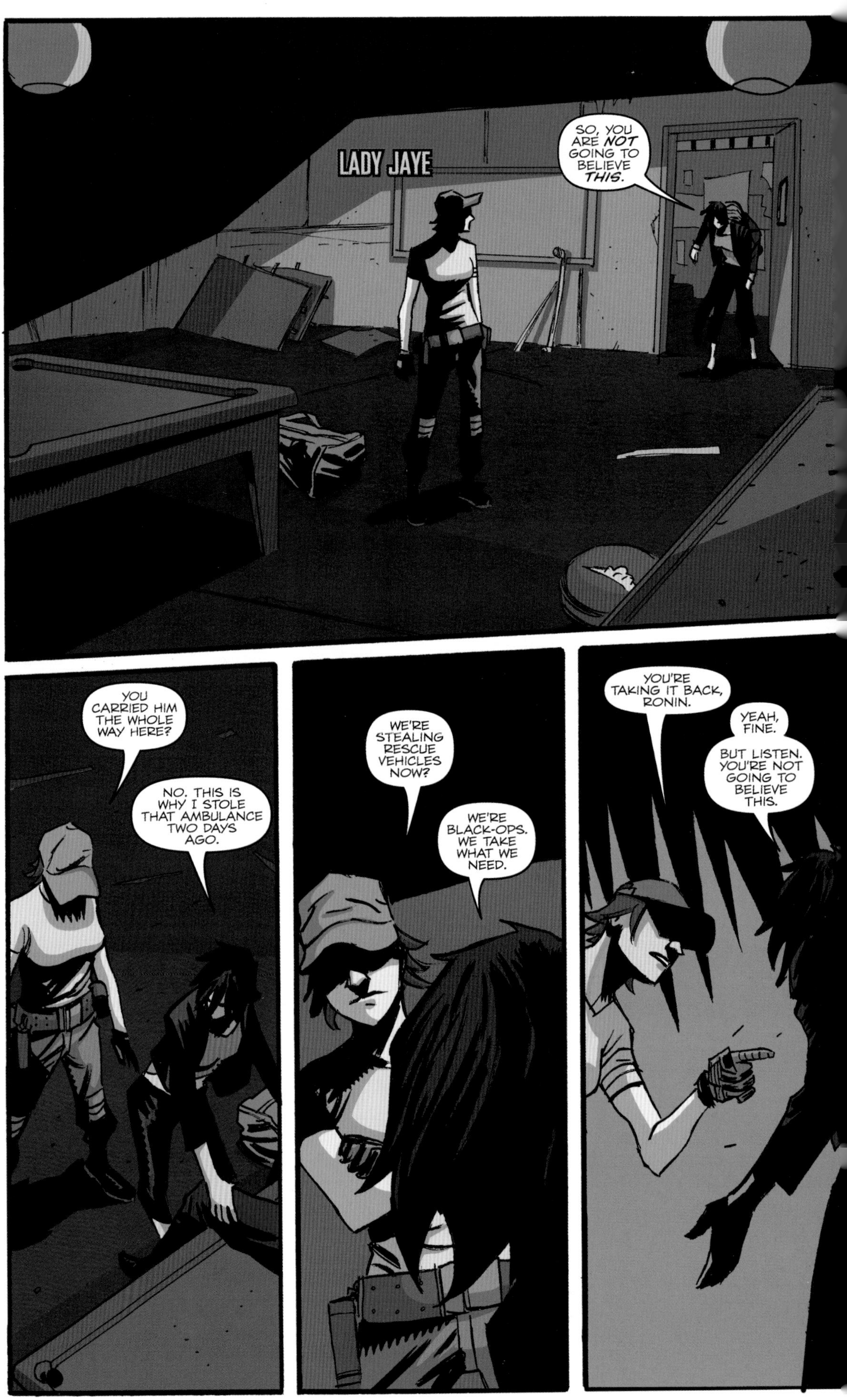
LADY JAYE
SO, YOU ARE NOT GOING TO BELIEVE THIS.
YOU CARRIED HIM THE WHOLE WAY HERE?
NO. THIS IS WHY I STOLE THAT AMBULANCE TWO DAYS AGO.
WE'RE STEALING RESCUE VEHICLES NOW?
WE'RE BLACK-OPS. WE TAKE WHAT WE NEED.
YOU'RE TAKING IT BACK, RONIN.
YEAH, FINE.
BUT LISTEN. YOU'RE NOT GOING TO BELIEVE THIS.

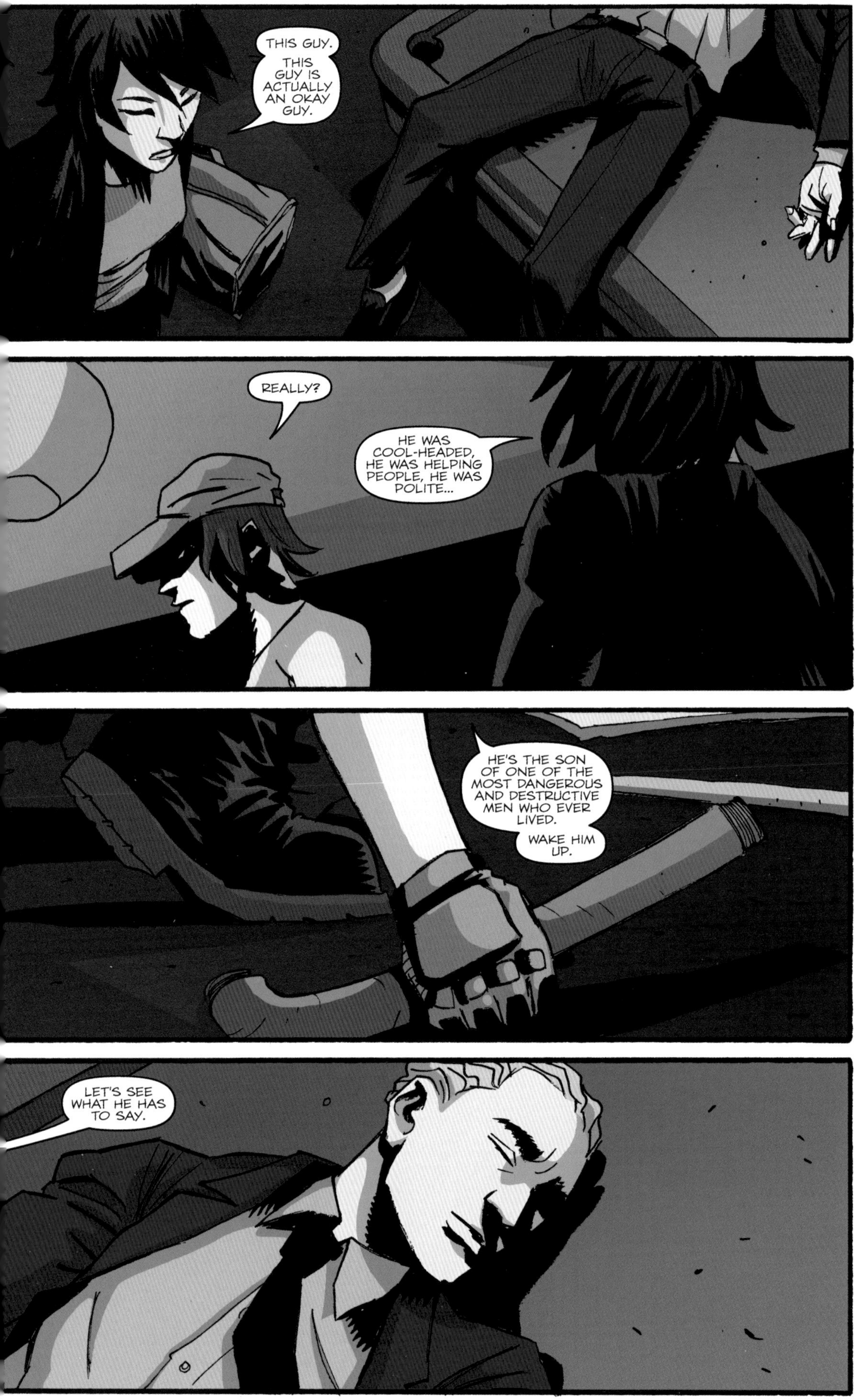
THIS GUY.
THIS GUY IS ACTUALLY AN OKAY GUY.
REALLY?
HE WAS COOL-HEADED, HE WAS HELPING PEOPLE, HE WAS POLITE...
HE'S THE SON OF ONE OF THE MOST DANGEROUS AND DESTRUCTIVE MEN WHO EVER LIVED.
WAKE HIM UP.
LET'S SEE WHAT HE HAS TO SAY.

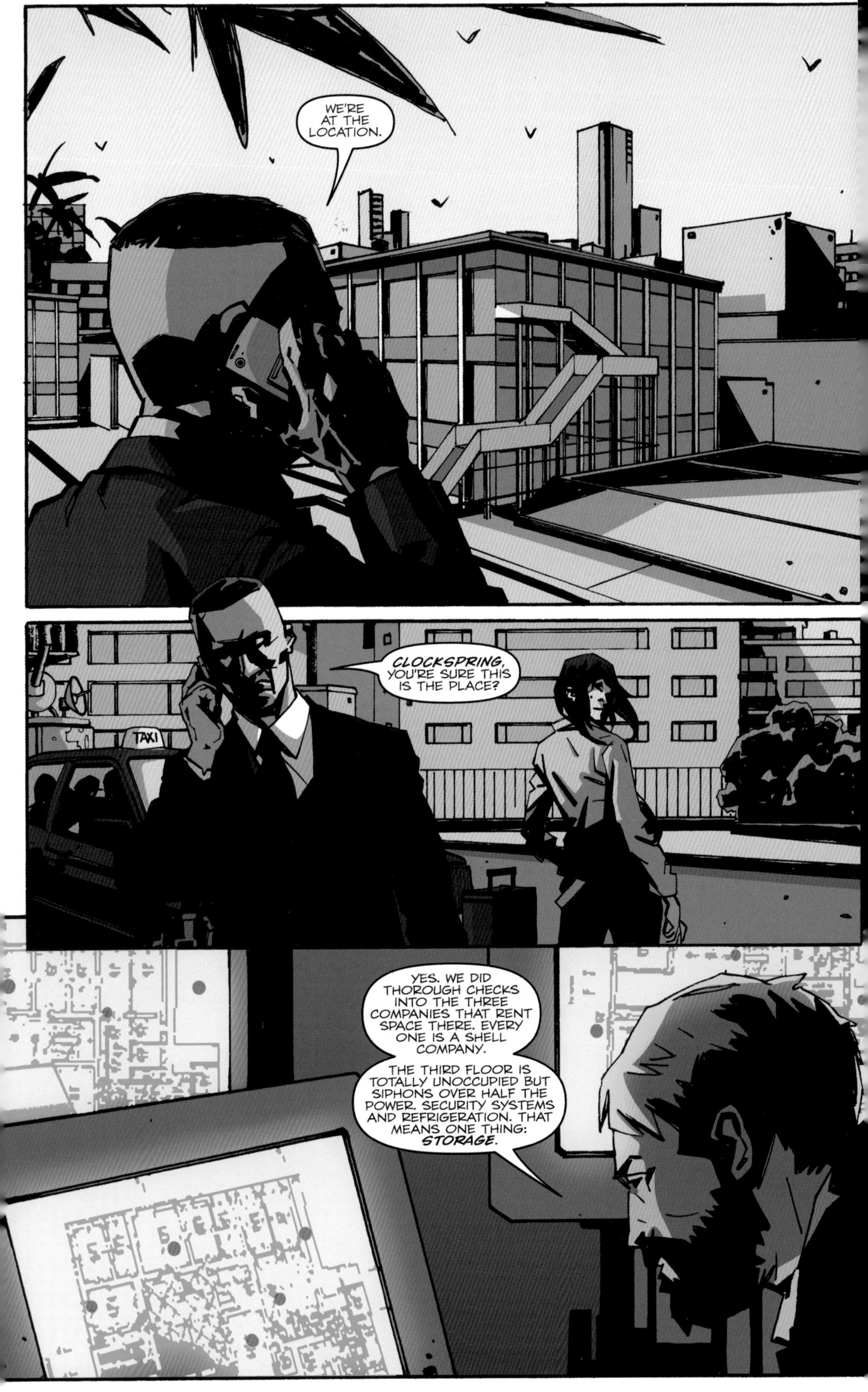
WE'RE AT THE LOCATION.
CLOCKSPRING, YOU'RE SURE THIS IS THE PLACE?
TAXI
YES. WE DID THOROUGH CHECKS INTO THE THREE COMPANIES THAT RENT SPACE THERE. EVERY ONE IS A SHELL COMPANY.
THE THIRD FLOOR IS TOTALLY UNOCCUPIED BUT SIPHONS OVER HALF THE POWER. SECURITY SYSTEMS AND REFRIGERATION. THAT MEANS ONE THING: STORAGE.

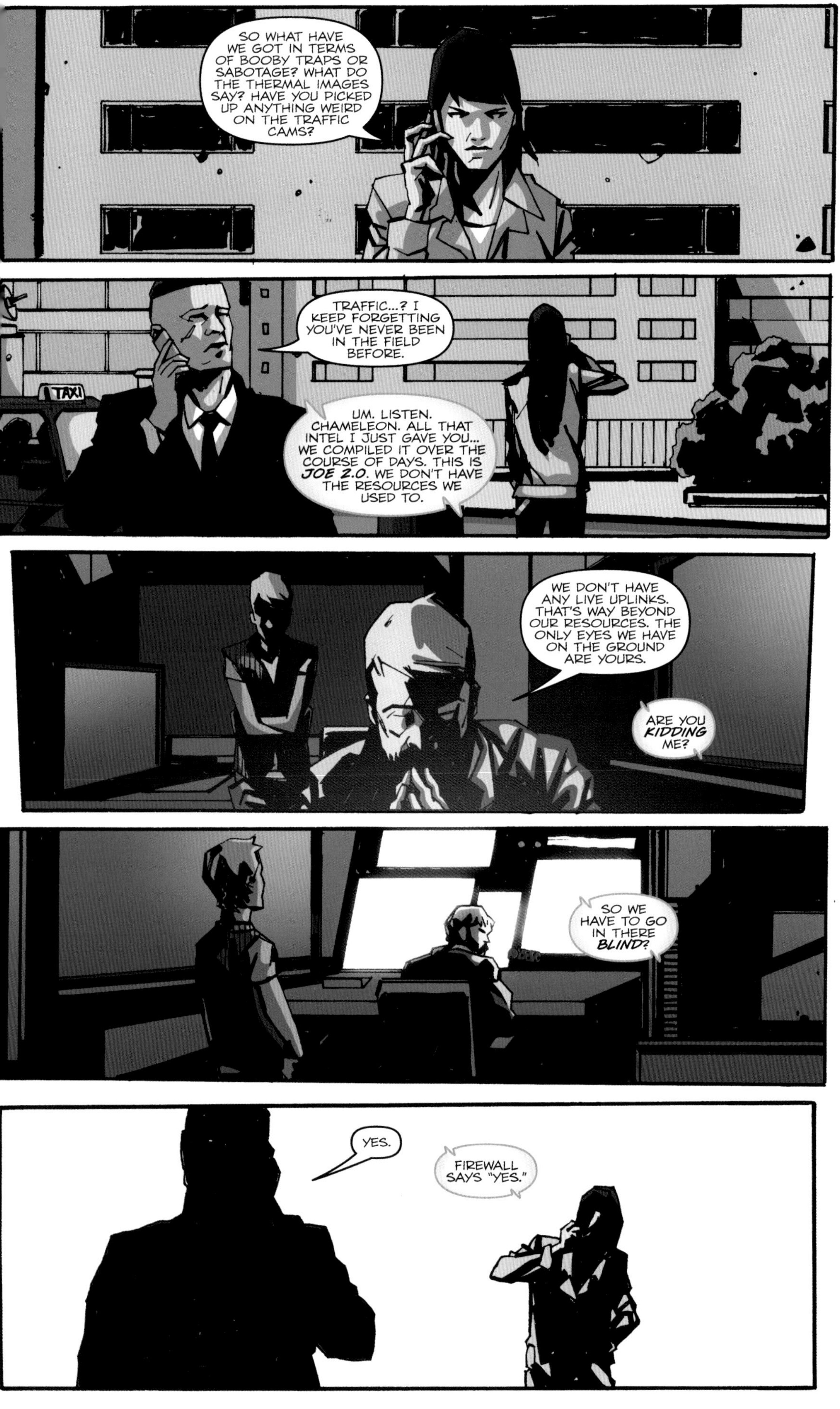
SO WHAT HAVE WE GOT IN TERMS OF BOOBY TRAPS OR SABOTAGE? WHAT DO THE THERMAL IMAGES SAY? HAVE YOU PICKED UP ANYTHING WEIRD ON THE TRAFFIC CAMS?
TAXI
TRAFFIC...? I KEEP FORGETTING YOU'VE NEVER BEEN IN THE FIELD BEFORE.
UM. LISTEN. CHAMELEON. ALL THAT INTEL I JUST GAVE YOU... WE COMPILED IT OVER THE COURSE OF DAYS. THIS IS *JOE 2.0*. WE DON'T HAVE THE RESOURCES WE USED TO.
WE DON'T HAVE ANY LIVE UPLINKS. THAT'S WAY BEYOND OUR RESOURCES. THE ONLY EYES WE HAVE ON THE GROUND ARE YOURS.
ARE YOU *KIDDING* ME?
SO WE HAVE TO GO IN THERE *BLIND*?
YES.
FIREWALL SAYS "YES."

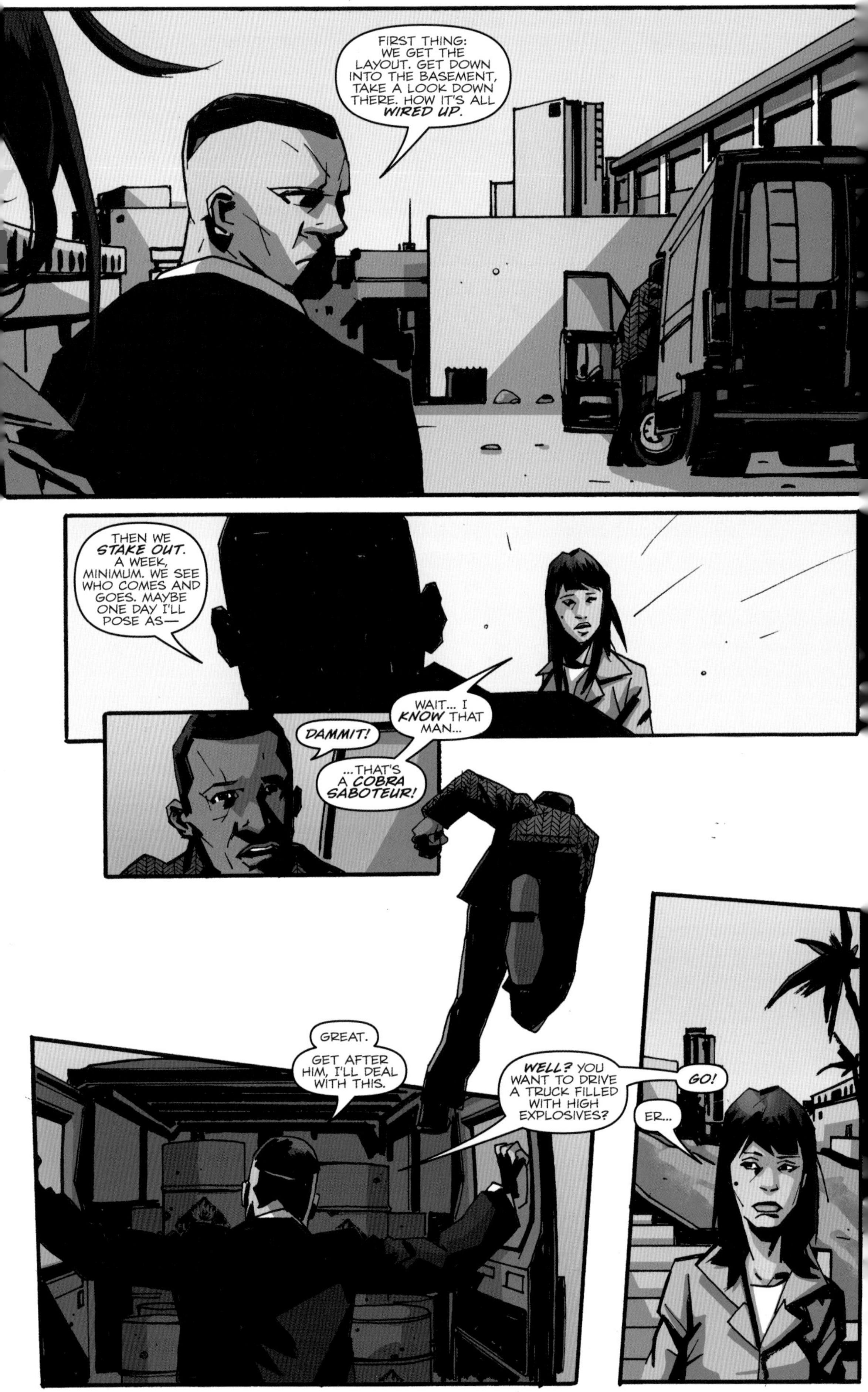
FIRST THING: WE GET THE LAYOUT. GET DOWN INTO THE BASEMENT, TAKE A LOOK DOWN THERE. HOW IT'S ALL WIRED UP.
THEN WE STAKE OUT. A WEEK, MINIMUM. WE SEE WHO COMES AND GOES. MAYBE ONE DAY I'LL POSE AS—
WAIT... I KNOW THAT MAN...
...THAT'S A COBRA SABOTEUR!
DAMMIT!
GREAT.
GET AFTER HIM, I'LL DEAL WITH THIS.
WELL? YOU WANT TO DRIVE A TRUCK FILLED WITH HIGH EXPLOSIVES?
GO!
ER...

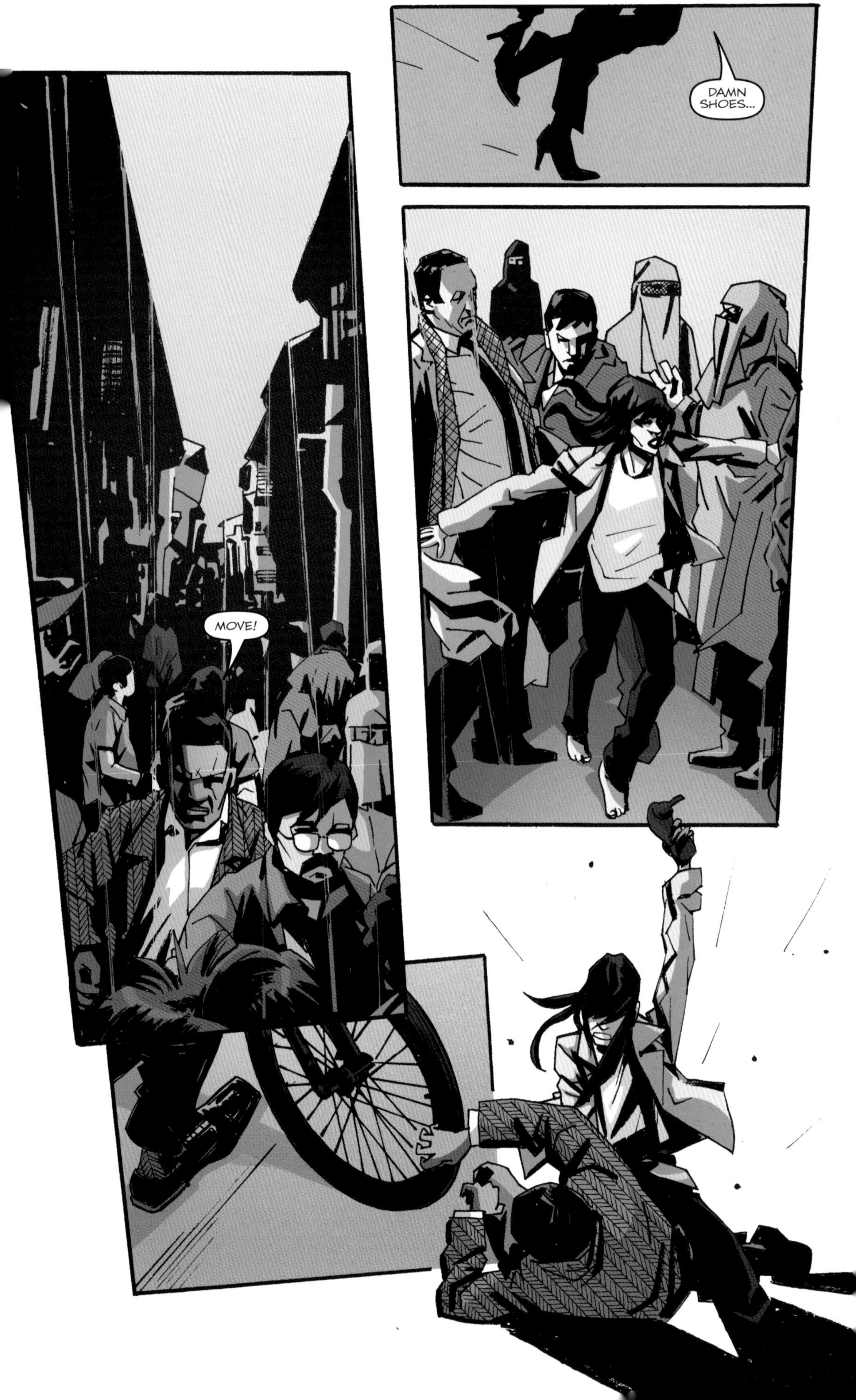
MOVE!
DAMN SHOES...

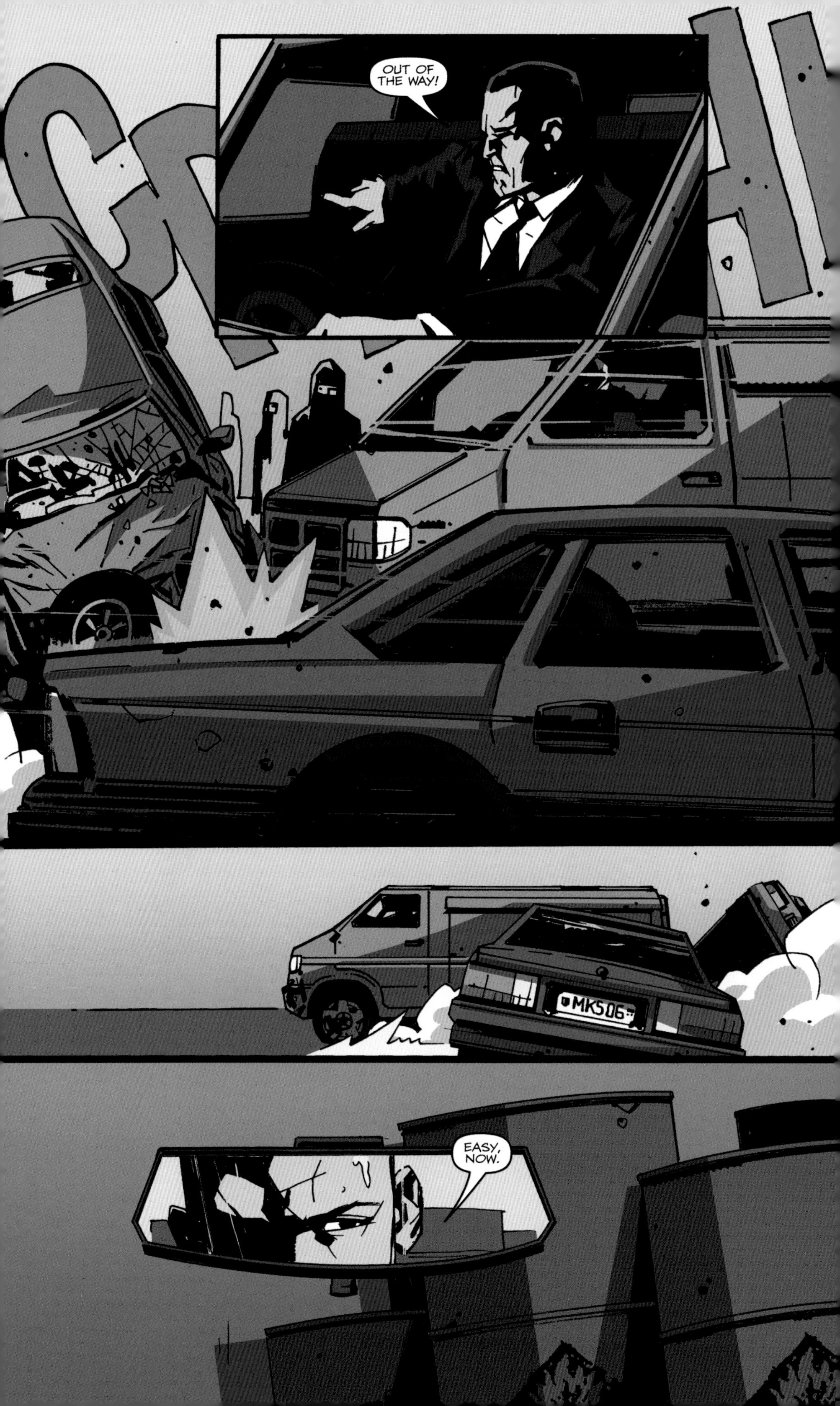
OUT OF THE WAY!
MKS 06
EASY, NOW.

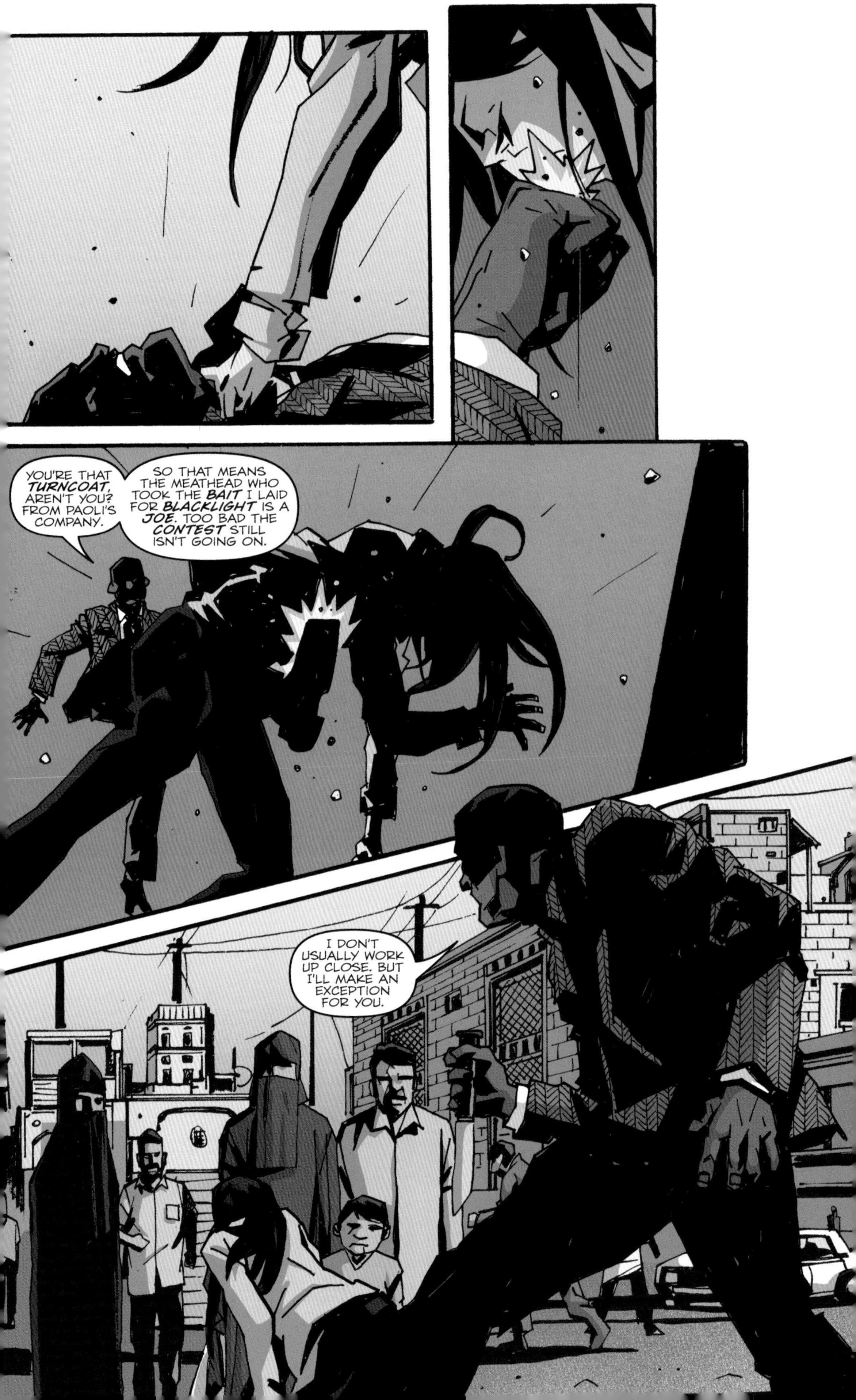
YOU'RE THAT TURNCOAT, AREN'T YOU? FROM PAOLI'S COMPANY.
SO THAT MEANS THE MEATHEAD WHO TOOK THE BAIT I LAID FOR BLACKLIGHT IS A JOE. TOO BAD THE CONTEST STILL ISN'T GOING ON.
I DON'T USUALLY WORK UP CLOSE. BUT I'LL MAKE AN EXCEPTION FOR YOU.

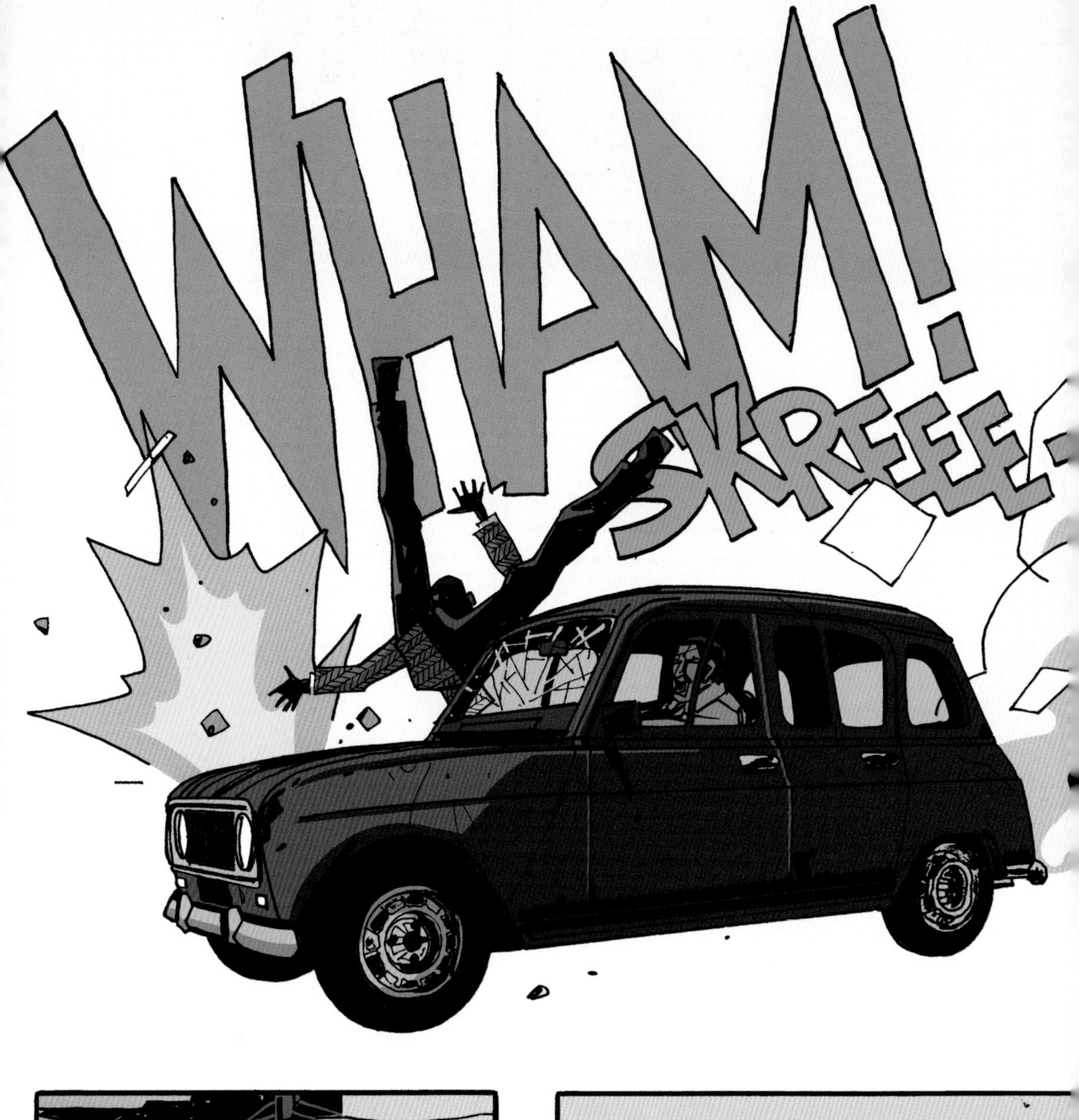
WHAM!
SKREEE-
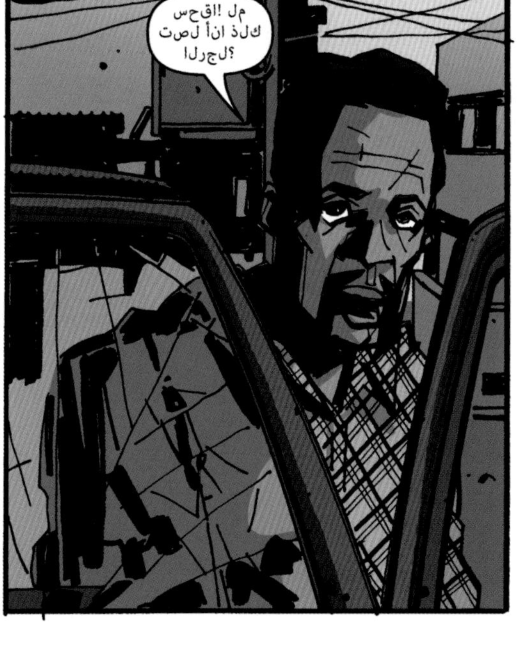
سحقا! لم
تصل أنا ذلك
الرجل؟
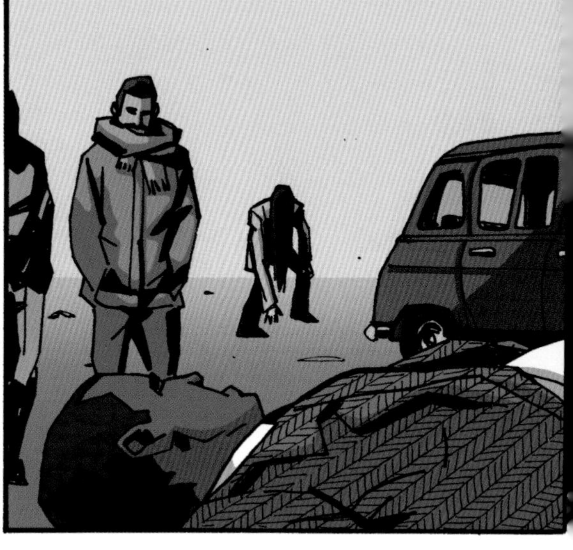

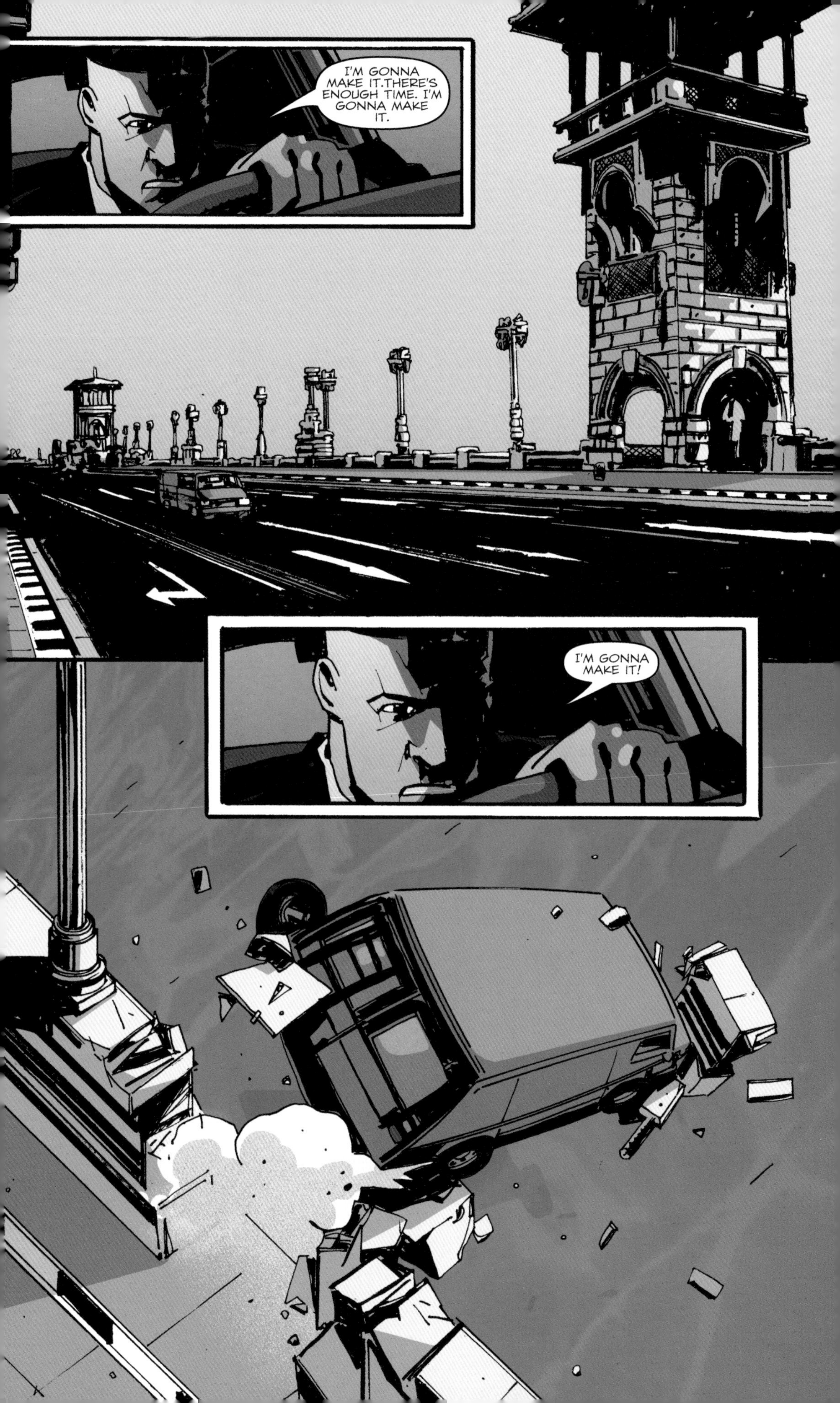
I'M GONNA MAKE IT.THERE'S ENOUGH TIME. I'M GONNA MAKE IT.
I'M GONNA MAKE IT!

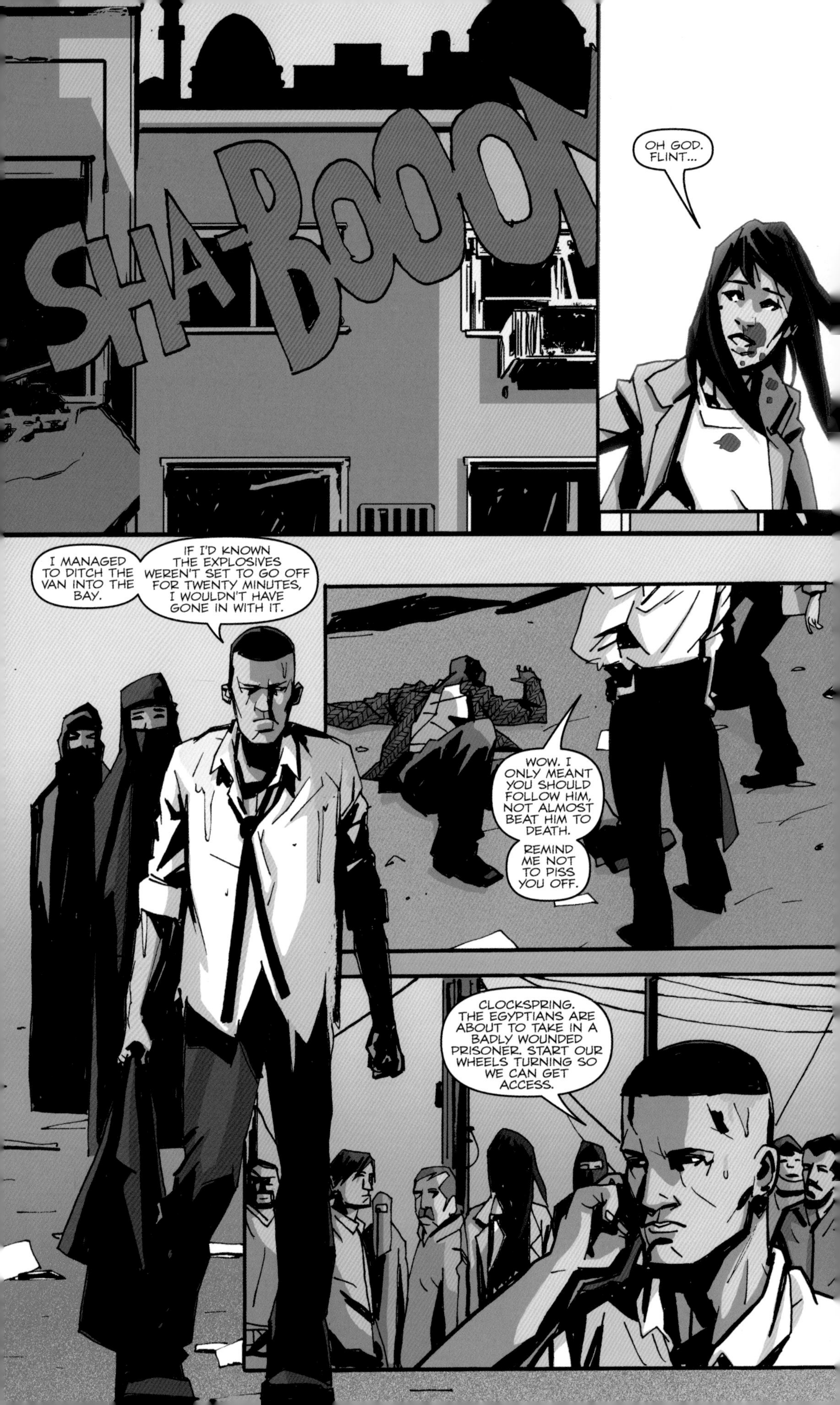
SHA-BOOOOM
OH GOD. FLINT...
I MANAGED TO DITCH THE VAN INTO THE BAY.
IF I'D KNOWN THE EXPLOSIVES WEREN'T SET TO GO OFF FOR TWENTY MINUTES, I WOULDN'T HAVE GONE IN WITH IT.
WOW. I ONLY MEANT YOU SHOULD FOLLOW HIM, NOT ALMOST BEAT HIM TO DEATH.
REMIND ME NOT TO PISS YOU OFF.
CLOCKSPRING. THE EGYPTIANS ARE ABOUT TO TAKE IN A BADLY WOUNDED PRISONER. START OUR WHEELS TURNING SO WE CAN GET ACCESS.

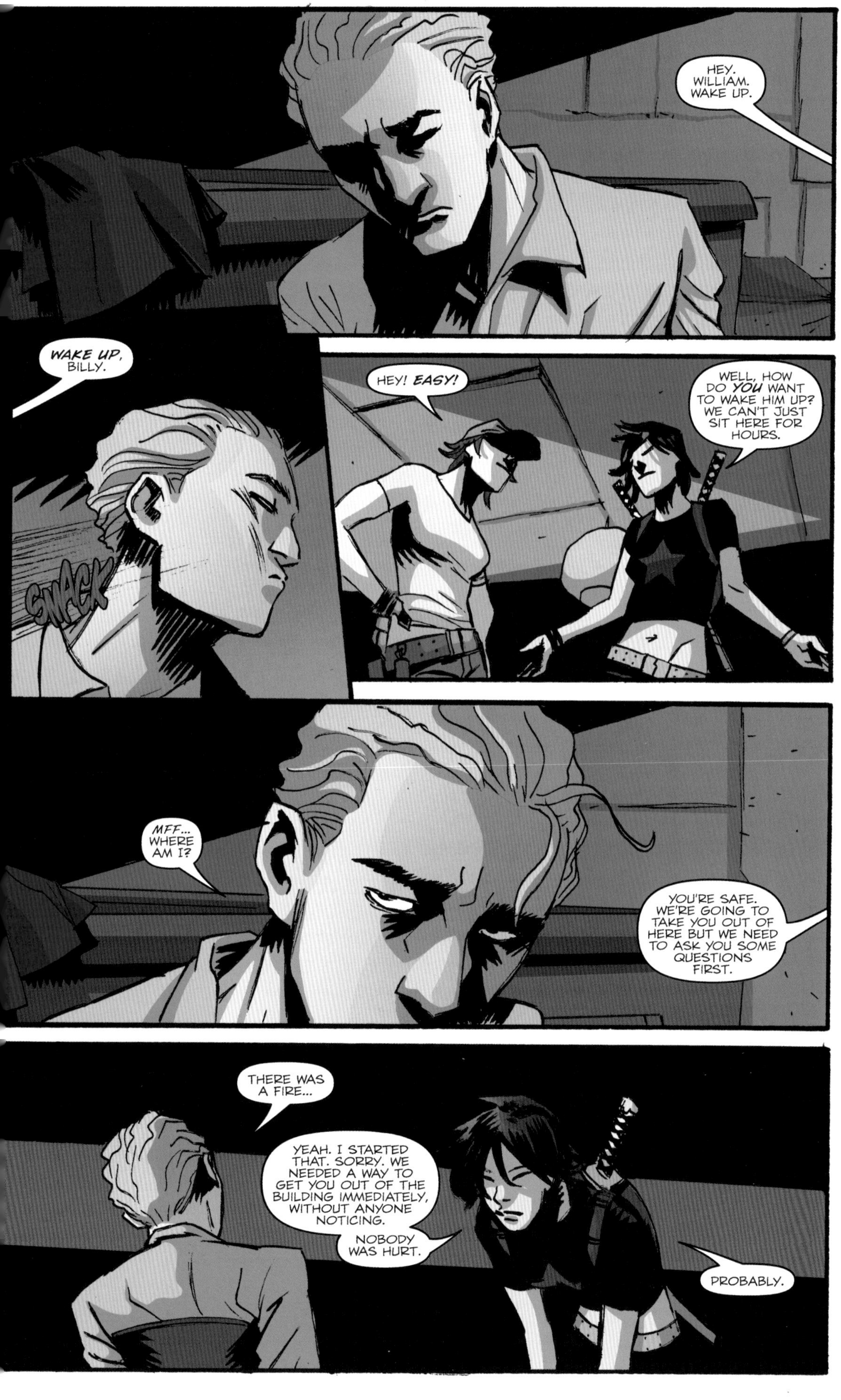
HEY. WILLIAM. WAKE UP.
WAKE UP, BILLY.
SMACK
HEY! EASY!
WELL, HOW DO YOU WANT TO WAKE HIM UP? WE CAN'T JUST SIT HERE FOR HOURS.
MFF... WHERE AM I?
YOU'RE SAFE. WE'RE GOING TO TAKE YOU OUT OF HERE BUT WE NEED TO ASK YOU SOME QUESTIONS FIRST.
THERE WAS A FIRE...
YEAH. I STARTED THAT. SORRY. WE NEEDED A WAY TO GET YOU OUT OF THE BUILDING IMMEDIATELY, WITHOUT ANYONE NOTICING.
NOBODY WAS HURT.
PROBABLY.

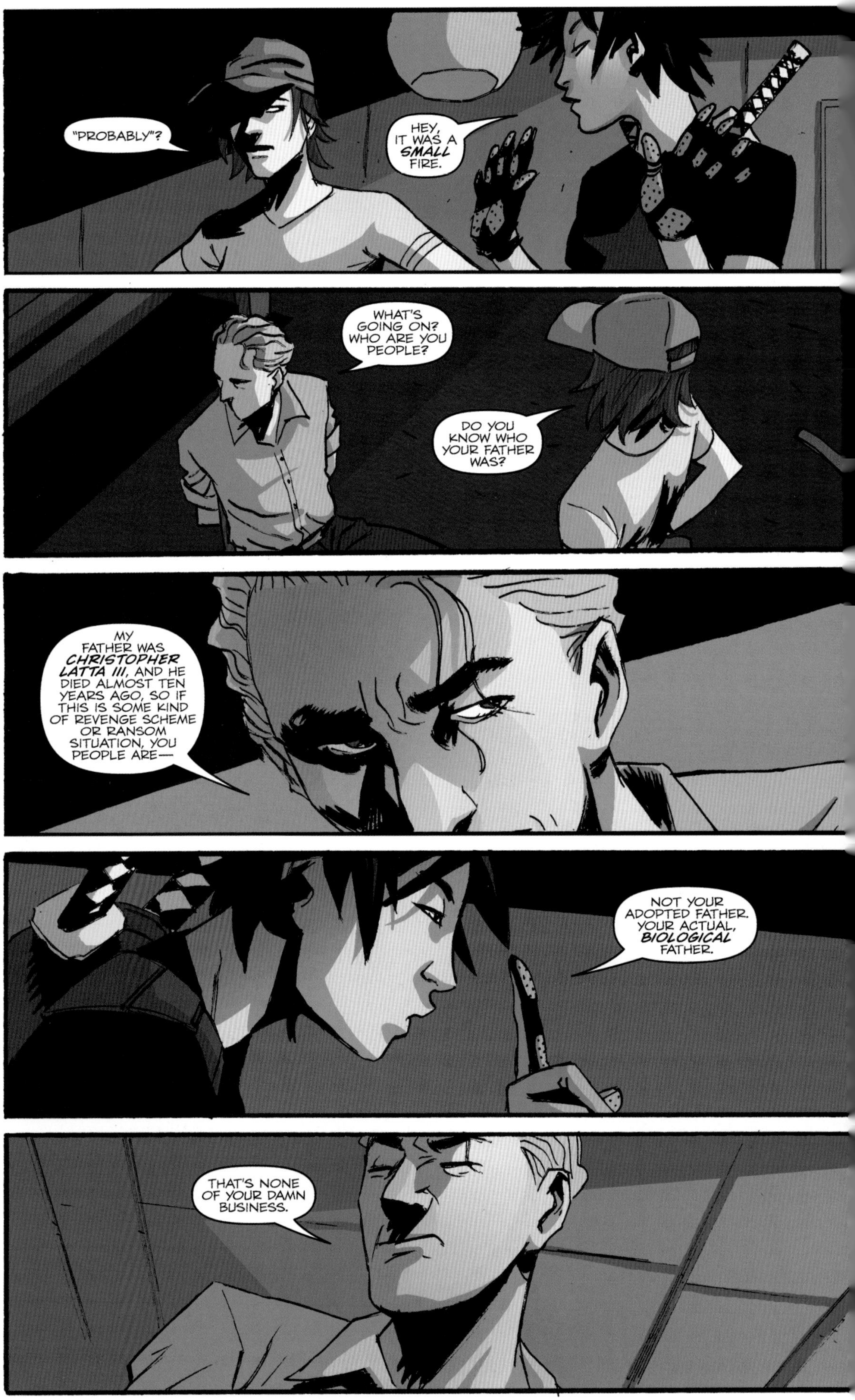
"PROBABLY"?
HEY, IT WAS A *SMALL* FIRE.
WHAT'S GOING ON? WHO ARE YOU PEOPLE?
DO YOU KNOW WHO YOUR FATHER WAS?
MY FATHER WAS *CHRISTOPHER LATTA III*, AND HE DIED ALMOST TEN YEARS AGO, SO IF THIS IS SOME KIND OF REVENGE SCHEME OR RANSOM SITUATION, YOU PEOPLE ARE—
NOT YOUR ADOPTED FATHER. YOUR ACTUAL, *BIOLOGICAL* FATHER.
THAT'S NONE OF YOUR DAMN BUSINESS.

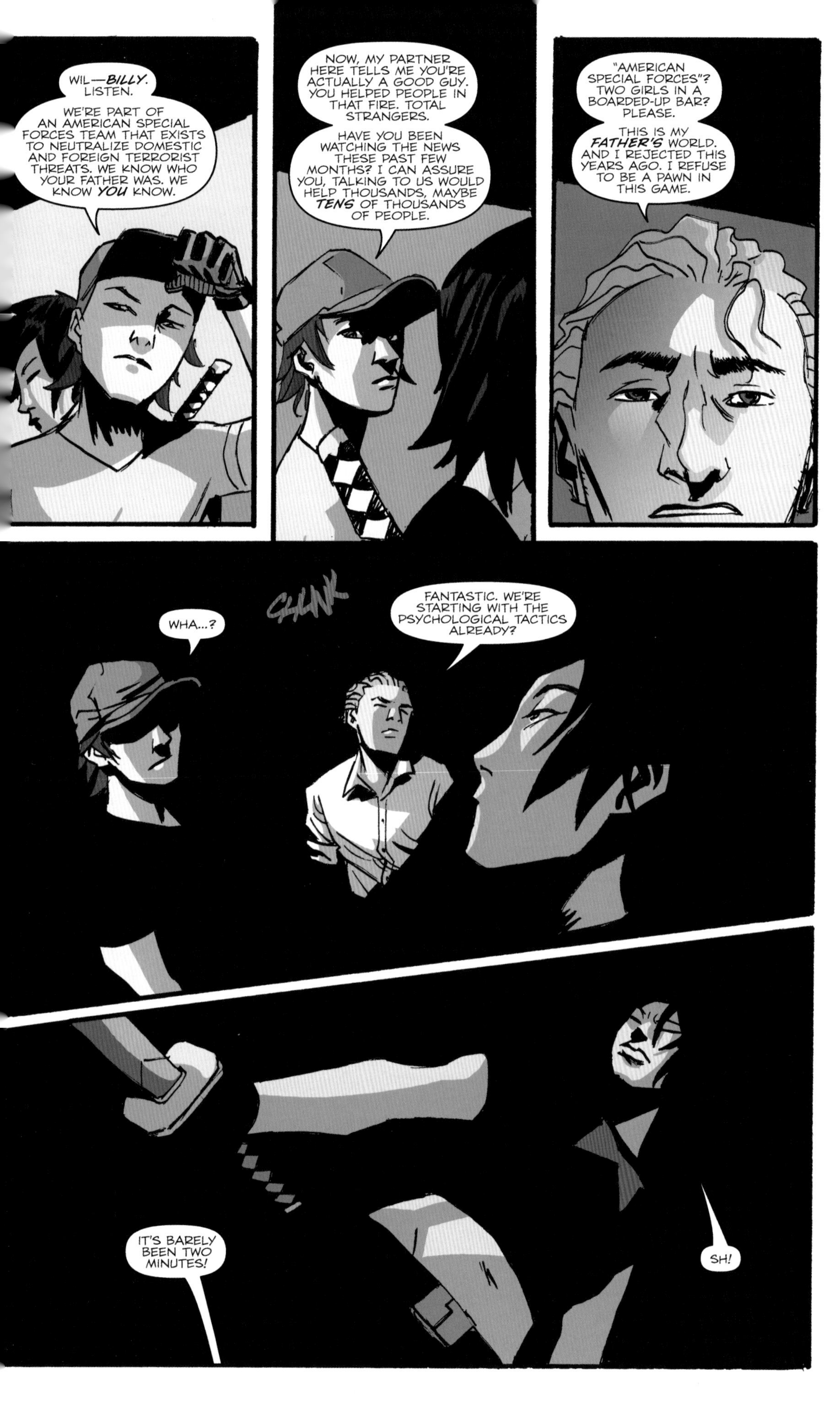
WIL—*BILLY*. LISTEN.
WE'RE PART OF AN AMERICAN SPECIAL FORCES TEAM THAT EXISTS TO NEUTRALIZE DOMESTIC AND FOREIGN TERRORIST THREATS. WE KNOW WHO YOUR FATHER WAS. WE KNOW *YOU* KNOW.
NOW, MY PARTNER HERE TELLS ME YOU'RE ACTUALLY A GOOD GUY. YOU HELPED PEOPLE IN THAT FIRE. TOTAL STRANGERS.
HAVE YOU BEEN WATCHING THE NEWS THESE PAST FEW MONTHS? I CAN ASSURE YOU, TALKING TO US WOULD HELP THOUSANDS, MAYBE *TENS* OF THOUSANDS OF PEOPLE.
"AMERICAN SPECIAL FORCES"? TWO GIRLS IN A BOARDED-UP BAR? PLEASE.
THIS IS MY *FATHER'S* WORLD. AND I REJECTED THIS YEARS AGO. I REFUSE TO BE A PAWN IN THIS GAME.
WHA...?
SHUNK
FANTASTIC. WE'RE STARTING WITH THE PSYCHOLOGICAL TACTICS ALREADY?
IT'S BARELY BEEN TWO MINUTES!
SH!

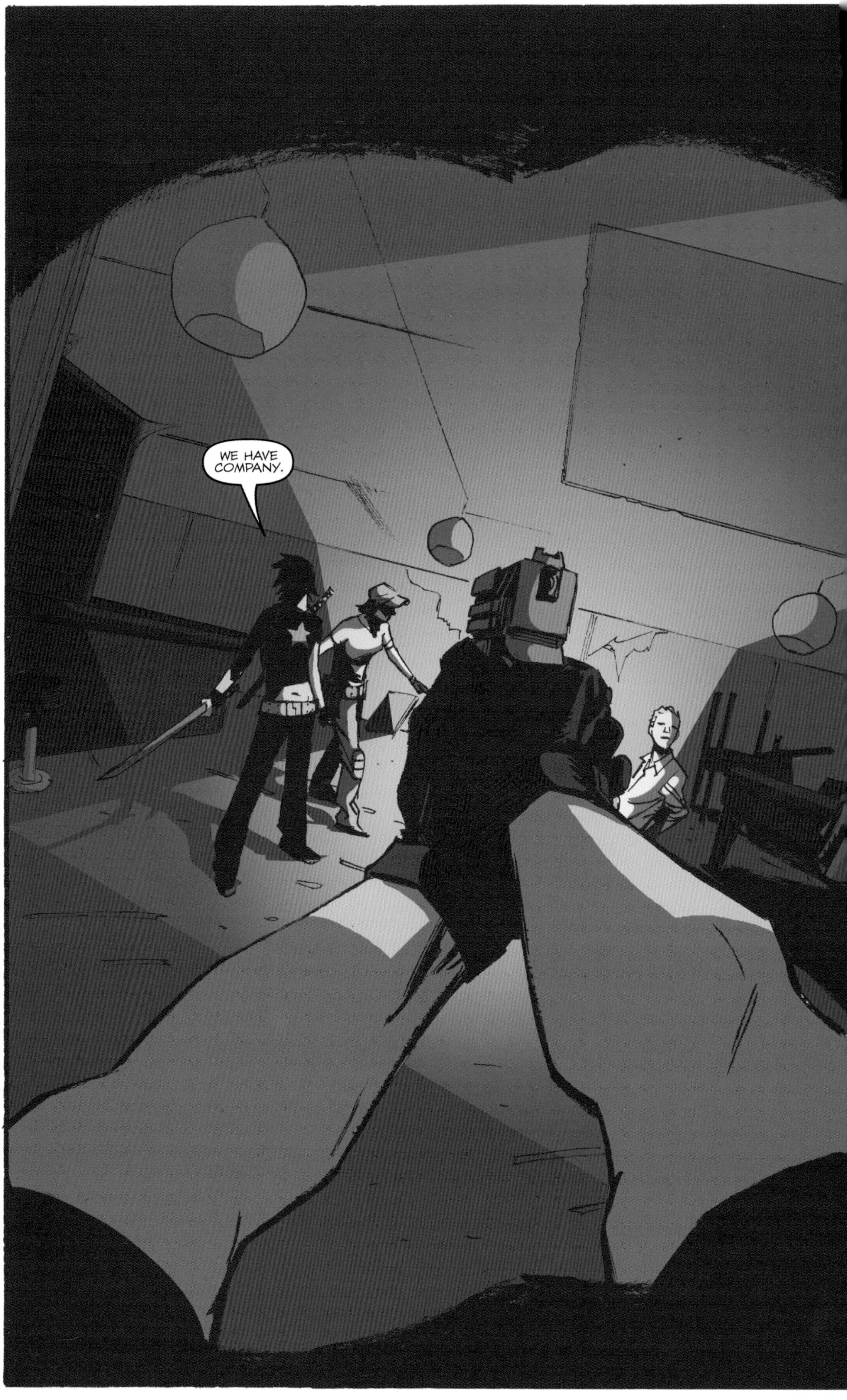
WE HAVE COMPANY.

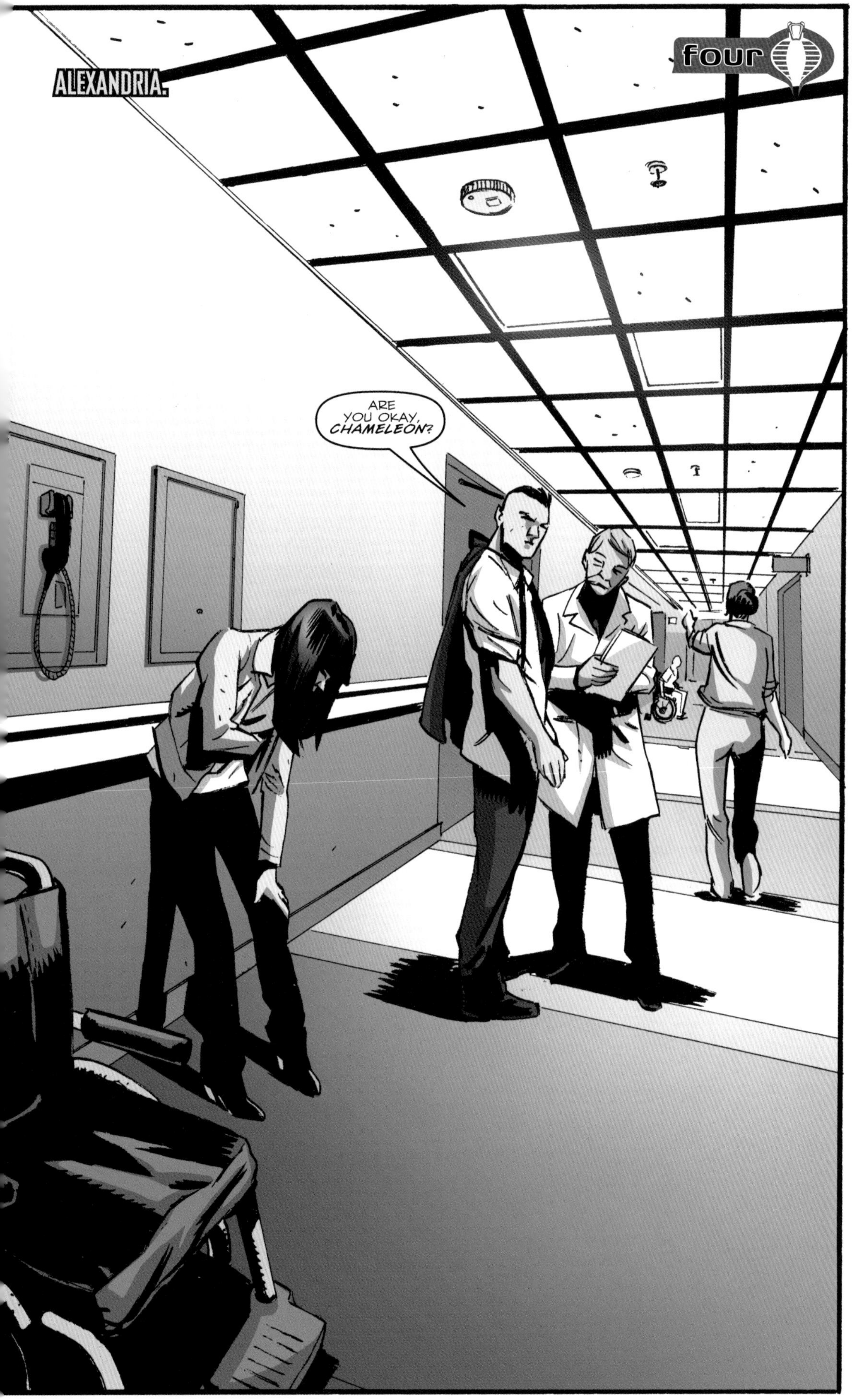
four
ALEXANDRIA.
ARE YOU OKAY, CHAMELEON?

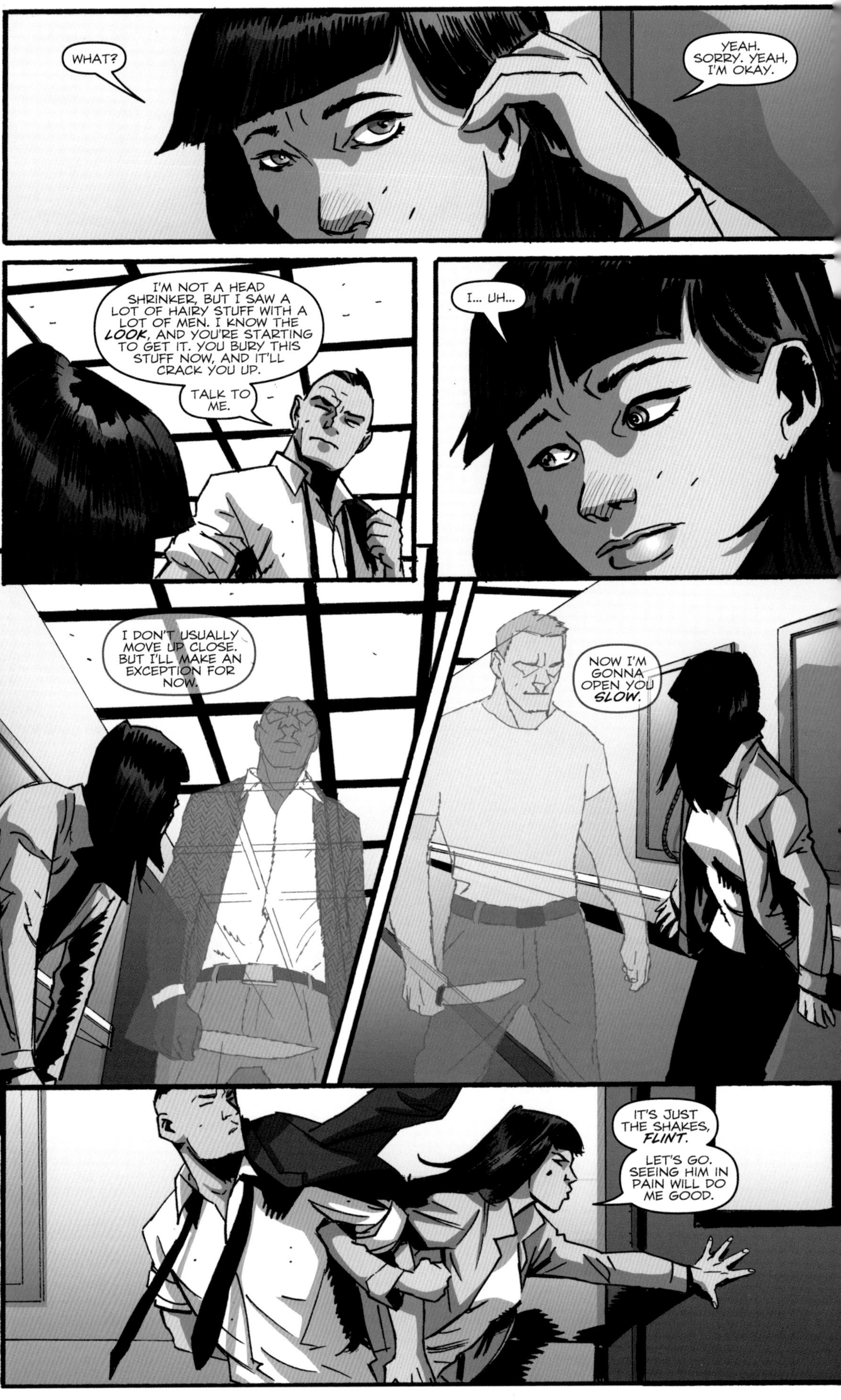
WHAT?
YEAH. SORRY. YEAH, I'M OKAY.
I'M NOT A HEAD SHRINKER, BUT I SAW A LOT OF HAIRY STUFF WITH A LOT OF MEN. I KNOW THE LOOK, AND YOU'RE STARTING TO GET IT. YOU BURY THIS STUFF NOW, AND IT'LL CRACK YOU UP.
TALK TO ME.
I... UH...
I DON'T USUALLY MOVE UP CLOSE. BUT I'LL MAKE AN EXCEPTION FOR NOW.
NOW I'M GONNA OPEN YOU SLOW.
IT'S JUST THE SHAKES, FLINT.
LET'S GO. SEEING HIM IN PAIN WILL DO ME GOOD.

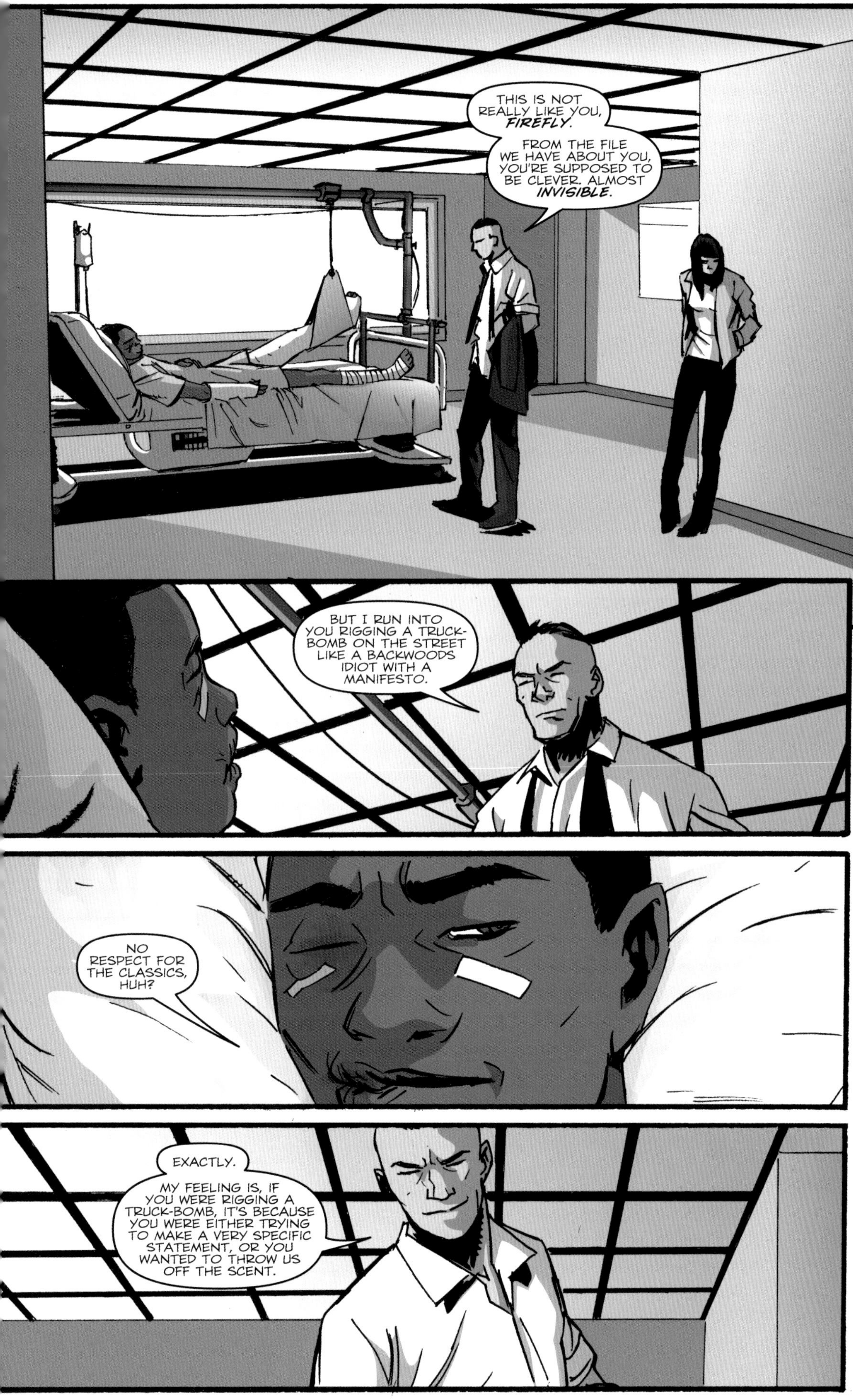
THIS IS NOT REALLY LIKE YOU, *FIREFLY*.
FROM THE FILE WE HAVE ABOUT YOU, YOU'RE SUPPOSED TO BE CLEVER. ALMOST *INVISIBLE*.
BUT I RUN INTO YOU RIGGING A TRUCK-BOMB ON THE STREET LIKE A BACKWOODS IDIOT WITH A MANIFESTO.
NO RESPECT FOR THE CLASSICS, HUH?
EXACTLY.
MY FEELING IS, IF YOU WERE RIGGING A TRUCK-BOMB, IT'S BECAUSE YOU WERE EITHER TRYING TO MAKE A VERY SPECIFIC STATEMENT, OR YOU WANTED TO THROW US OFF THE SCENT.

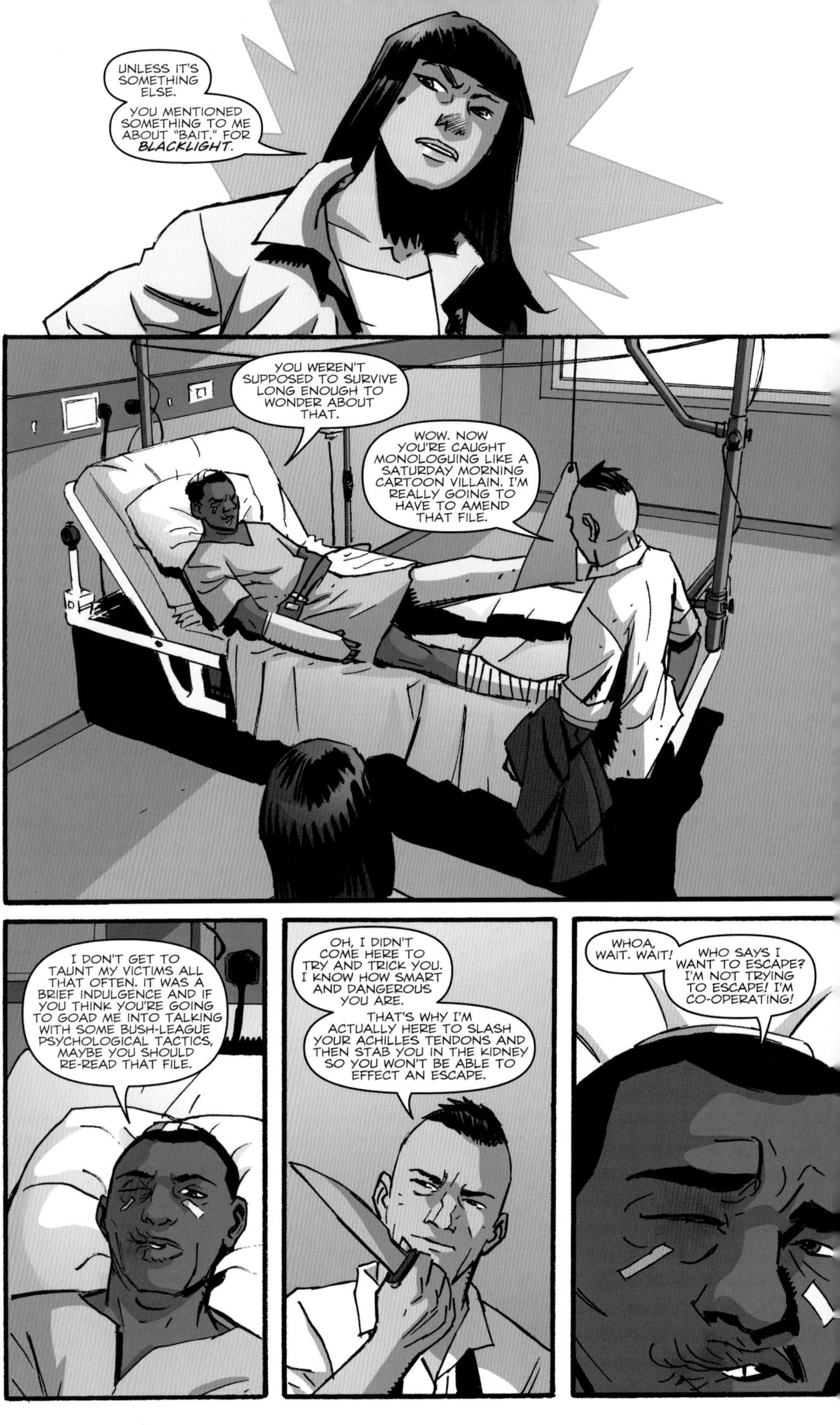
UNLESS IT'S SOMETHING ELSE.
YOU MENTIONED SOMETHING TO ME ABOUT "BAIT." FOR *BLACKLIGHT*.
YOU WEREN'T SUPPOSED TO SURVIVE LONG ENOUGH TO WONDER ABOUT THAT.
WOW. NOW YOU'RE CAUGHT MONOLOGUING LIKE A SATURDAY MORNING CARTOON VILLAIN. I'M REALLY GOING TO HAVE TO AMEND THAT FILE.
I DON'T GET TO TAUNT MY VICTIMS ALL THAT OFTEN. IT WAS A BRIEF INDULGENCE AND IF YOU THINK YOU'RE GOING TO GOAD ME INTO TALKING WITH SOME BUSH-LEAGUE PSYCHOLOGICAL TACTICS, MAYBE YOU SHOULD RE-READ THAT FILE.
OH, I DIDN'T COME HERE TO TRY AND TRICK YOU. I KNOW HOW SMART AND DANGEROUS YOU ARE.
THAT'S WHY I'M ACTUALLY HERE TO SLASH YOUR ACHILLES TENDONS AND THEN STAB YOU IN THE KIDNEY SO YOU WON'T BE ABLE TO EFFECT AN ESCAPE.
WHOA, WAIT. WAIT!
WHO SAYS I WANT TO ESCAPE? I'M NOT TRYING TO ESCAPE! I'M CO-OPERATING!

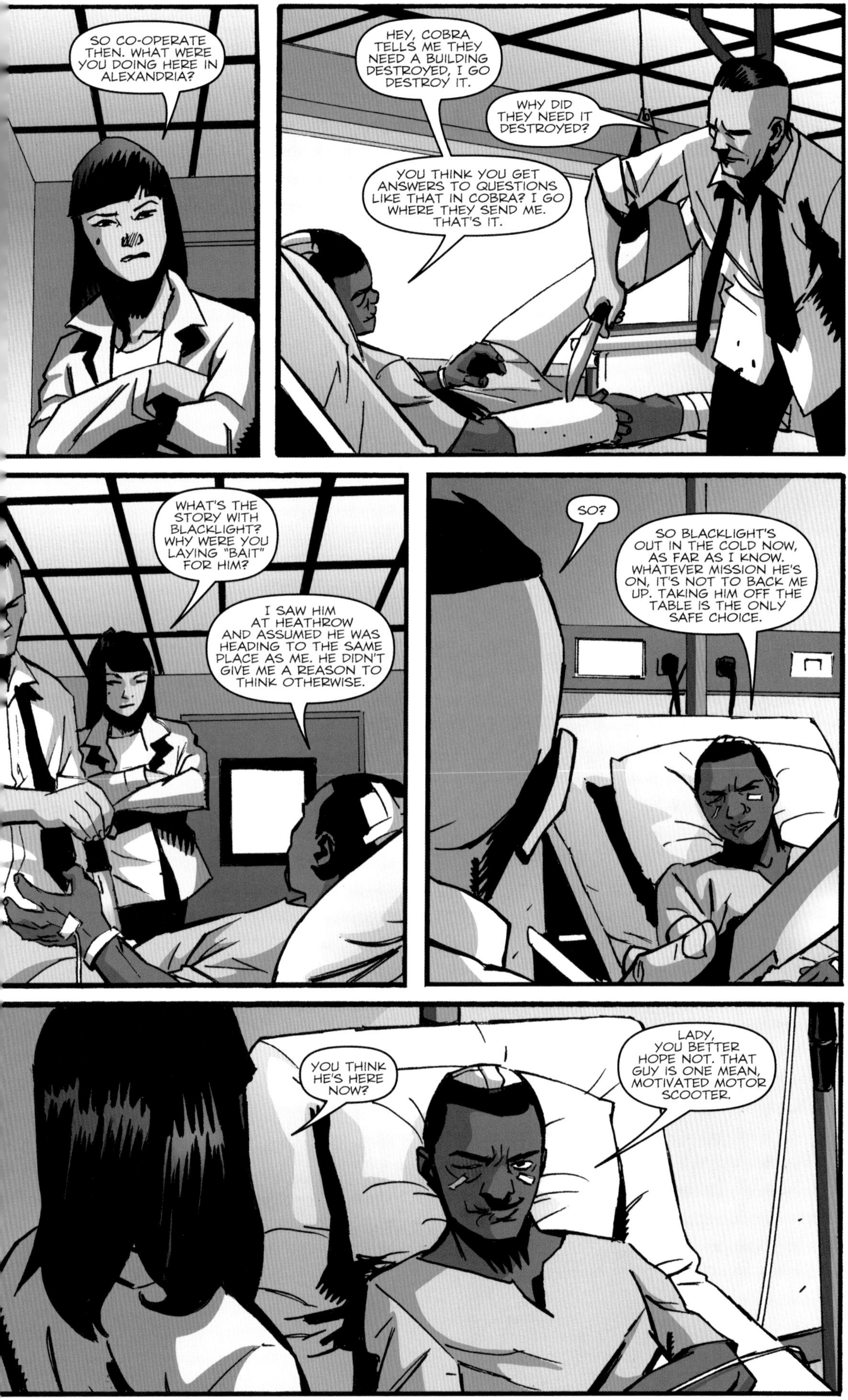
SO CO-OPERATE THEN. WHAT WERE YOU DOING HERE IN ALEXANDRIA?
HEY, COBRA TELLS ME THEY NEED A BUILDING DESTROYED, I GO DESTROY IT.
WHY DID THEY NEED IT DESTROYED?
YOU THINK YOU GET ANSWERS TO QUESTIONS LIKE THAT IN COBRA? I GO WHERE THEY SEND ME. THAT'S IT.
WHAT'S THE STORY WITH BLACKLIGHT? WHY WERE YOU LAYING "BAIT" FOR HIM?
I SAW HIM AT HEATHROW AND ASSUMED HE WAS HEADING TO THE SAME PLACE AS ME. HE DIDN'T GIVE ME A REASON TO THINK OTHERWISE.
SO?
SO BLACKLIGHT'S OUT IN THE COLD NOW, AS FAR AS I KNOW. WHATEVER MISSION HE'S ON, IT'S NOT TO BACK ME UP. TAKING HIM OFF THE TABLE IS THE ONLY SAFE CHOICE.
YOU THINK HE'S HERE NOW?
LADY, YOU BETTER HOPE NOT. THAT GUY IS ONE MEAN, MOTIVATED MOTOR SCOOTER.

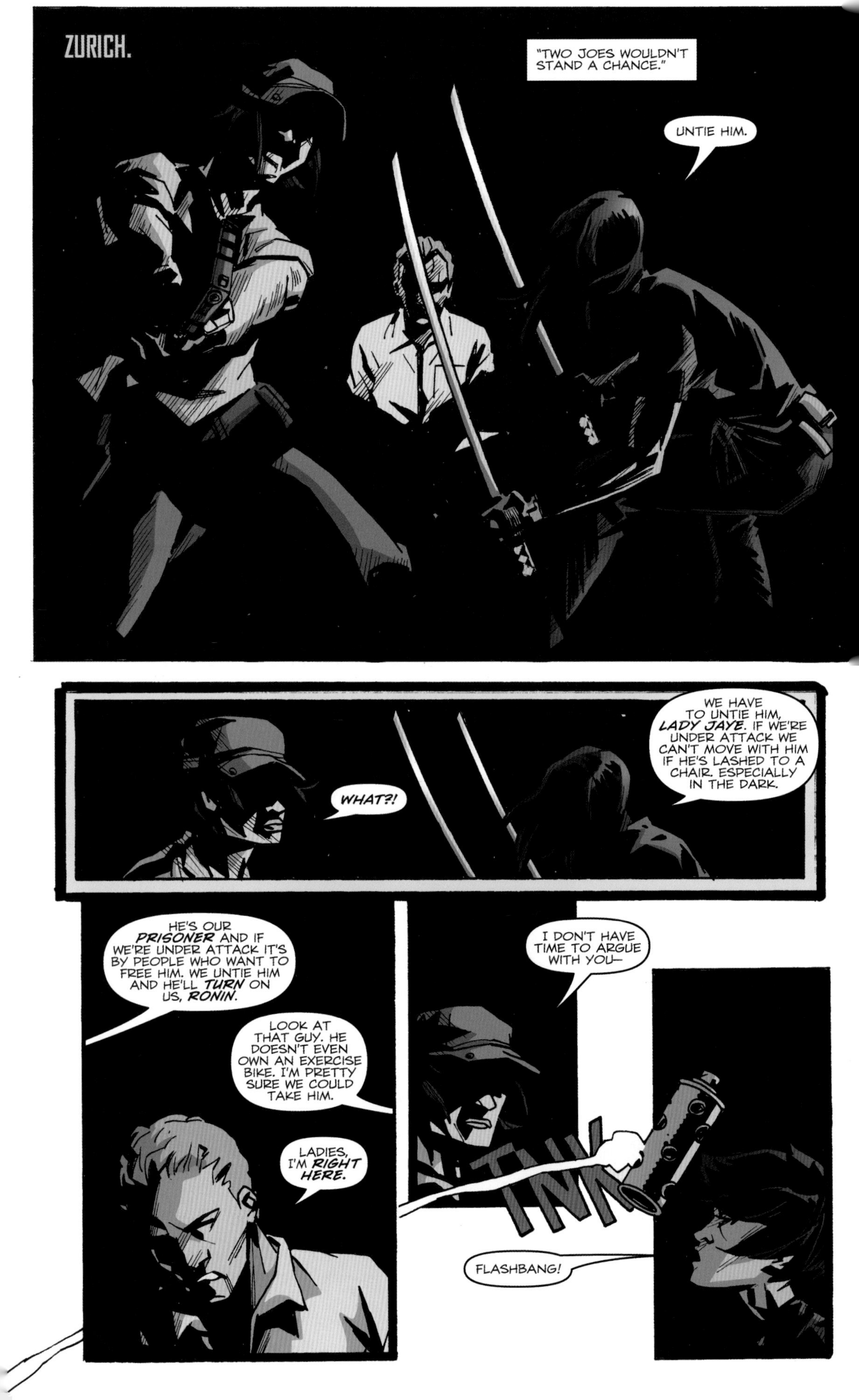
ZURICH.
"TWO JOES WOULDN'T STAND A CHANCE."
UNTIE HIM.
WHAT?!
WE HAVE TO UNTIE HIM, LADY JAYE. IF WE'RE UNDER ATTACK WE CAN'T MOVE WITH HIM IF HE'S LASHED TO A CHAIR. ESPECIALLY IN THE DARK.
HE'S OUR PRISONER AND IF WE'RE UNDER ATTACK IT'S BY PEOPLE WHO WANT TO FREE HIM. WE UNTIE HIM AND HE'LL TURN ON US, RONIN.
LOOK AT THAT GUY. HE DOESN'T EVEN OWN AN EXERCISE BIKE. I'M PRETTY SURE WE COULD TAKE HIM.
LADIES, I'M RIGHT HERE.
I DON'T HAVE TIME TO ARGUE WITH YOU—
TINK
FLASHBANG!

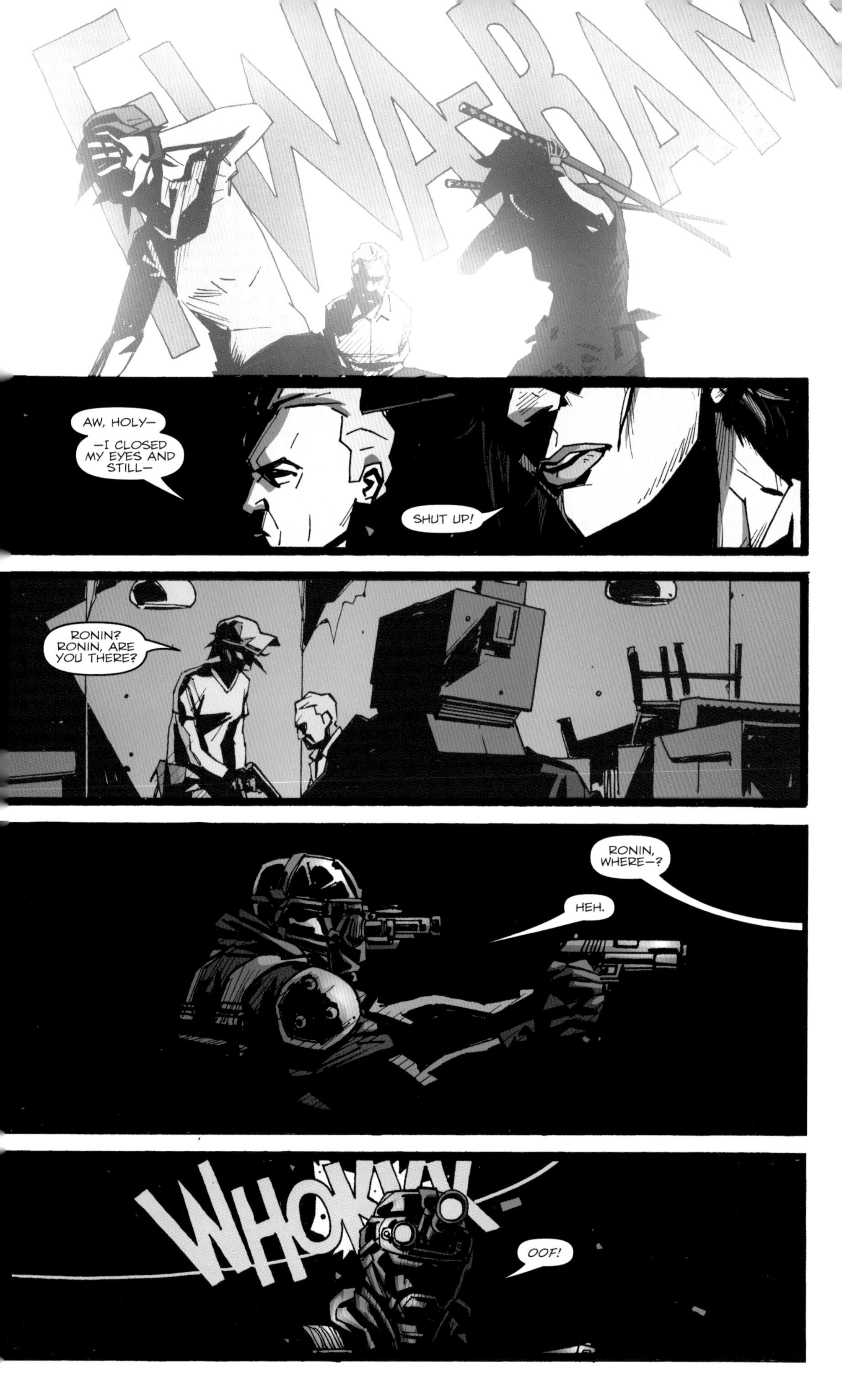
AW, HOLY—
—I CLOSED MY EYES AND STILL—
SHUT UP!
RONIN? RONIN, ARE YOU THERE?
RONIN, WHERE—?
HEH.
OOF!

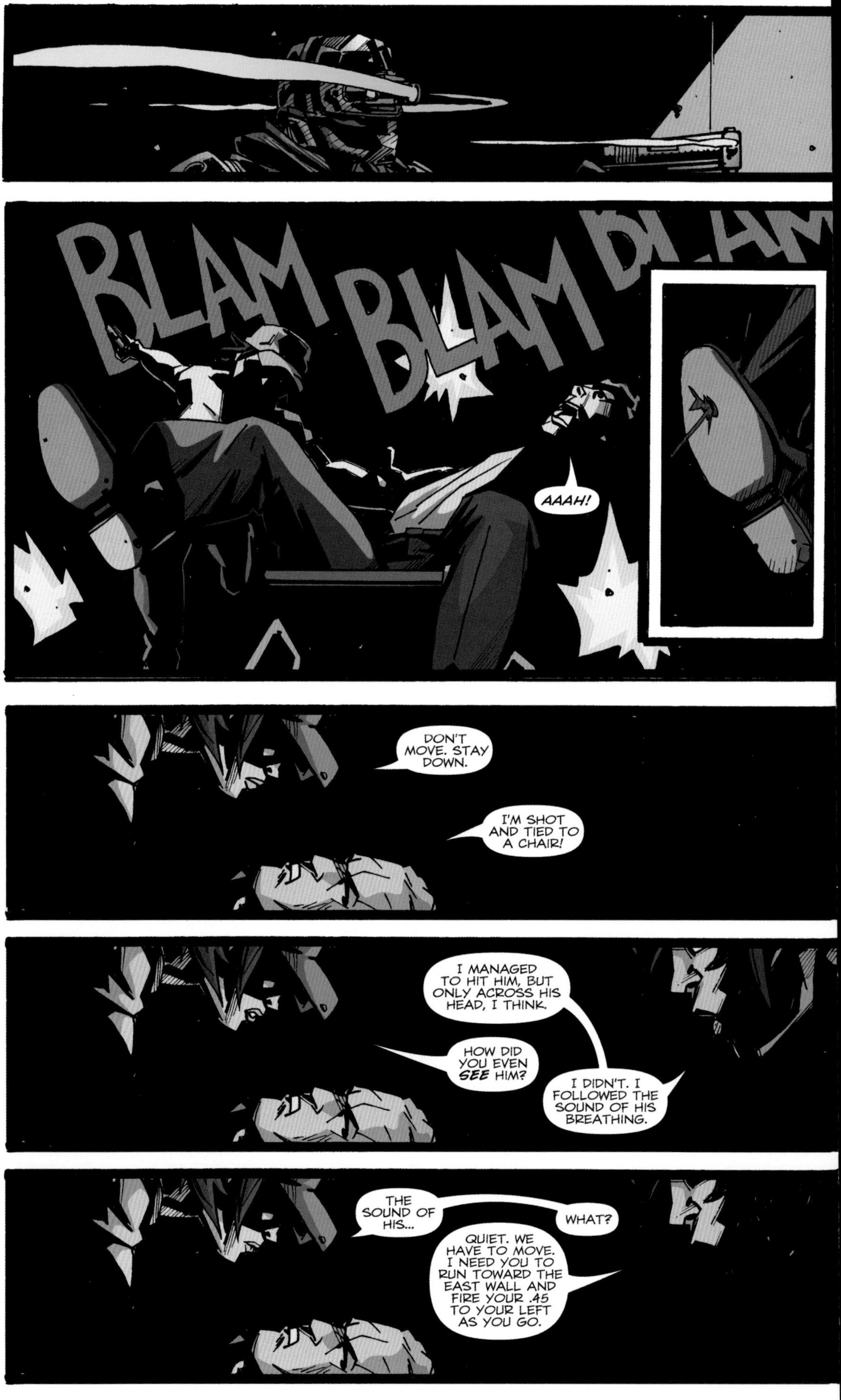
BLAM BLAM BLAM
AAAH!
DON'T MOVE. STAY DOWN.
I'M SHOT AND TIED TO A CHAIR!
I MANAGED TO HIT HIM, BUT ONLY ACROSS HIS HEAD, I THINK.
HOW DID YOU EVEN SEE HIM?
I DIDN'T. I FOLLOWED THE SOUND OF HIS BREATHING.
THE SOUND OF HIS...
WHAT?
QUIET. WE HAVE TO MOVE. I NEED YOU TO RUN TOWARD THE EAST WALL AND FIRE YOUR .45 TO YOUR LEFT AS YOU GO.

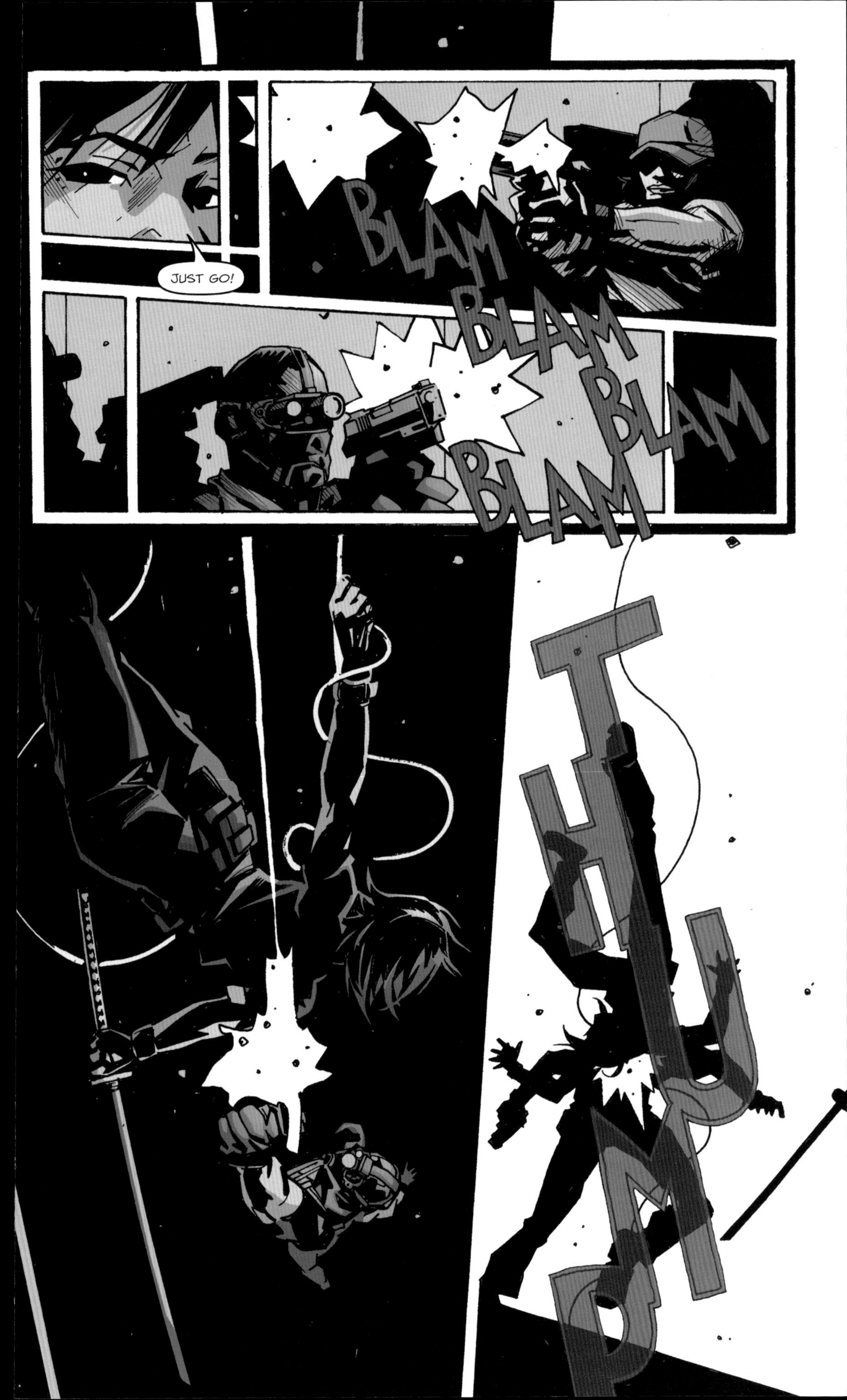
JUST GO!
BLAM
BLAM
BLAM
BLAM
BLAM
THUMP

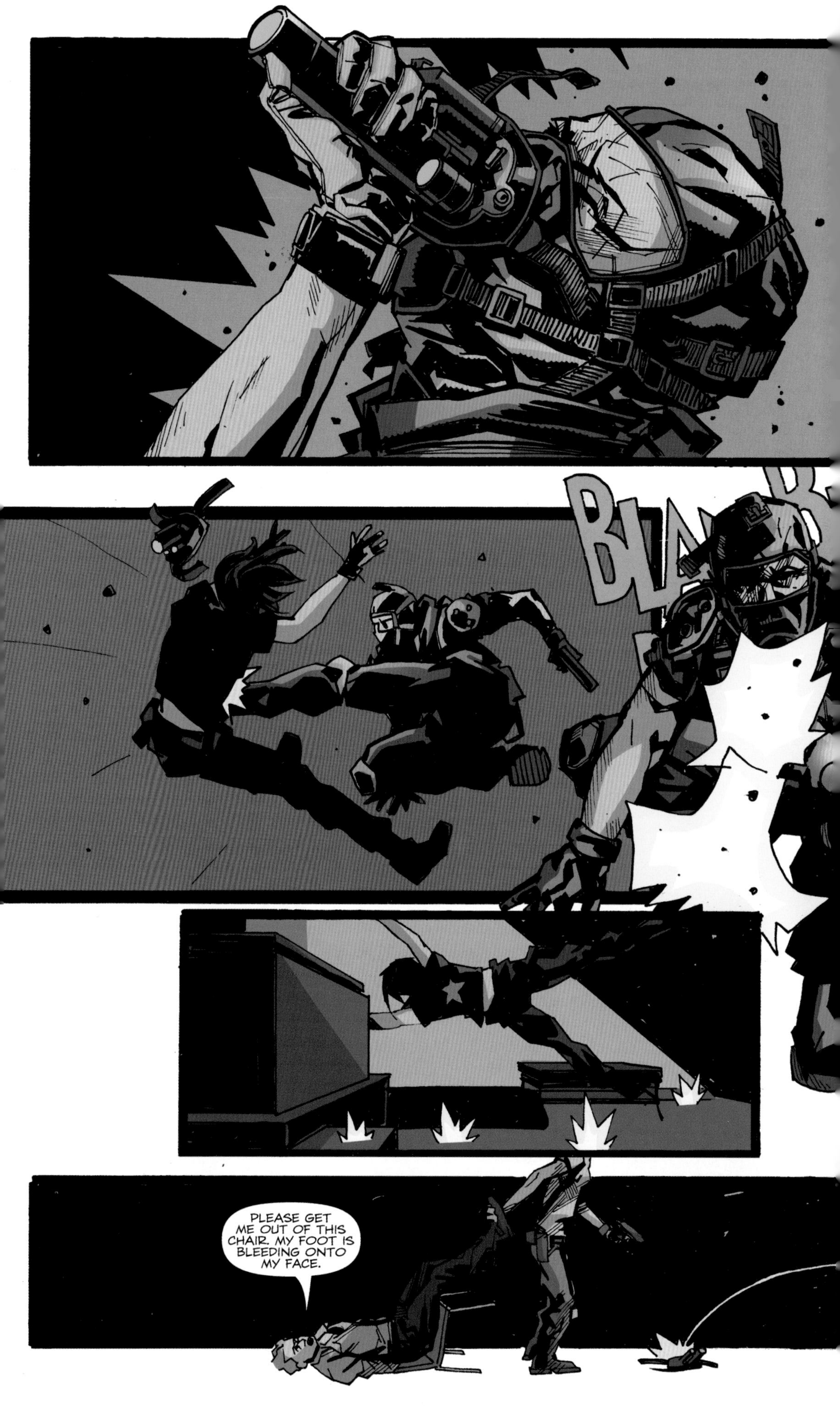
PLEASE GET ME OUT OF THIS CHAIR. MY FOOT IS BLEEDING ONTO MY FACE.

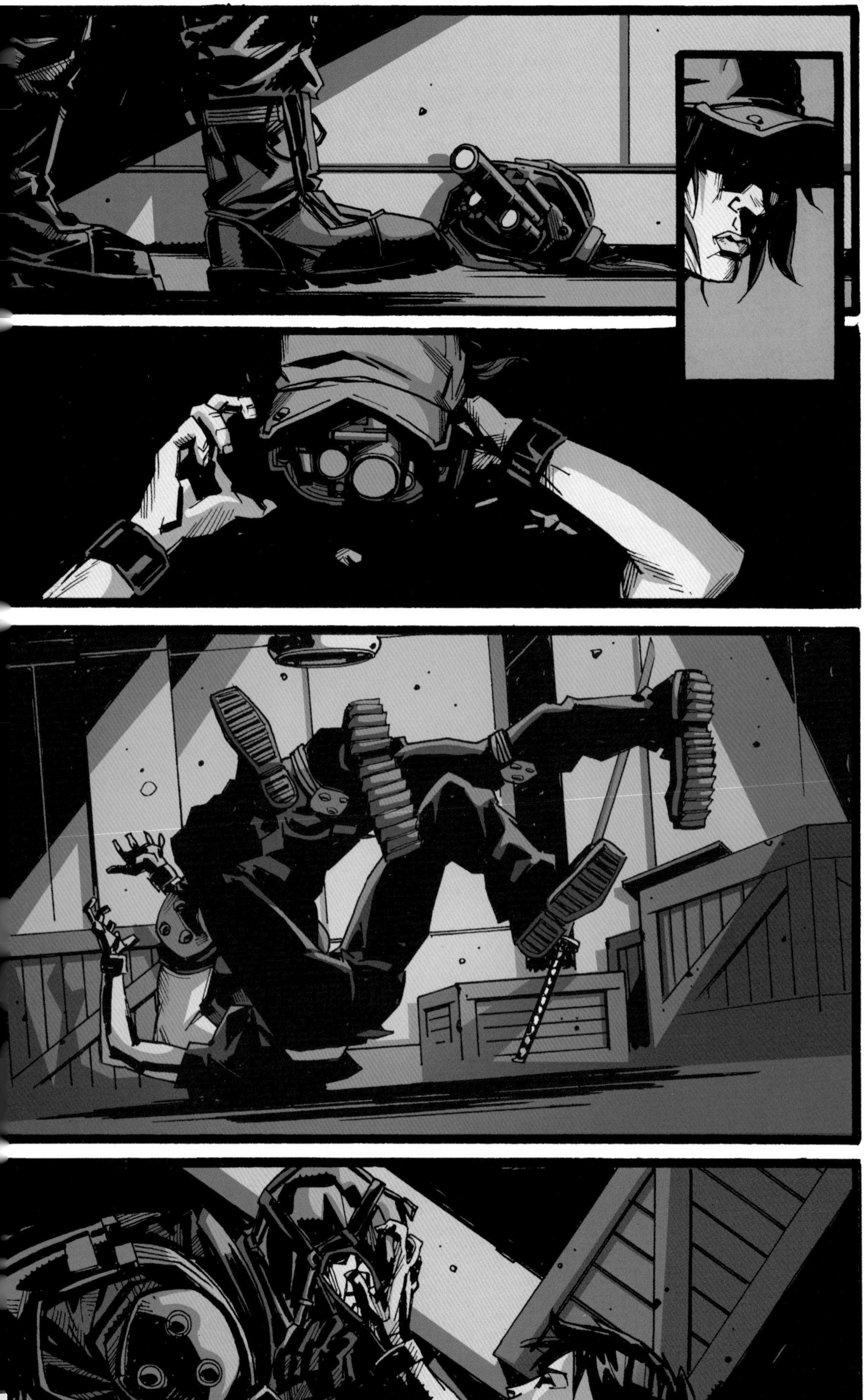

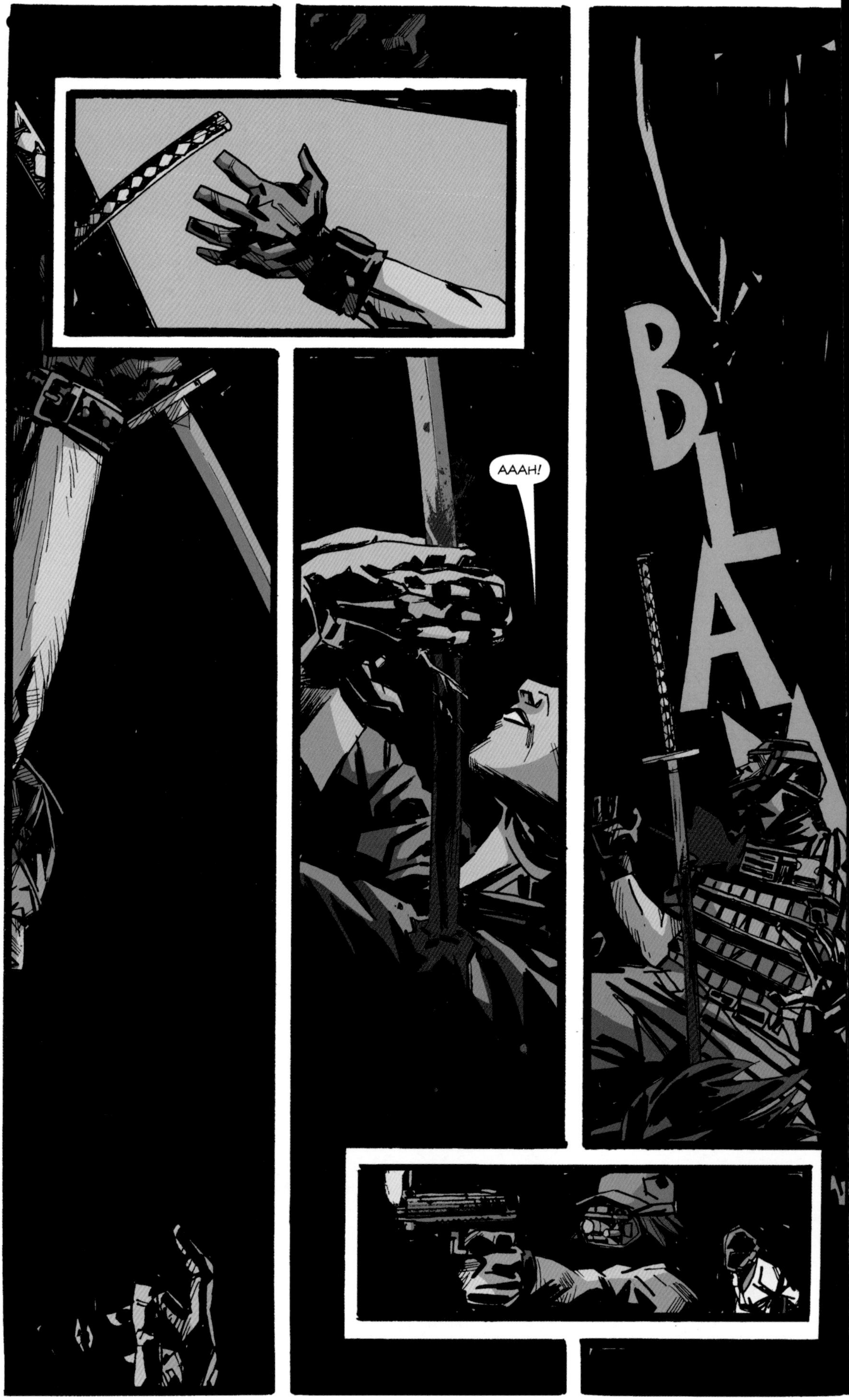
AAAH!
BLA

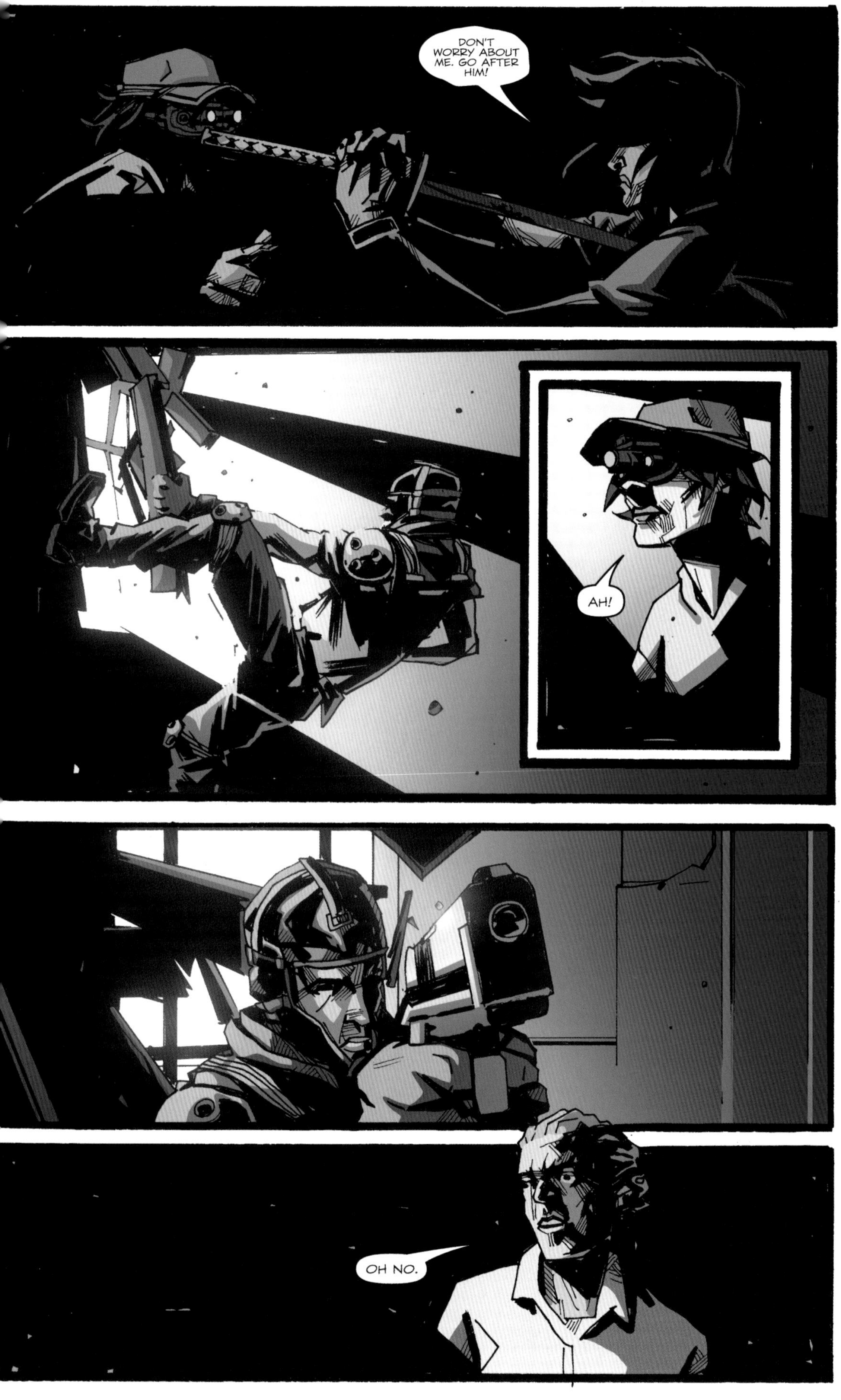
DON'T WORRY ABOUT ME. GO AFTER HIM!
AH!
OH NO.

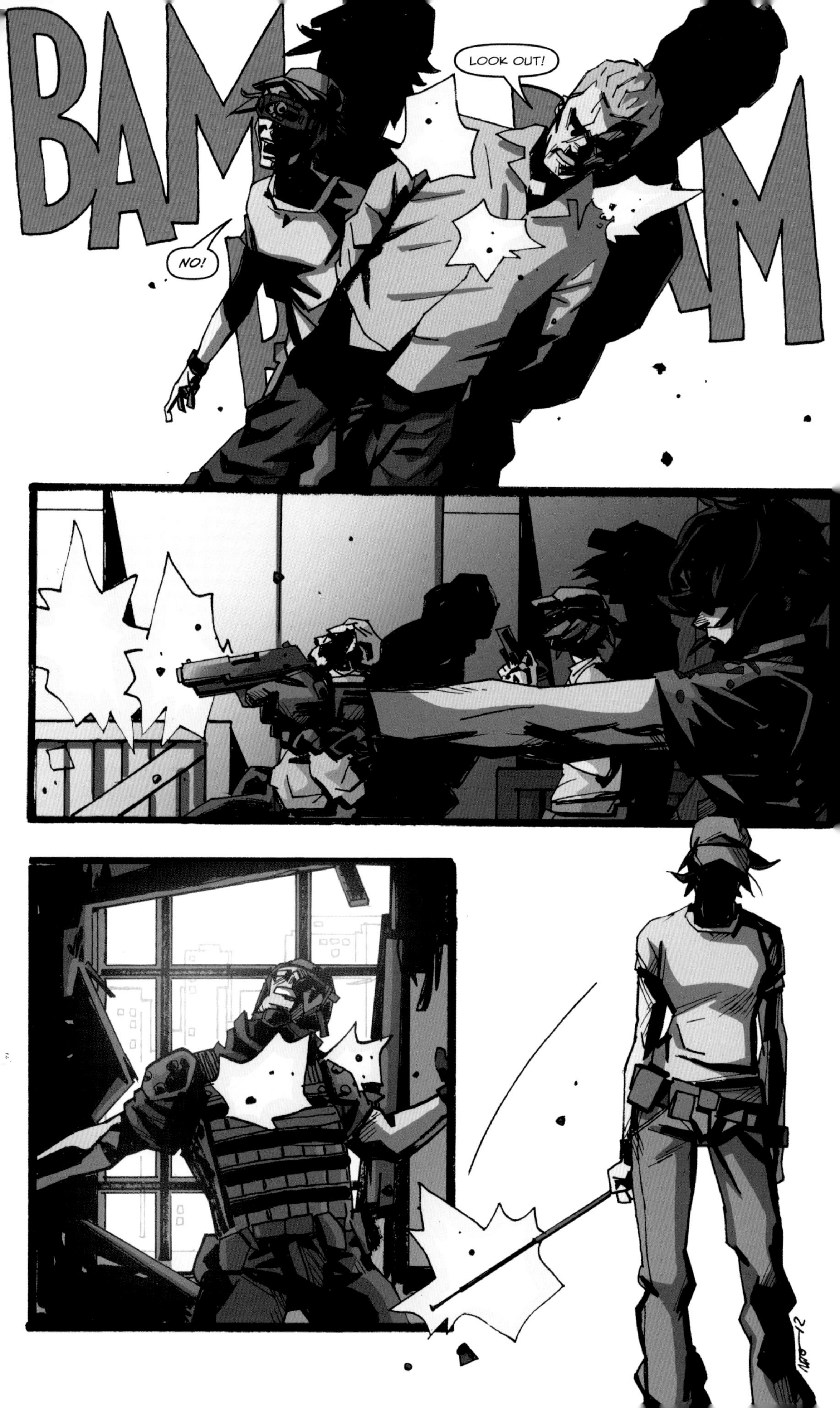
BAM
LOOK OUT!
NO!
BAM

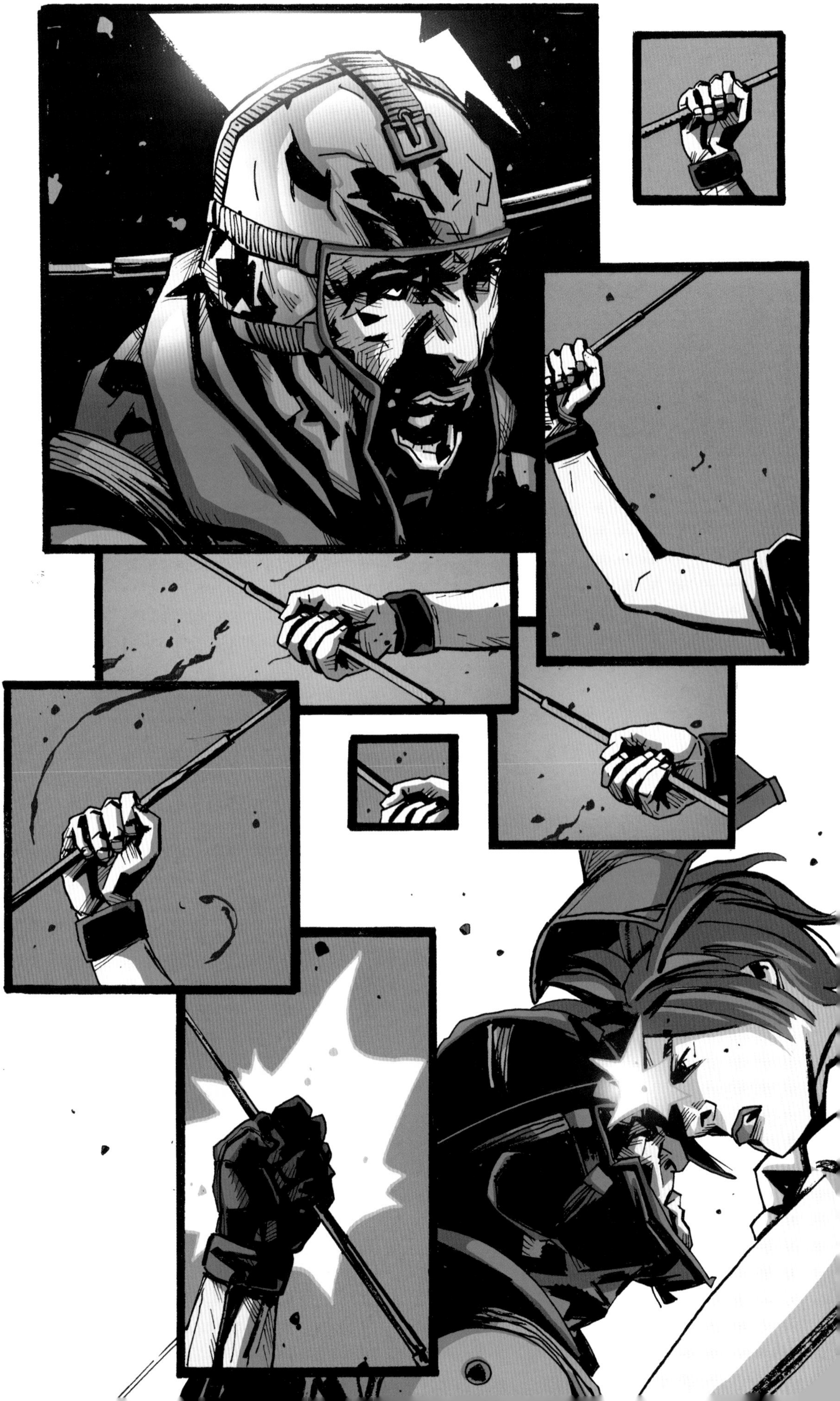

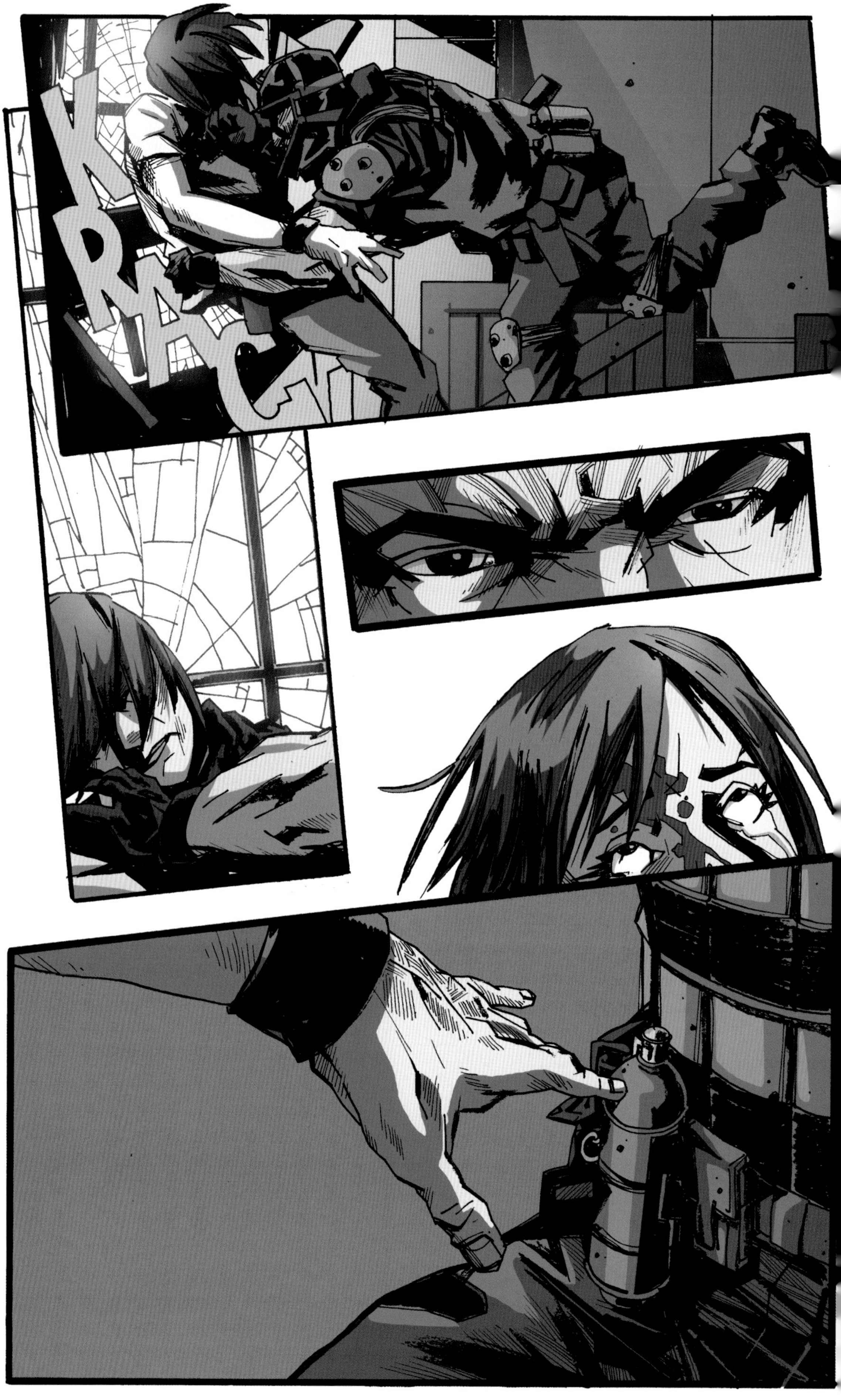
KRAC

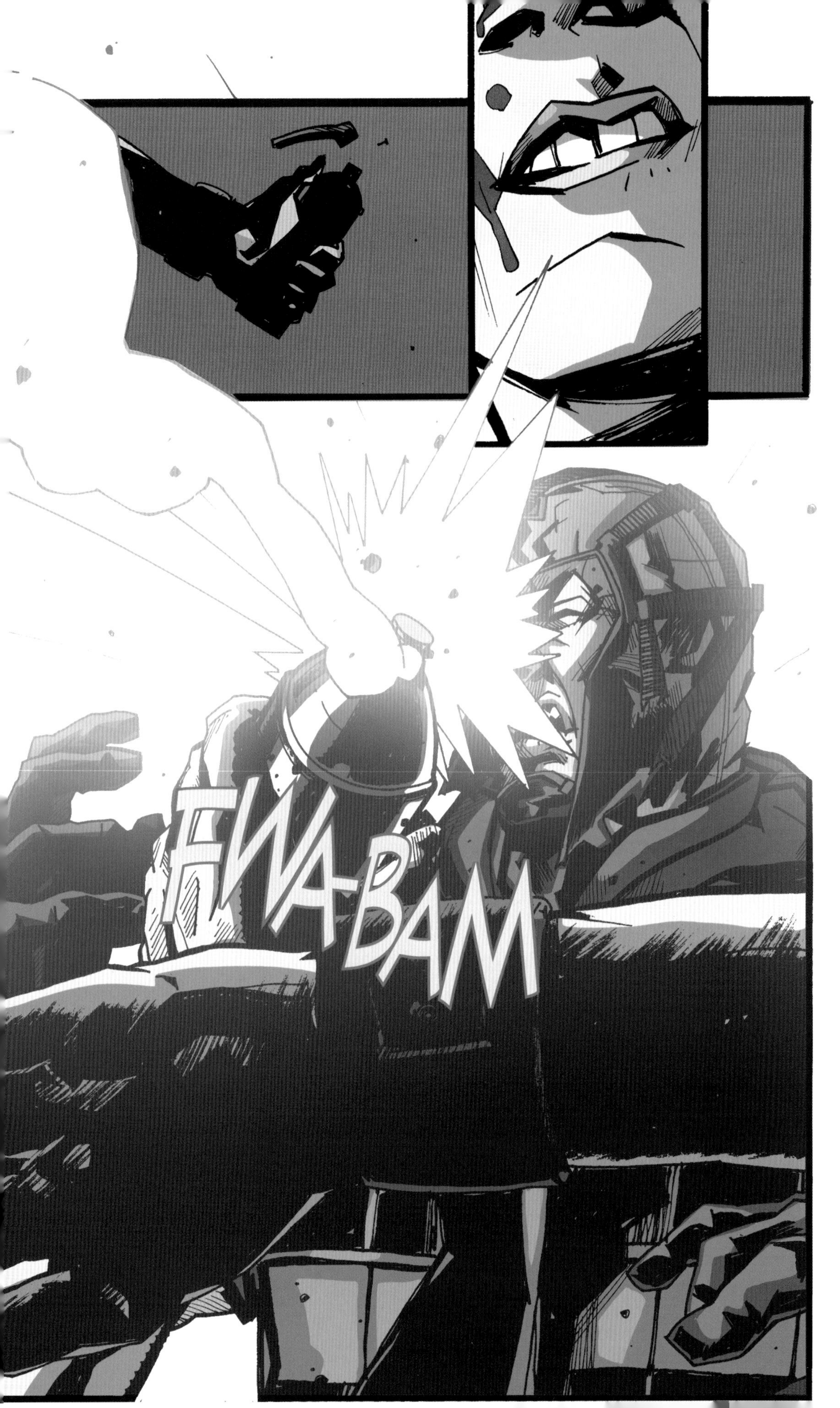
FWA-BAM

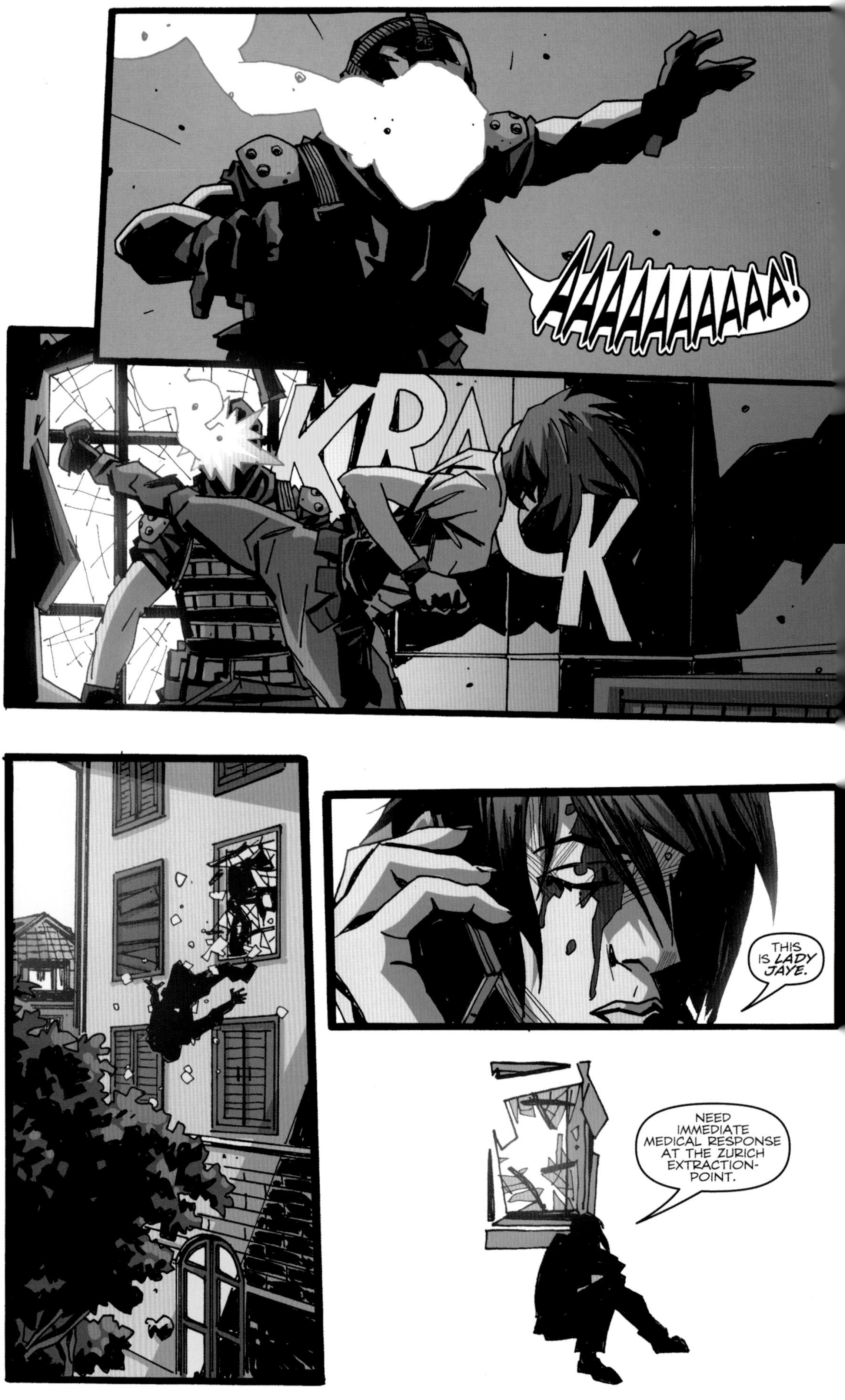
AAAAAAAAAA!
KRACK
THIS IS *LADY JAYE.*
NEED IMMEDIATE MEDICAL RESPONSE AT THE ZURICH EXTRACTION-POINT.

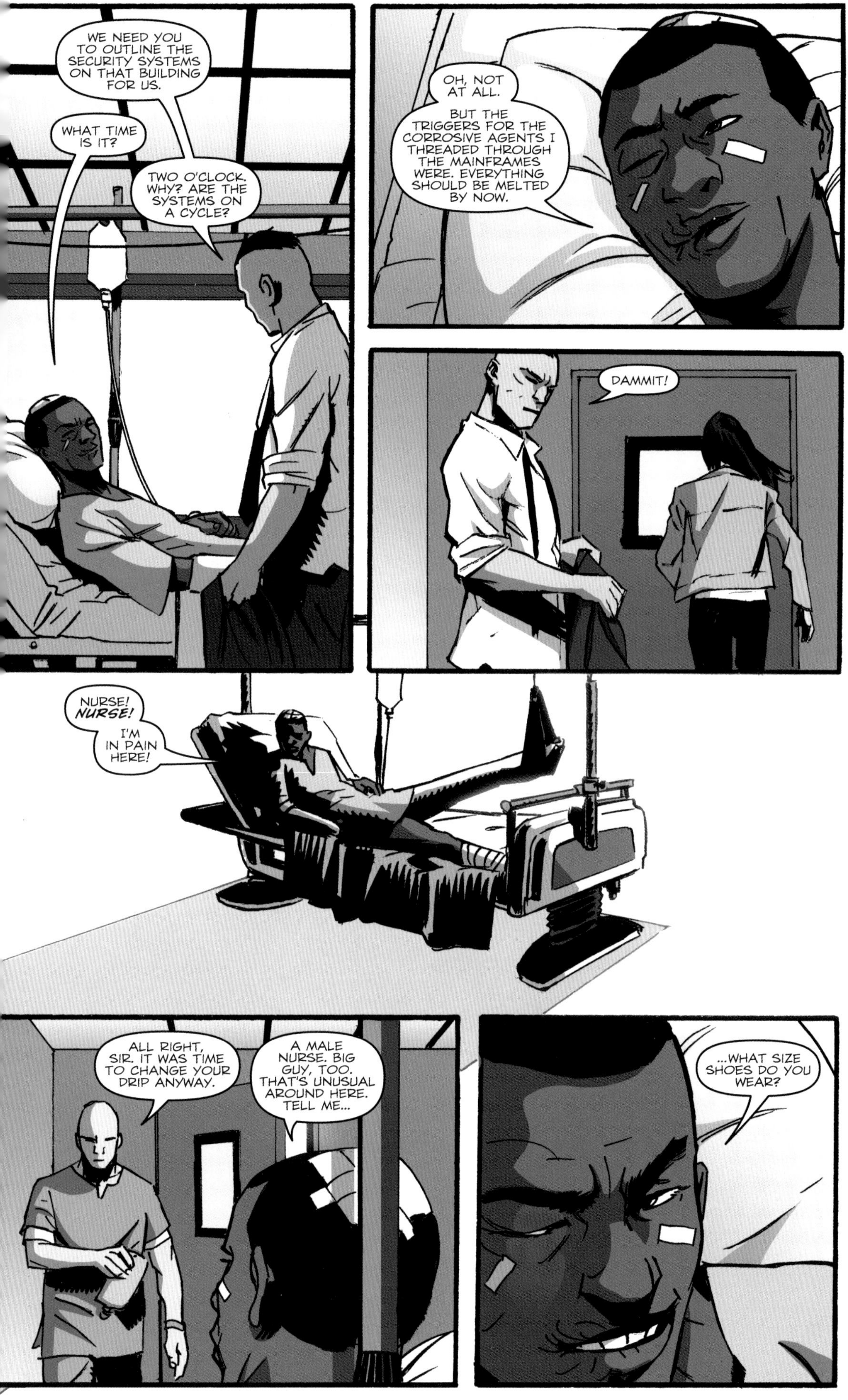
WE NEED YOU TO OUTLINE THE SECURITY SYSTEMS ON THAT BUILDING FOR US.
WHAT TIME IS IT?
TWO O'CLOCK. WHY? ARE THE SYSTEMS ON A CYCLE?
OH, NOT AT ALL.
BUT THE TRIGGERS FOR THE CORROSIVE AGENTS I THREADED THROUGH THE MAINFRAMES WERE. EVERYTHING SHOULD BE MELTED BY NOW.
DAMMIT!
NURSE! ***NURSE!***
I'M IN PAIN HERE!
ALL RIGHT, SIR. IT WAS TIME TO CHANGE YOUR DRIP ANYWAY.
A MALE NURSE. BIG GUY, TOO. THAT'S UNUSUAL AROUND HERE. TELL ME...
...WHAT SIZE SHOES DO YOU WEAR?

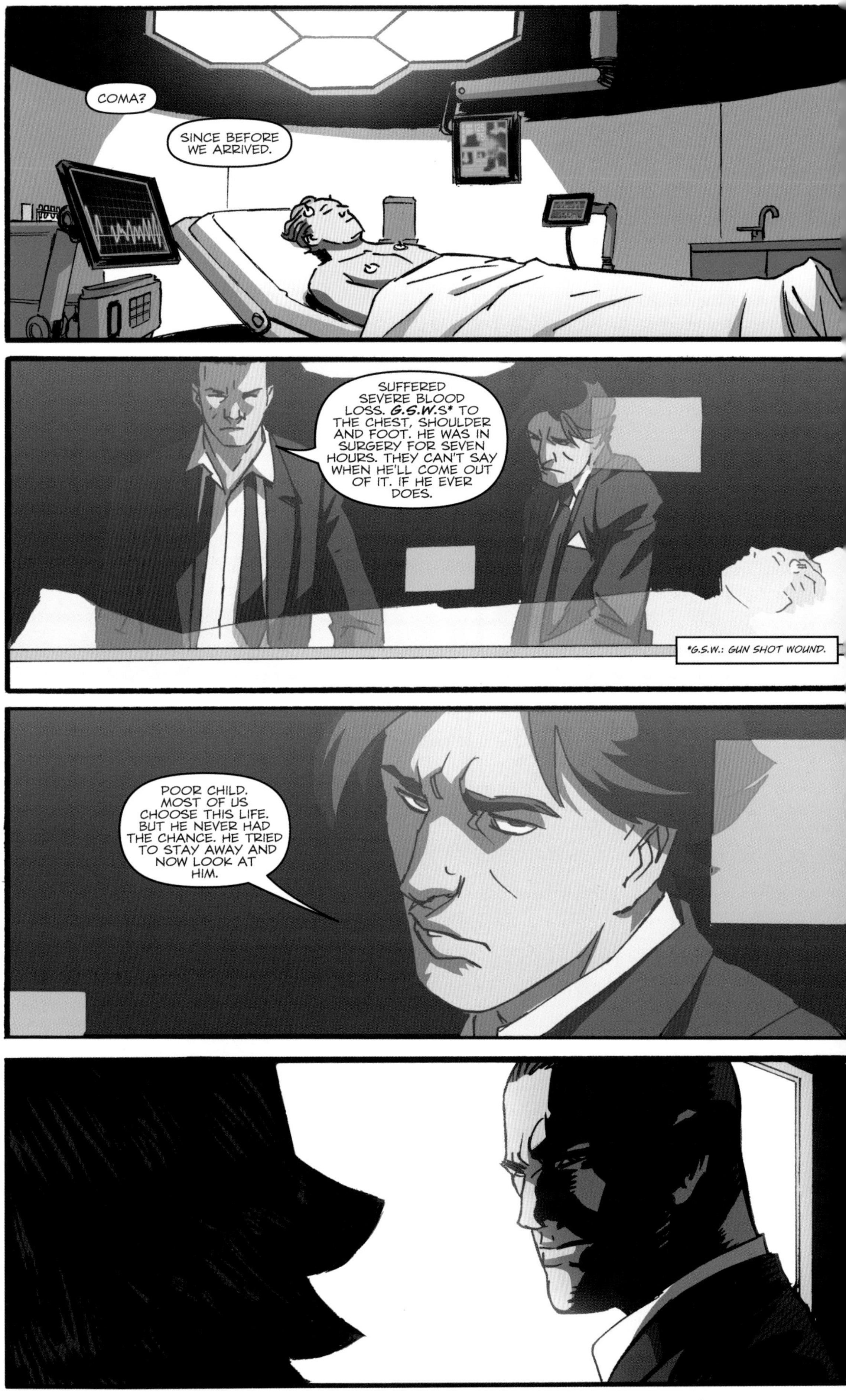
COMA?
SINCE BEFORE WE ARRIVED.
SUFFERED SEVERE BLOOD LOSS. G.S.W.S* TO THE CHEST, SHOULDER AND FOOT. HE WAS IN SURGERY FOR SEVEN HOURS. THEY CAN'T SAY WHEN HE'LL COME OUT OF IT. IF HE EVER DOES.
*G.S.W.: GUN SHOT WOUND.
POOR CHILD. MOST OF US CHOOSE THIS LIFE. BUT HE NEVER HAD THE CHANCE. HE TRIED TO STAY AWAY AND NOW LOOK AT HIM.

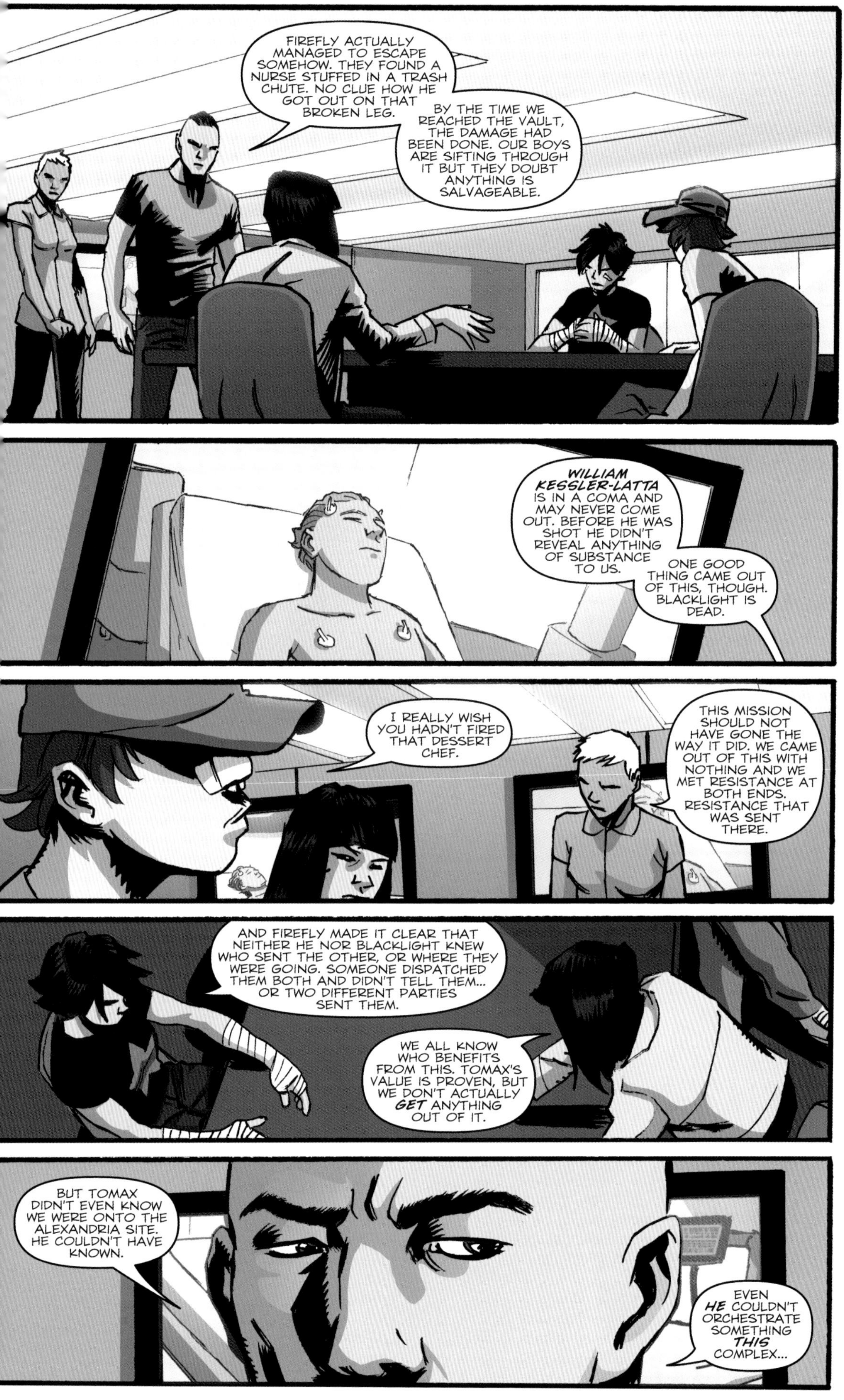

FIREFLY ACTUALLY MANAGED TO ESCAPE SOMEHOW. THEY FOUND A NURSE STUFFED IN A TRASH CHUTE. NO CLUE HOW HE GOT OUT ON THAT BROKEN LEG.
BY THE TIME WE REACHED THE VAULT, THE DAMAGE HAD BEEN DONE. OUR BOYS ARE SIFTING THROUGH IT BUT THEY DOUBT ANYTHING IS SALVAGEABLE.
WILLIAM KESSLER-LATTA IS IN A COMA AND MAY NEVER COME OUT. BEFORE HE WAS SHOT HE DIDN'T REVEAL ANYTHING OF SUBSTANCE TO US.
ONE GOOD THING CAME OUT OF THIS, THOUGH. BLACKLIGHT IS DEAD.
I REALLY WISH YOU HADN'T FIRED THAT DESSERT CHEF.
THIS MISSION SHOULD NOT HAVE GONE THE WAY IT DID. WE CAME OUT OF THIS WITH NOTHING AND WE MET RESISTANCE AT BOTH ENDS. RESISTANCE THAT WAS SENT THERE.
AND FIREFLY MADE IT CLEAR THAT NEITHER HE NOR BLACKLIGHT KNEW WHO SENT THE OTHER, OR WHERE THEY WERE GOING. SOMEONE DISPATCHED THEM BOTH AND DIDN'T TELL THEM... OR TWO DIFFERENT PARTIES SENT THEM.
WE ALL KNOW WHO BENEFITS FROM THIS. TOMAX'S VALUE IS PROVEN, BUT WE DON'T ACTUALLY GET ANYTHING OUT OF IT.
BUT TOMAX DIDN'T EVEN KNOW WE WERE ONTO THE ALEXANDRIA SITE. HE COULDN'T HAVE KNOWN.
EVEN HE COULDN'T ORCHESTRATE SOMETHING THIS COMPLEX...

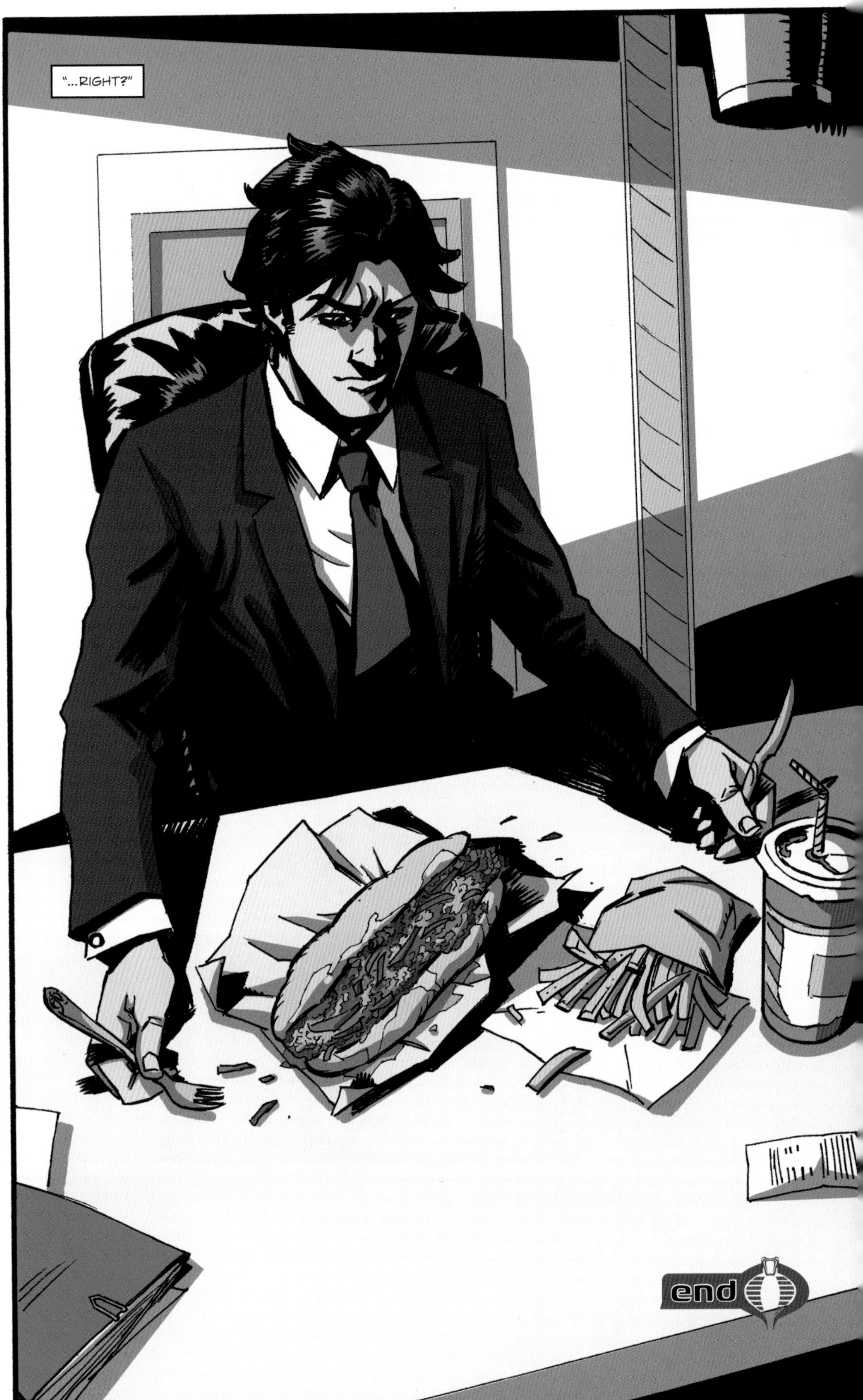
"...RIGHT?"
end

ART GALLERY

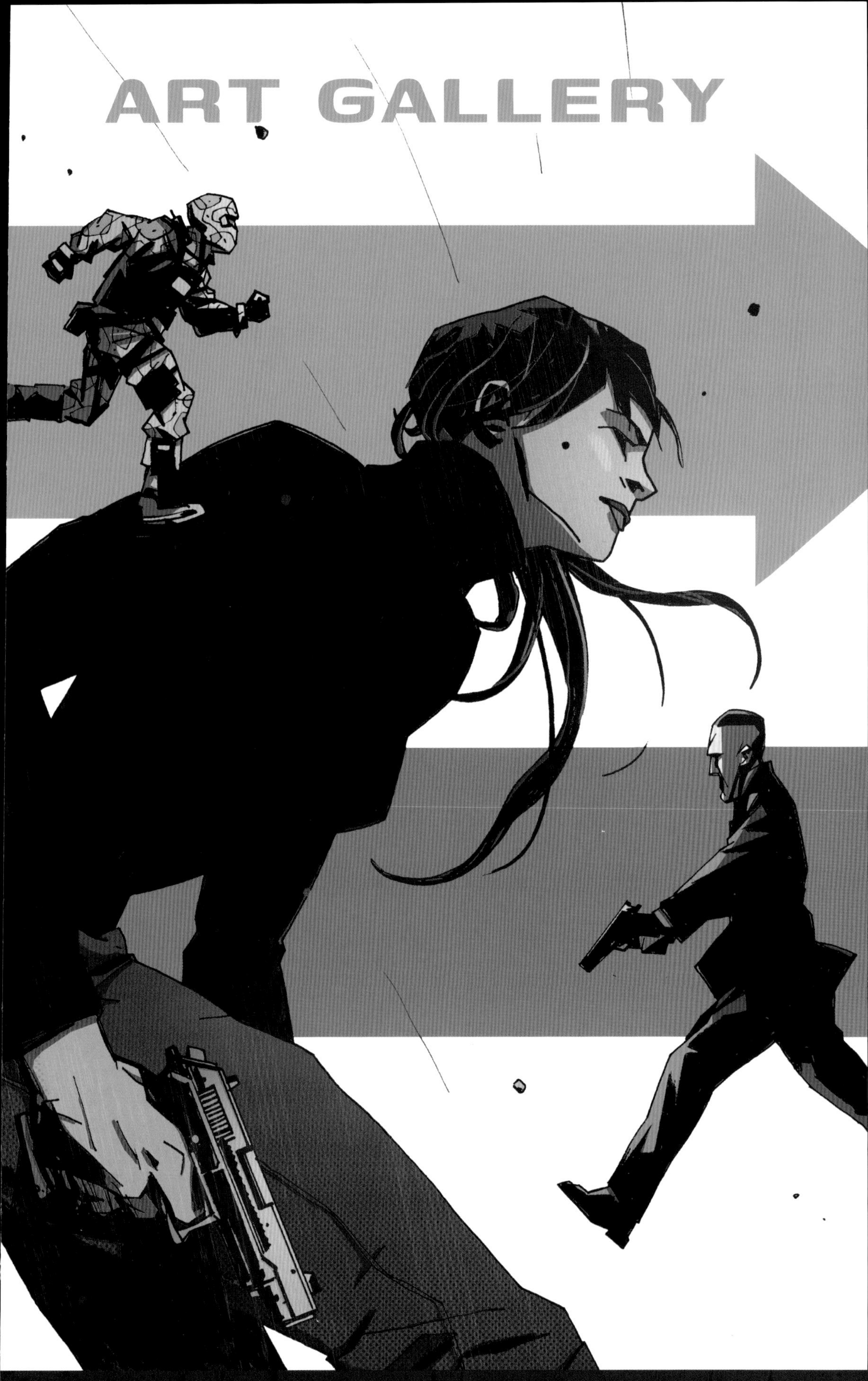

ART BY ANTONIO FUSO

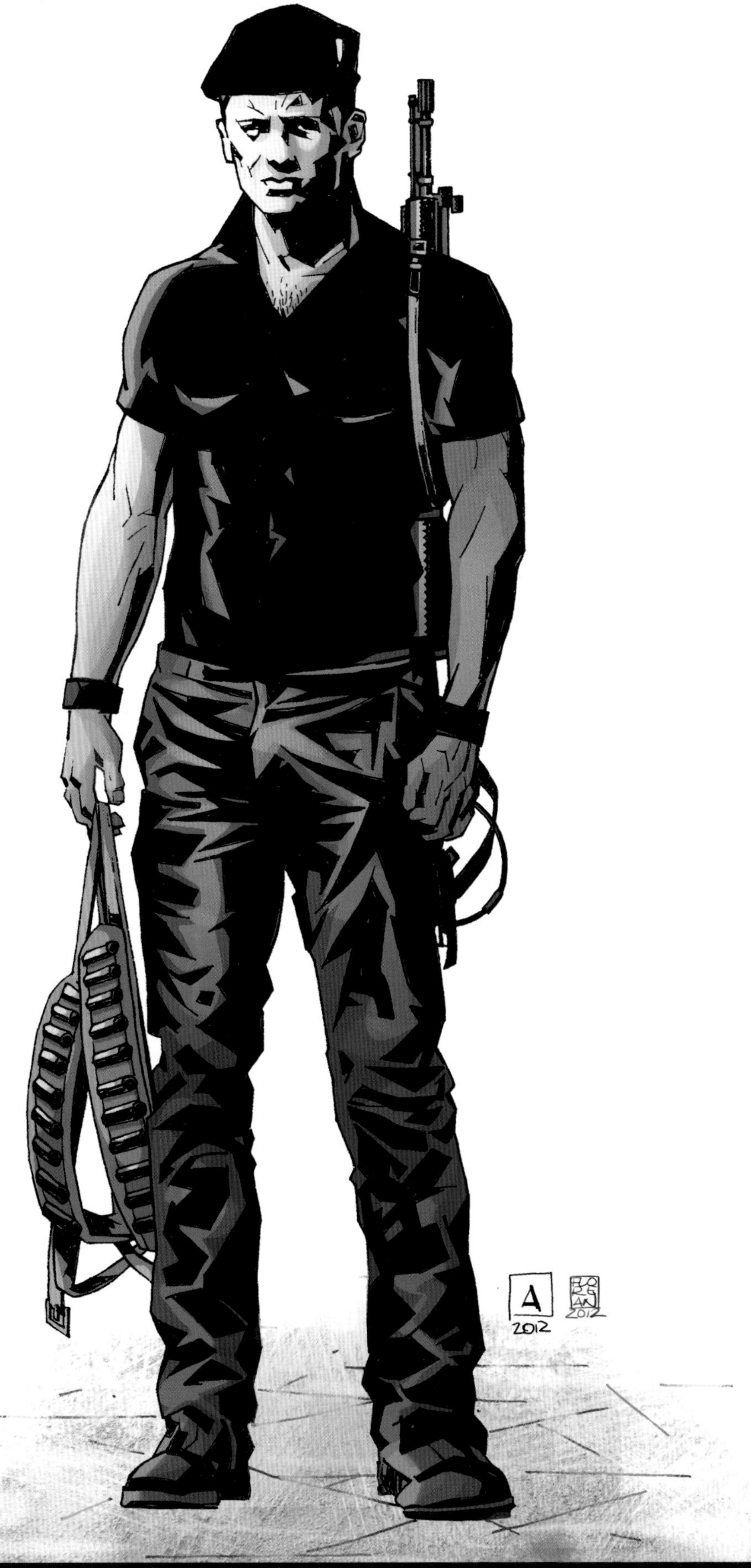
A
2012

ART BY **ANTONIO FUSO** • COLORS BY **ARIANNA FLOREAN**

ART BY **ANTONIO FUSO** • COLORS BY **ARIANNA FLOREAN**

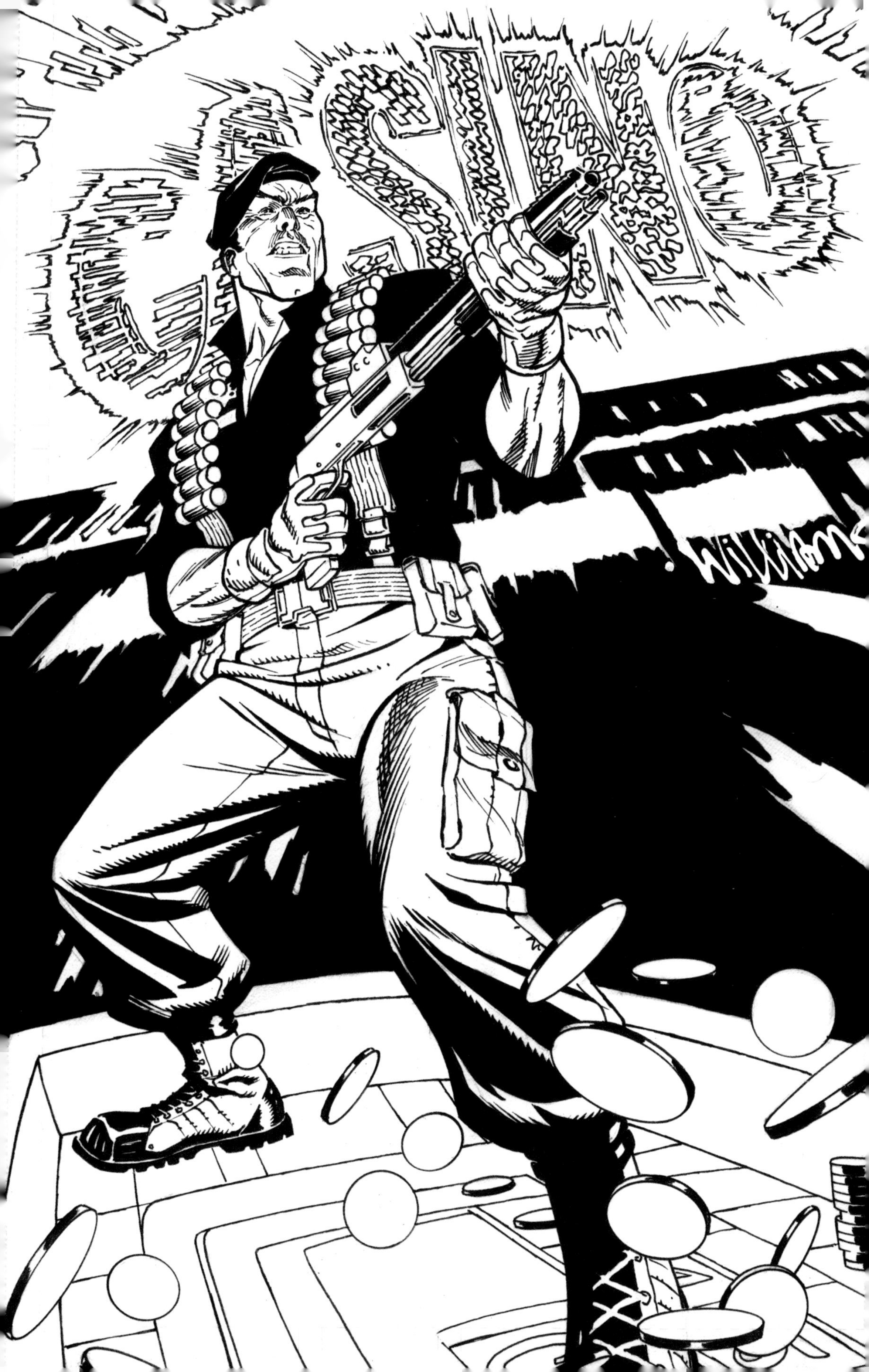
CASINO
Williams

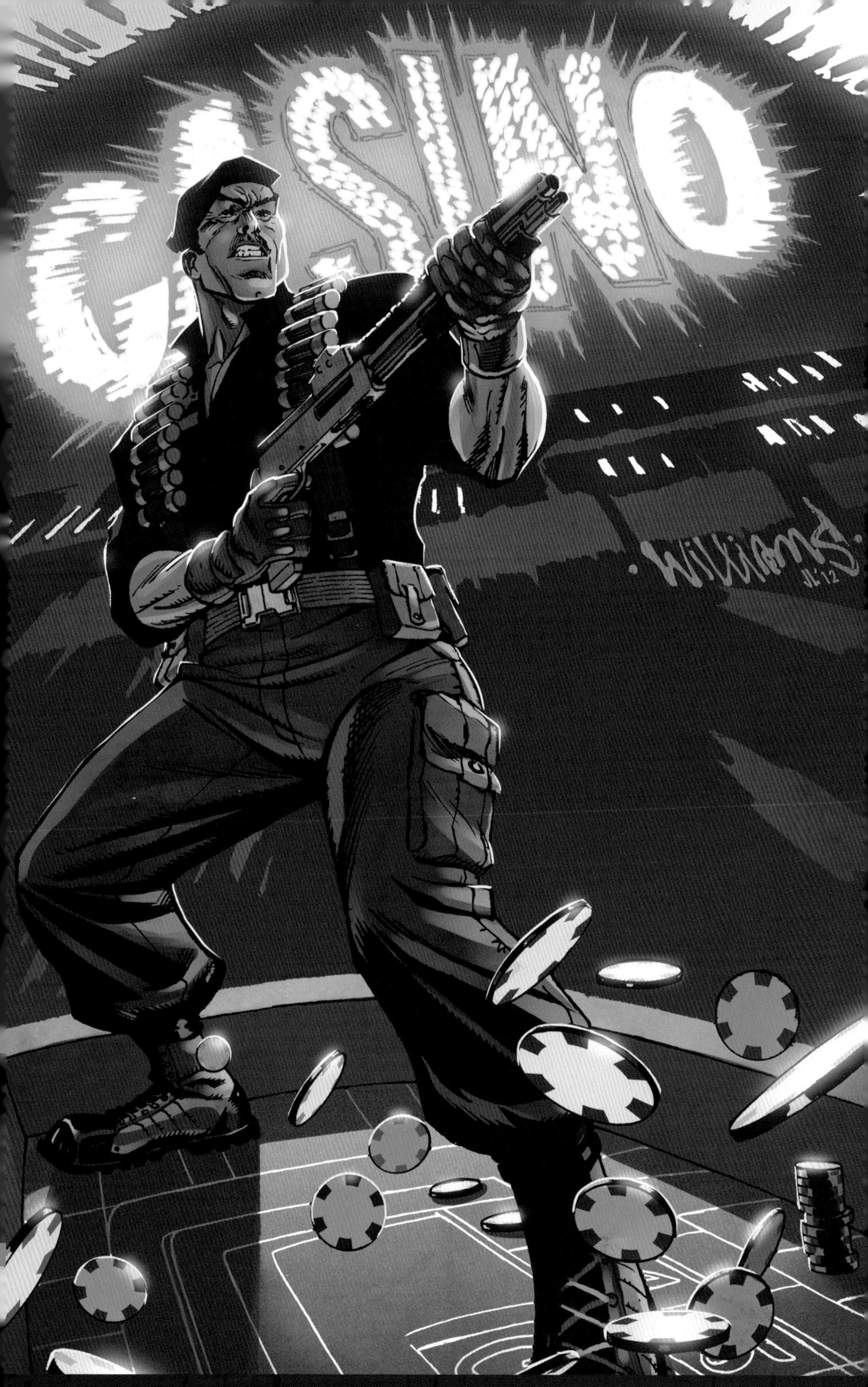
CASINO

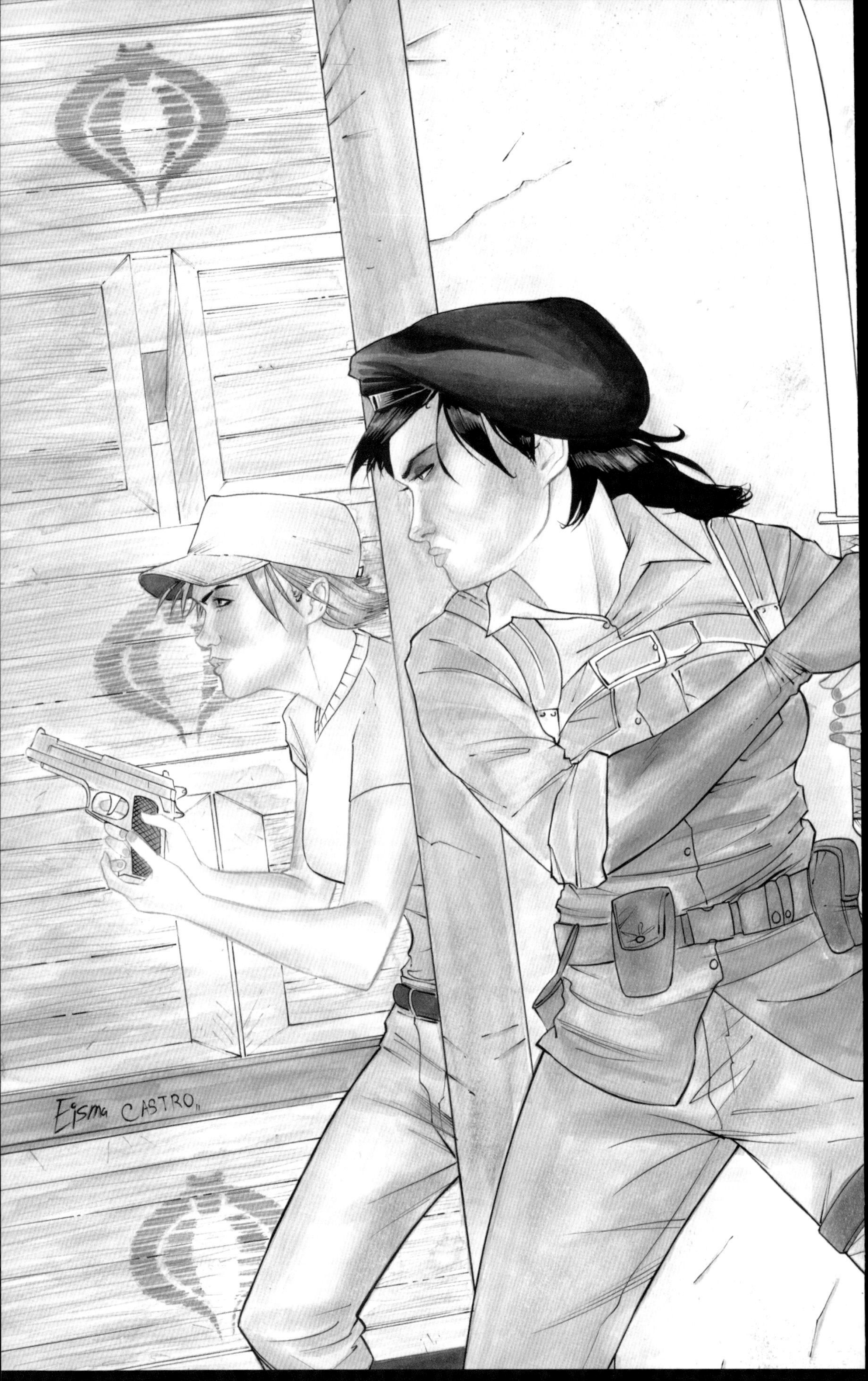
Eisma CASTRO

ART BY **JOE EISMA** AND **JUAN CASTRO**

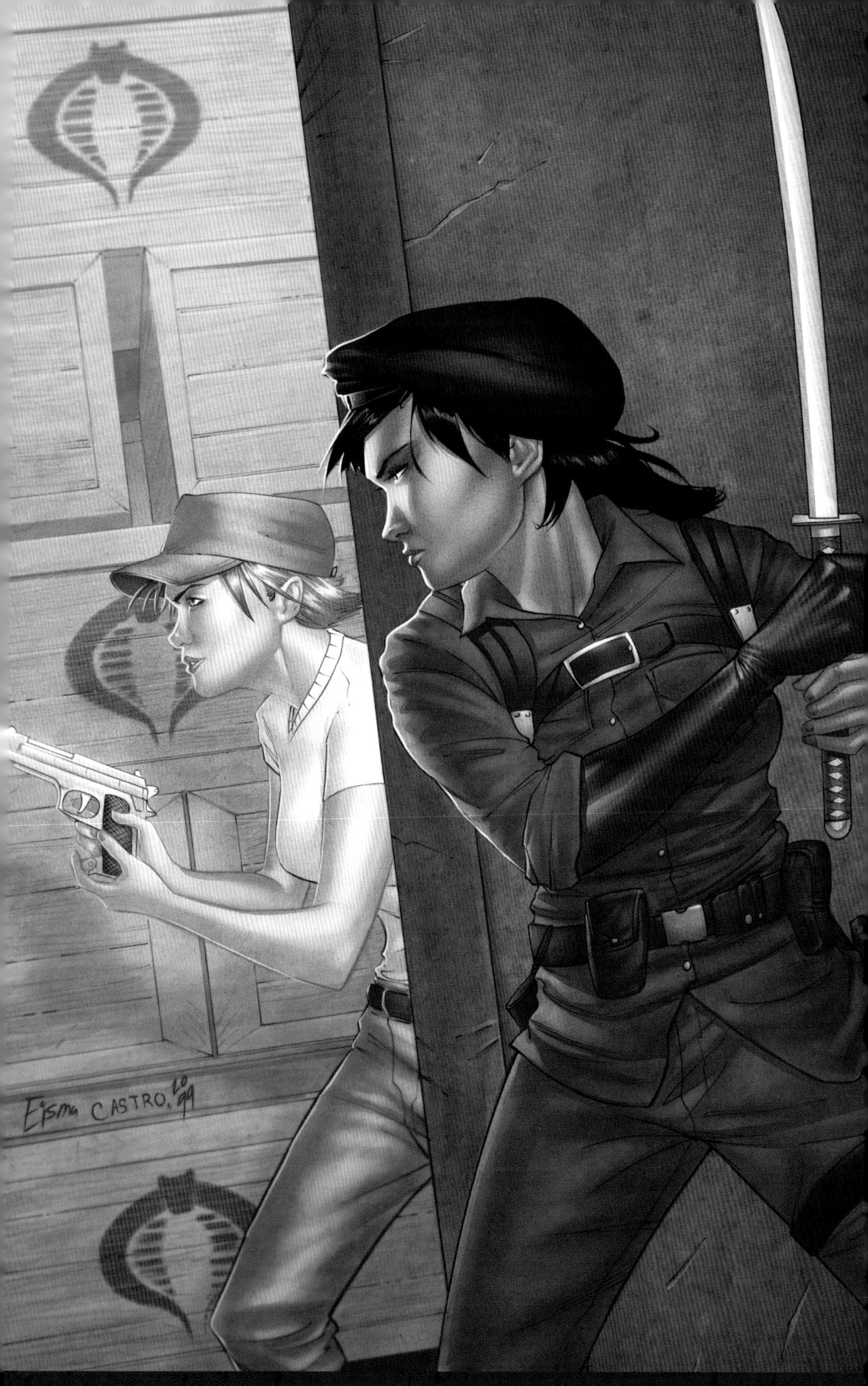
Eisma CASTRO 10.99

ART BY JOE EISMA AND JUAN CASTRO • COLORS BY SIMON GOUGH

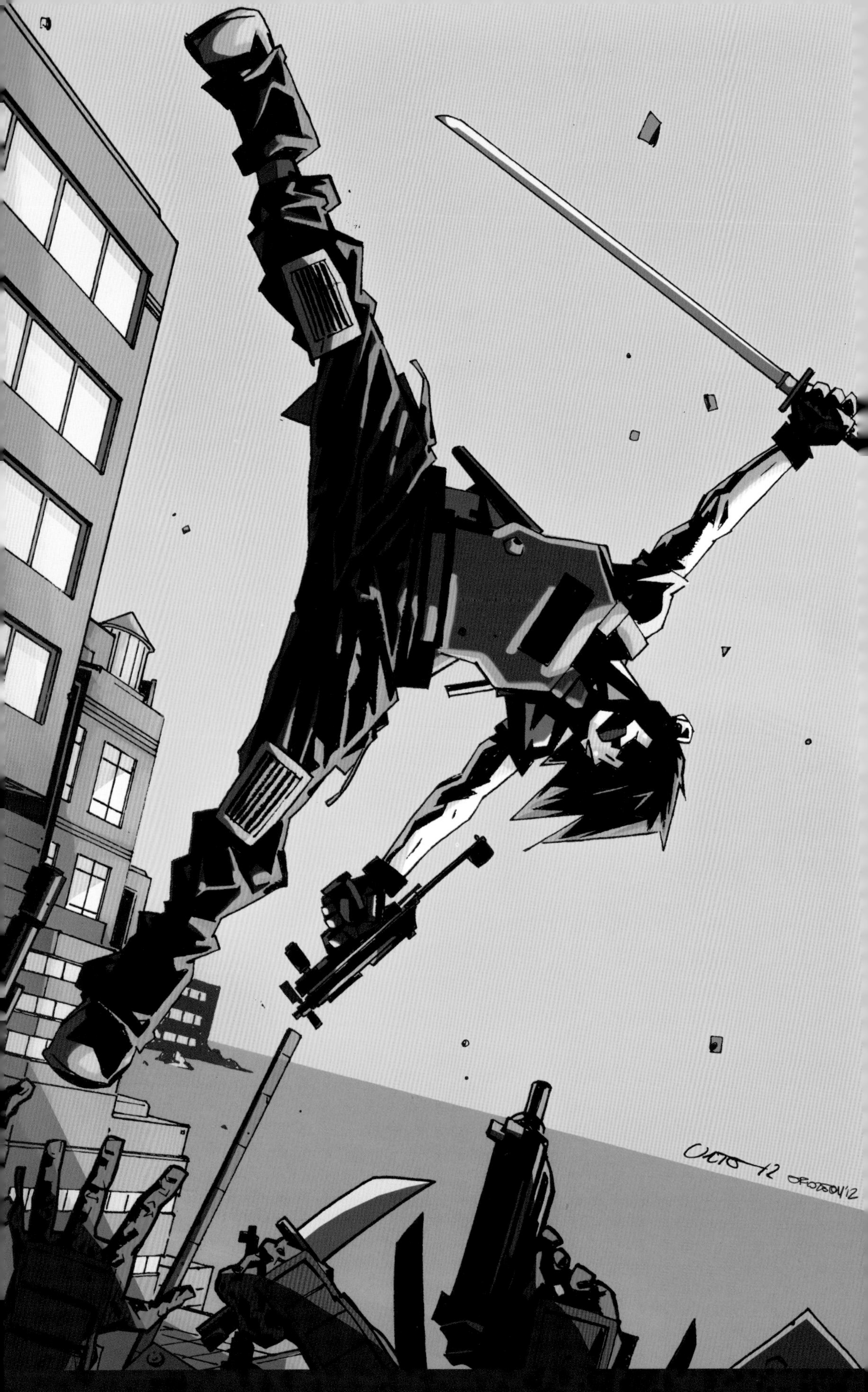

ART BY ANTONIO FUSO • COLORS BY ARIANNA FLOREAN

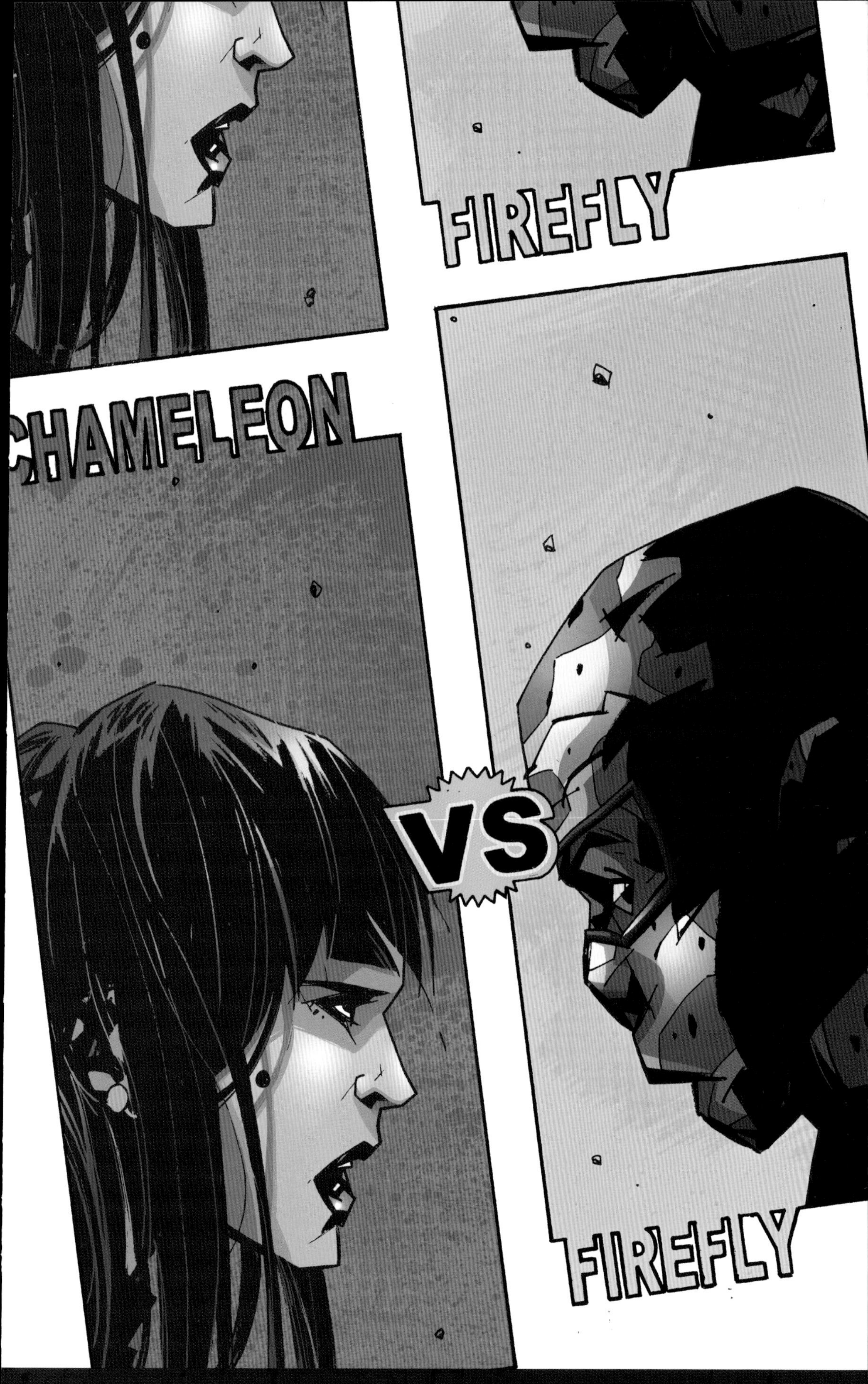
FIREFLY
CHAMELEON
VS
FIREFLY

ART BY **ANTONIO FUSO** • COLORS BY **ARIANNA FLOREAN**

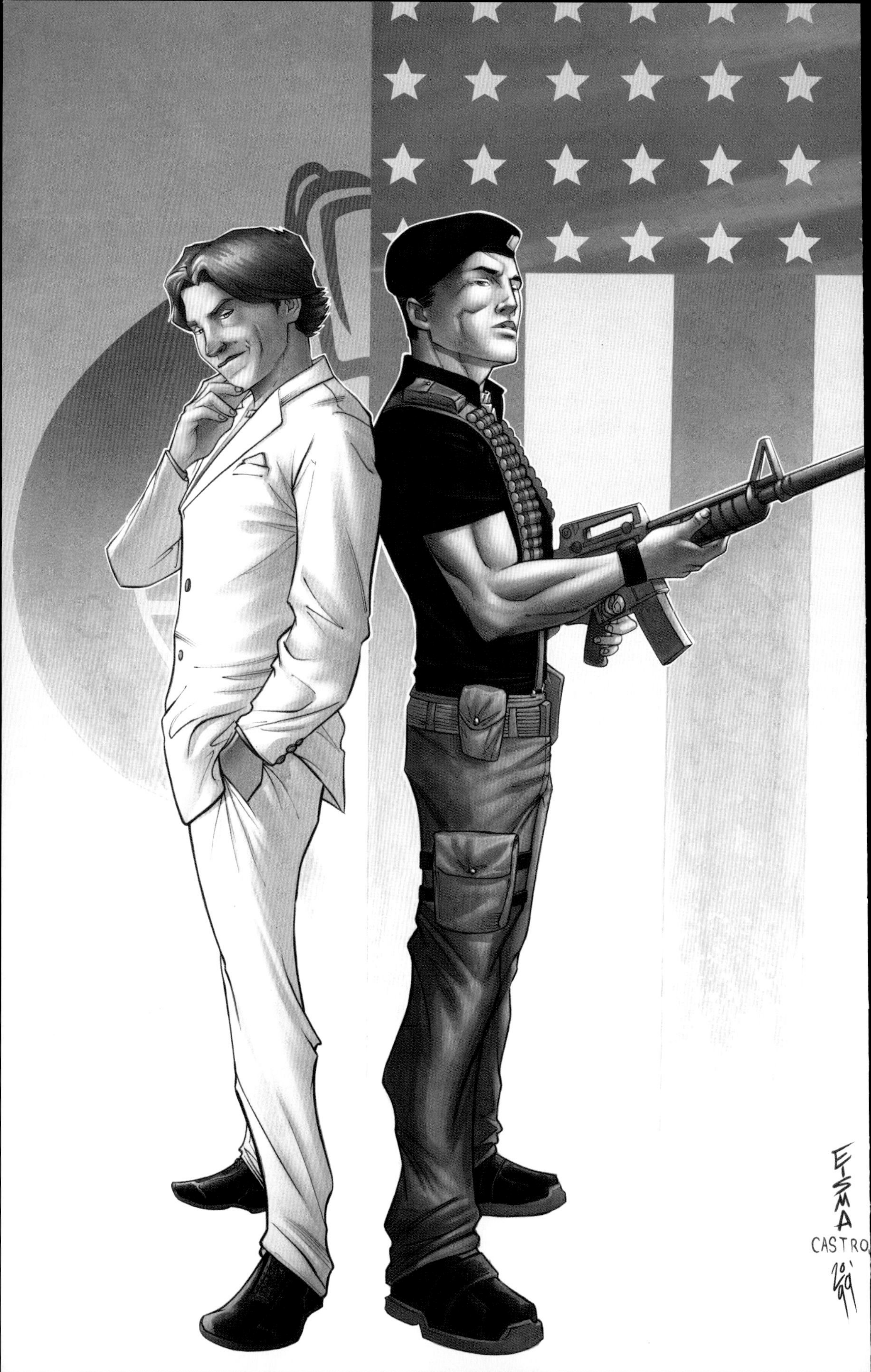
EISMA
CASTRO
20'09

ART BY **JOE EISMA** AND **JUAN CASTRO** • COLORS BY **SIMON GOUGH**

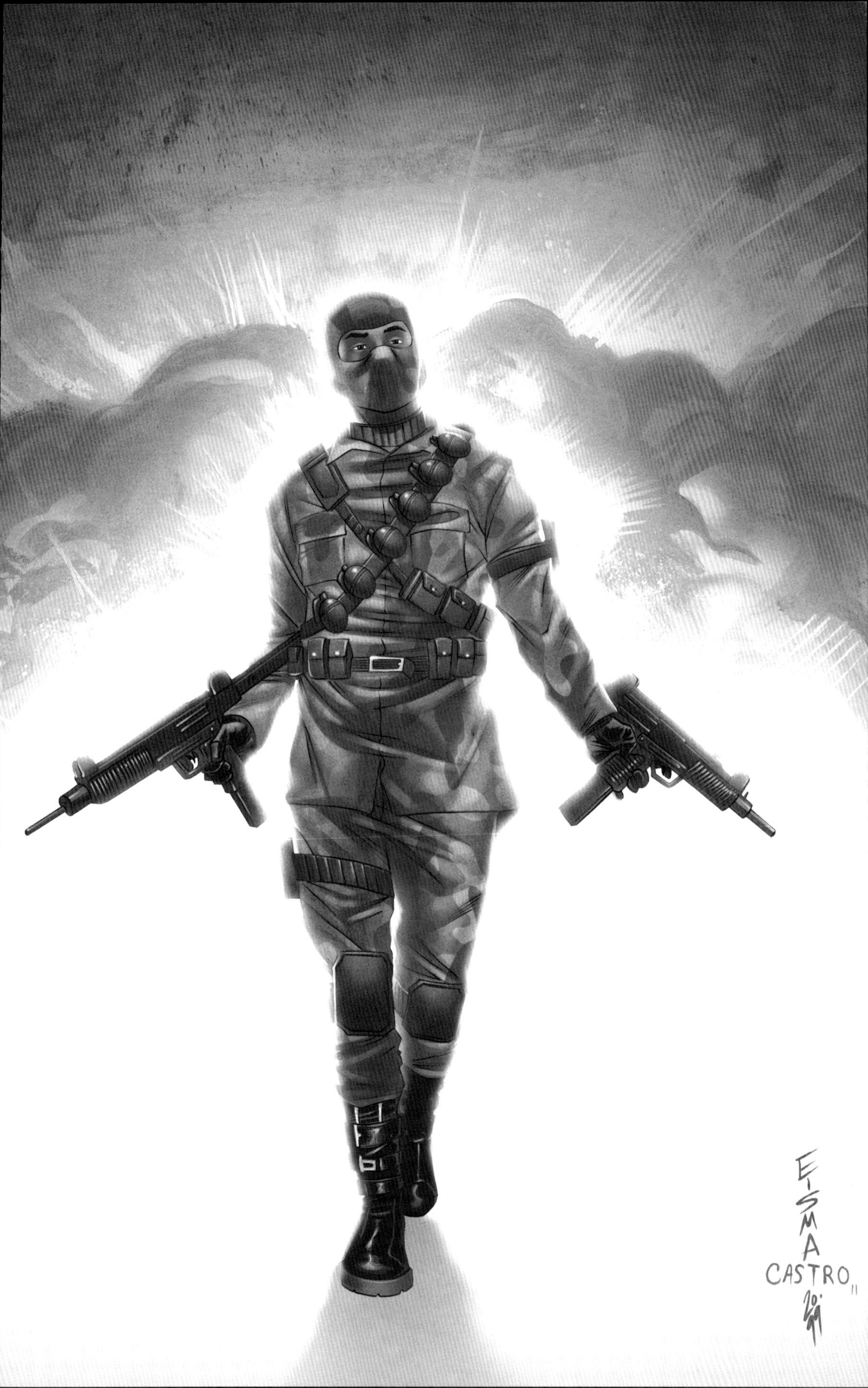
EISMA
CASTRO
2011

ART BY **JOE EISMA** AND **JUAN CASTRO** • COLORS BY **SIMON GOUGH**

JOIN THE MISSION!

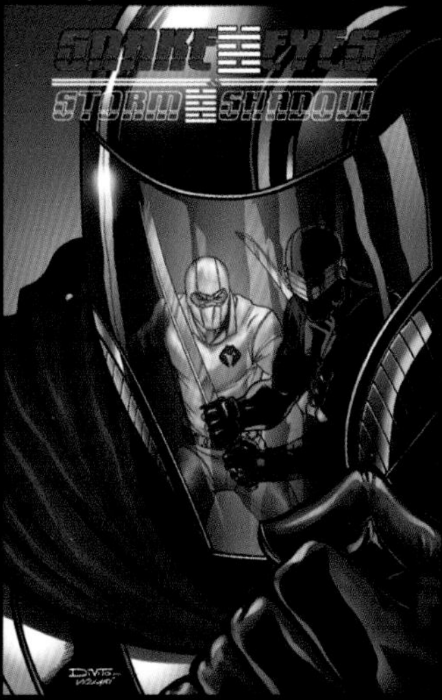
STORM SHADOW

SNAKE EYES / STORM SHADOW
ISBN: 978-1-61377-419-9

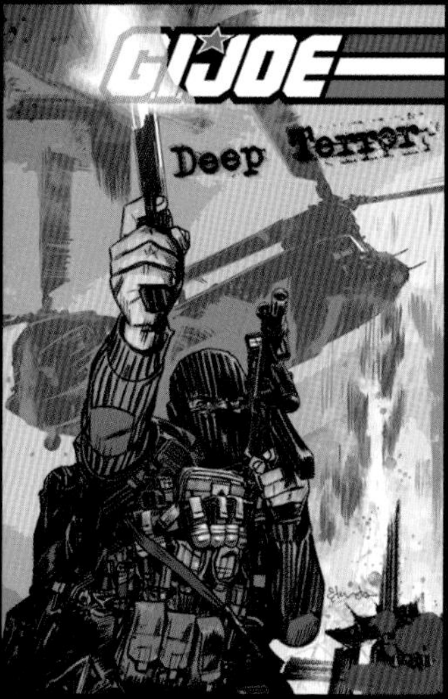
G.I. JOE
Deep Terror

G.I. JOE: DEEP TERROR
ISBN: 978-1-61377-511-0

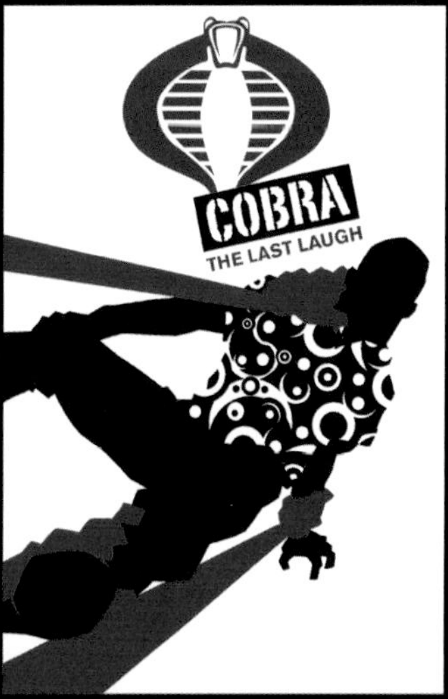
COBRA
THE LAST LAUGH

COBRA: LAST LAUGH
ISBN: 978-1-61377-523-3

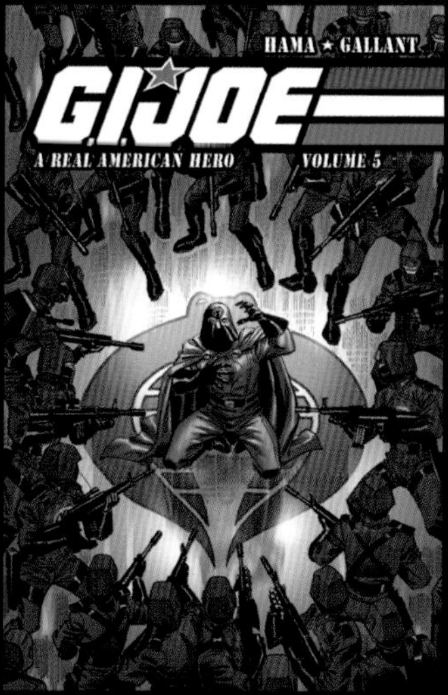
HAMA ★ GALLANT
G.I. JOE
A REAL AMERICAN HERO
VOLUME 5

G.I. JOE: A REAL AMERICAN HERO, VOL. 5
ISBN: 978-1-61377-486-1

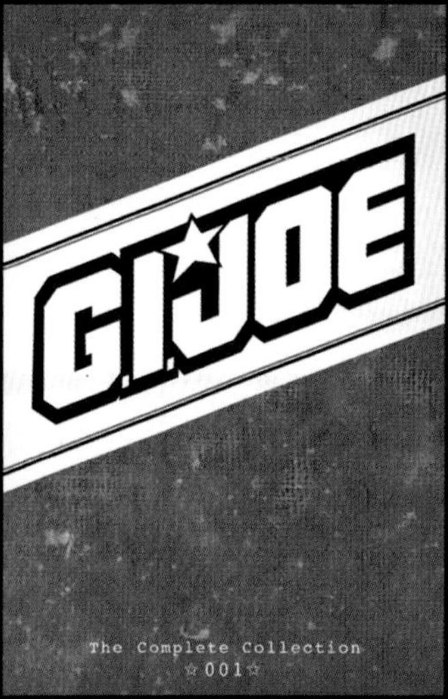
G.I. JOE
The Complete Collection
☆001☆

G.I. JOE: THE COMPLETE COLLECTION, VOL. 1
ISBN: 978-1-61377-396-3

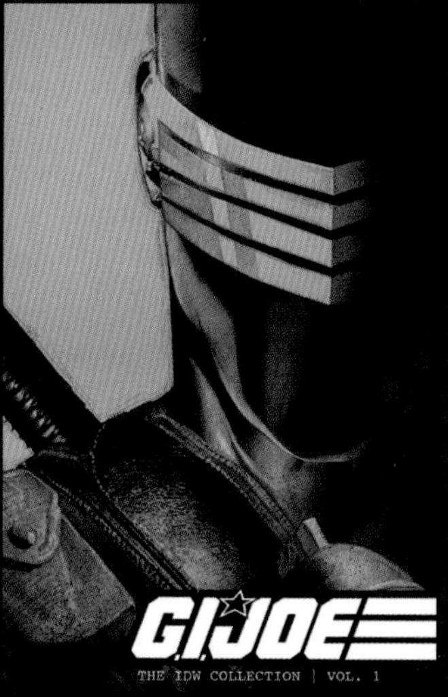
G.I. JOE
THE IDW COLLECTION | VOL. 1

G.I. JOE: THE IDW COLLECTION, VOL. 1
ISBN: 978-1-61377-549-3

IDW
Licensed By: Hasbro

WWW.IDWPUBLISHING.COM

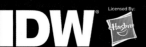